The Beasts

by

Braxton DeGarmo

Christen Haus Publishing

COPYRIGHT

DEDICATION

To believers everywhere. Christ is coming. Just as in the days of Noah, the world doesn't suspect a thing. Yet, He'll be here sooner than anyone expects, and for His followers, He keeps no secrets.

Matthew 13:11
To you it has been given to know the secrets of the kingdom of heaven, but to them it has not been given.

Matthew 24:32-33
From the fig tree learn its lesson: as soon as its branch becomes tender and puts out its leaves, you know that summer is near. So also, when you see all these things, you know that he is near, at the very gates.

1 Thessalonians 5:4
But you are not in darkness, brothers, for that day to surprise you like a thief.

Revelation 13:1-15

And I saw a beast rising out of the sea, with ten horns and seven heads, with ten diadems on its horns and blasphemous names on its heads.

And the beast that I saw was like a leopard; its feet were like a bear's, and its mouth was like a lion's mouth. And to it the dragon gave his power and his throne and great authority.

One of its heads seemed to have a mortal wound, but its mortal wound was healed, and the whole earth marveled as they followed the beast.

And they worshiped the dragon, for he had given his authority to the beast, and they worshiped the beast, saying, "Who is like the beast, and who can fight against it?"

And the beast was given a mouth uttering haughty and blasphemous words, and it was allowed to exercise authority for forty-two months.

It opened its mouth to utter blasphemies against God, blaspheming his name and his dwelling, that is, those who dwell in heaven. Also it was allowed to make war on the saints and to conquer them. And authority was given it over every tribe and people and language and nation, and all who dwell on earth will worship it, everyone whose name has not been written before the foundation of the world in the book of life of the Lamb who was slain.

If anyone has an ear, let him hear: If anyone is to be taken captive, to captivity he goes; if anyone is to be slain with the sword, with the sword must he be slain. Here is a call for the endurance and faith of the saints.

Then I saw another beast rising out of the earth. It had two horns like a lamb and it spoke like a dragon.

It exercises all the authority of the first beast in its presence, and makes the earth and its inhabitants worship the first beast, whose mortal wound was healed. It performs great signs, even making fire come down from heaven to earth in front of people, and by the signs that it is allowed to work in the presence of the beast it deceives those who dwell on earth, telling them to make an image for the beast that was wounded by the sword and yet lived. And it was allowed to give breath to the image of the beast, so that the image of the beast might even speak and might cause those who would not worship the image of the beast to be slain.

ONE

"Incoming! We've got another one coming up from the ER, doc!"

Dr. Caleb Wahlburg took another deep breath as he tore off his blood-splattered surgical gown and gloves and raced down the hall of the Labor & Delivery ward to grab a clean set. As he ran, he seemed to be in an endless hallway filled with stretchers holding women in various stages of pregnancy, all of them in distress. Gurney after gurney. He dodged pools of blood forming across the floor, dripping from many of the gurneys, and adding to the obstacle course he found himself combating.

A moment later, he seemed teleported back into the operating suite, his protective gear again splashed with the red liquid of life. Another young mother-to-be crying and screaming for the baby she was losing. Exhausted nurses worked like automatons to assist but were no longer numb to the loss of life filling their ward. Their wails matched those of the patients. L&D was supposed to be a happy place; a place filled with new life and parents in love with their freshly delivered bundles of joy.

"Incoming! We've got another one coming up from the ER,

doc!"

In that instant, he found himself again rushing down the hall in search of clean gear, dodging stretchers and blood, only to find no more clean gowns. And then, he was back in the operating suite. Gurneys lined the room as he began to deal with yet one more stillbirth.

"Incoming! We've got another . . ."

He awoke in a sweat. The nightmare had returned.

Aric Afton picked up his book bag and jacket from his desk and opened the door to his dorm room.

"See you at lunch," he said as he looked back to his roommate, Robert.

"I'll be there unless something comes up."

Aric nodded and closed the door behind him. He smiled to himself. Lunch on Wednesdays had evolved into a growing Bible study among the Christian youth group on campus. And while they faced some opposition from the LGBTQ+ and BLM crowds that once claimed the central residence hall as their own fiefdom, that resistance had been minimal during the past year and a half. Aric couldn't help but ponder that turn of events every Wednesday morning as he left for class. *God is good!* he thought, and in his mind, he heard Jess respond, "All the time."

Jessica Larson and her brother Chris were in different classes from Aric this semester. Aric missed seeing her each morning, so the Wednesday lunch sessions were doubly special to him. Their relationship had grown in ways that still surprised him.

Reflecting on Robert, he, too, had surprised Aric. A confused young man who once insisted upon being called Bobbi and crossdressed flamboyantly, Bobbi had been sicced on Aric by the LGBTQ+ crowd to drive him from the dorm during the short January term in the middle of the 2020-2021 school year. Now, just over eighteen months later with a new school year in progress, Robert refused to respond to the name Bobbi and nothing feminine could be found in their dorm room. In fact, he had become the "perfect" roommate for Aric, to the point that Aric and Robert had agreed to room together yet again for the year.

And for the past four weeks on Wednesday mornings, Robert had said the same thing. And every Wednesday at lunch he showed up. Aric anticipated that he would soon join the group at church on Sundays, too.

Aric decided to take the elevator down and waited for it. As the door opened, he found Toni riding inside. Toni had been another part of the "team" dedicated to driving Aric from the dorm. The guy identified by the pronouns they/them and was openly gay. As recently as the previous spring semester, Toni would have bolted from the elevator rather than ride in it with Aric. Today, he nodded a subtle greeting and didn't move from the back of the box.

"Hey, Toni, I like the purple. Was it hard to make the switch?"

Toni had been known for his neon pink hair, most commonly worn in a spike over the top of his head. Now a deep, plum-purple color topped his head.

"Yeah. A bit."

Aric's brow flinched up in surprise for a microsecond.

While the guy no longer ran in the opposite direction and offered the occasional nod in greeting, these were the first words spoken to Aric since a confrontation in the dining hall two previous Januarys ago.

Aric decided to brave the waters, figuratively speaking, by asking, "So, have you seen or heard from Ashley?"

Toni glowered. "Don't ask me about that traitor."

With that, the door opened on the first floor, and the guy swished out of the elevator.

Aric raised his brow and shook his head in mild disbelief. Ashley Love had been a resident advisor at the dorm that fateful January. Few would have guessed "her" to be a trans activist whose birth name was Sam Cooke. His depression ultimately led to a suicide attempt by jumping into the icy waters off the Kenosha lighthouse pier. Aric had been there with Jess, who was taking photographs. It was then that he had braved the waters, literally, and saved "her." That was also when he first learned as fact that she was a he. Prior to that, he'd only heard the rumors.

After that incident, Ashley left the college. But now, rumors swirled once again about a return to campus. Yet, this time they also whispered that he'd had an encounter with God in those icy waters and was back to being Sam. If Sam had returned to campus, Aric had not encountered him.

"Aric!"

He smiled at the sound of Jess's voice behind him. He stopped and turned to see her rushing toward him. On rare occasions that semester, they found themselves heading to class at the same time, despite being in different ones. This was one of those serendipitous days.

She walked up to him and kissed him on the cheek. Serendipity indeed. A public kiss was rarer than meeting up before class.

"Wow. To what do I owe that special honor?"

She stepped back and looked at him in surprise. "What? You don't know? I would think you'd be the first to know."

"Know what?" He felt truly confused.

"You really don't know, do you?"

He shook his head.

"Hmmm. Maybe I shouldn't spoil the surprise."

"Too late for that. You have to tell me now."

Jess started to speak when Dean Schmitz's secretary approached them, waving an envelope in her hands. Aric, Jess, and Chris had all been called to the dean of students' office that previous January at risk of being charged with hate speech. However, that incident had been cleared up thanks to Robert.

"Aric! Aric Afton! Wait up!"

The two of them stopped and waited upon the woman.

What now? wondered Aric.

The woman caught her breath and proceeded to say, "This is for you." She held out the envelope. "The dean asked me to also convey his congratulations."

Aric had no idea what was going on, but the look on Jess's face suggested that she did.

"Open it." She smiled.

Aric complied, as the dean's secretary turned and headed back to the admin building. Inside, he found another envelope embossed in gold. *A wedding invitation?* he wondered. That's what it reminded him of. Instead, as he opened it, he discovered an announcement as well as an invitation. He was to receive the Mayor's Award for Courage and was invited to a special reception in his honor.

"The Mayor's Award for Courage? What's that?" He looked at Jess who appeared radiant. "And how did you know?"

She teased her right index fingernail along his jaw. "From what I've heard, the award's a new one, and you're its first recipient. My dad's got several friends in city hall and the police department. That's how I heard, but I thought you already knew. Sorry."

"No problem. You can spoil my surprises anytime." He leaned into her and kissed her fully on the lips.

Now, she was the surprised one.

"It says, plus one. Hey, maybe I could ask Kels—" He grinned, as she punched him in the arm. "I mean, would you like to be my plus one?"

"You bet," she replied. "I wouldn't want it any other way."

Aric pondered Jess's comment that this was a new award. Had his crazy, knee-jerk reaction to a suicidal individual's jumping into the icy waters by the lighthouse truly been an act of courage deserving an award? Plus, the incident had occurred almost two years earlier. Why now?

More than that, though, was that the mayor's left-leaning, "Woke" policies would seem to rule Aric out as the award's first recipient. Was the man aware that he, Aric, was a white, faith-filled, cis-gendered, heterosexual, Christian conservative? He didn't tick off a single intersection.

But then he recalled the story of Mordecai and Ahasuerus in the Bible. Mordecai, Esther's uncle had foiled an assassination plot against the king. Sometime later, the king sought to honor someone who had performed a service for him. It had been such a long time since Mordecai's revelation of the plot that it required a search of the archives to reveal his name. In that story, the timing served God's purpose. Aric trusted that this upcoming award would also serve God's purposes.

TWO

Werner Koch sat back in the leather seat of the private Gulfstream G550 as it went wheels up above the Duebendorf military base near Zürich, Switzerland. He had permission from the highest level to utilize the landing strip there whenever he traveled to Davos, which was a one-hour helicopter flight from the base.

The attendant brought him a celebratory glass of Egon Müller Scharzhofberger Riesling Trockenbeerenauslese. Only special negotiants via auction could obtain this wine, and fewer still could afford its $12,000 per bottle price.

He nodded. "Thank you, Anna."

He sat back in his seat and savored the wine while calculating the flight time. They would reach their cruising speed of 550 knots shortly, which would give them a flight time of just over seven hours. With the six-hour time zone change, to his advantage, he would arrive just an hour or so later in the day than their take-off. In time for dinner. He loved traveling west. With his current destination, he could get seven hours of work completed on the flight but end up losing only one hour of his day.

As the jet leveled off and the attendant informed him they were at cruising altitude, he opened his briefcase. He wanted to be prepared for his private meeting with President Sidon and his national security adviser, Jim Salk, the next morning. As director of the World Order Council, he was the face of what some detractors would call the Deep State. But he was more than a distinguished visage; he saw himself as a visionary and as a savior of both mankind and the planet. World leaders changed their schedules to meet with him. Those who crossed him found their lives taking a sudden turn . . . and not for the better.

No, he didn't see himself as a global dictator. He preferred the image of being a global facilitator. The planet was expending its resources faster than anyone had ever anticipated. With a global population of just over eight billion people—and increasing at the rate of 63 million a year—many non-sustainable resources were already scarce and could soon become very difficult to find. Likewise, the population was causing an overheating of the world, with melting ice caps and rising sea levels. Pacific island nations were in peril and threatened with extinction. Coastal cities worldwide were likely to experience devastating floods.

He and the council had the answers, and he had been the one chosen to effect those answers. However, these solutions were not easy ones. Population growth could not simply be curtailed. The population needed to be reduced, significantly. The global use of resources required better control, which meant private land ownership, private ownership of companies that used such natural resources, and even private, individual family homes all had to be eliminated or come under the control of those who could manage them wisely under the guidelines of the council.

He smiled as he reflected upon the results of the weekend G20 meeting at Davos. As the traditional meeting place of the World Order Council, the city had evolved into becoming the de facto capital of the world. He couldn't think of a more beautiful city to stake that claim. Stretched out along the Landwasser Valley, the city was the highest resort town in the Alps. Snowcapped mountains and ski slopes surrounded them in the winter when the forum was held, but summer held equally as many activities for visitors. This past weekend, the autumn colors had been at their peak.

As he opened the first file for review, his laptop signaled an incoming video call. His top aide, Edvin Bergstedt, appeared on the screen. Werner still marveled at the technology that allowed his satellite communications to operate so superbly that Edvin seemed to be sitting across from him.

"Good morning, sir."

"Good afternoon, Edvin." He smiled at the man's momentary look of confusion.

"Um, oh, yes, sir. I wasn't thinking about the time zone difference." He straightened up in his chair and looked directly into the webcam. "I've heard that the meetings went well. Did you get the concessions you sought?"

"Enough of them. All of the nations involved are in agreement, but the timetables vary. We couldn't agree on a single target date."

"Yes, sir. My sources told me that the U.S. hesitated the most."

"Your sources were correct. Their negotiators agreed in principle, but they could not fully commit because the administration has yet to attain the level of control they seek. Plus, their Republican opponents continue to insist that their constitution requires senate approval for all treaties. They need to secure the senate and make it filibuster-proof."

"And so, they don't want to rock any boats with the upcoming election."

"True." Werner knew that those elections were simply theater and that they would have the senate seats required. Much money had been spent to develop the voting software, build ballot printing companies, put their judges in critical offices, and more in order to reach that goal.

And, they had learned from the 2020 election. Don't win so spectacularly that even the common citizen might question the results. The upcoming election results would be much closer and less questionable. They expected a few run-off elections and several recounts, as well as lawsuits challenging the results. Still, the end result would give them the senate.

Then, with the senate secured, the new global pandemic health regulations would become a reality. Yes, they would promote them initially as a means of curtailing the spread of the next pandemic. And true, they would have many who oppose them, but the regulations would prevail. Those same opponents would decry the potential "slippery slope," but there would be nothing slippery about it. The true intent of the regulation changes was to make them mandatory, not advisory; to give the WHO global power that superseded all national regulatory bodies; and to impose an international identity card that could control access to food, energy, banking, and more. Those who opposed them would find themselves on the outside of society. And if they starved, they starved. The world needed fewer mouths.

"Sir, I have your usual suite at the Willard reserved, and a car with your usual driver will be available 24 hours a day. He will meet you at the private terminal at DCA upon arrival. Your security team will be there round-the-clock as well."

"Thank you, Edvin." He much preferred flying into Reagan National over Dulles, and despite the limited number of private flights allowed into DCA, he was among those with top priority. "You have been as proficient as usual. What about the other task I gave you?"

"Thank you, sir. The second task has been a bit more daunting."

"Do you have an update for me?"

"Well, sir, our team has been working ardently to replicate the AlterNet software from CCS. It seems that when Wallace Chamberlain died, the event triggered the complete erasure of the software, their business records, and personnel files. And I do mean complete erasure with the data overwritten with gibberish zeros and ones."

That much Werner already knew, but he was a patient man. He waited for his aide to continue.

"Since we last discussed this, we have successfully traced a handful of CCS personnel through data at the IRS and FBI, which did the individual security screens and issued clearances. Two individuals stood out as likely members of the original coding team, a Sam Renner and a Rebecca Stiles. Ms. Stiles, now Olsen, tells us she did little of the actual coding and was largely responsible for the database architecture and certain search algorithms. The majority of coding was done by Renner and a man named Adam Afton, as far as she knew. She informed us that Renner was dead. We confirmed that to be so, and apparently, he was killed by Chamberlain's man, Buckner, who is also no longer with us. Ms. Olsen welcomed the opportunity to join our team and help us reproduce the program."

Werner sighed. Wallace Chamberlain had indeed been a thorn in their sides. He was a valuable asset because of AlterNet's surveillance capabilities. That is until his predilection for underage girls got in the way. Had they known he had "insurance" set up to protect him—a protocol for deleting his software—he might still be alive. Yet, somehow, if he had made known to someone that such "insurance" existed, that person had failed to inform those above him who made the decisions.

There was also a better than 50-50 chance that Chamberlain had been bluffing. Maybe there had been no such insurance. Maybe someone else deleted the program. Either way, the original program was gone. That was water under the bridge.

"What about this Adam Afton?"

"That's where we're stymied, sir. Either that was a fake name, or this individual was the genius behind AlterNet, and he's done a very, very good job at erasing his existence. There are no tax records, FBI records, or NSA records on an Adam Afton. Nothing. Ms. Olsen told us he once mentioned St. Louis, so we've searched birth records, property and tax records, auto licenses, and more in St. Louis city, the county, and all adjacent counties in Missouri and Illinois, as well as state records."

Werner frowned. Was anyone *that* good at erasing their existence? There was always a chink in one's armor. Somewhere.

"Did Ms. Olsen say anything else?"

"She did. He was always very closed about his family, but she was sure he had a brother and a couple of sisters. And something happened that caused him to become an alcoholic. All she heard were rumors, but the talk was he was fired for using AlterNet to try to find a daughter who had been kidnapped. She figured that the kidnapping was what started his drinking. That seems to be a reasonable speculation but it's still just that, speculation."

Werner nodded. "True, but that sounds like something to work with."

"Agree, sir. So, we've been chasing that. If he worked at CCS, he would have to have resided in Virginia, Maryland, or DC. We've checked state, local, and FBI records for kidnappings of young girls in those locales. Lots of disappearances, with few proven kidnappings. None with the Afton surname. We also hit a dead end with the FBI's national database."

This was not the news Werner had hoped to hear. They needed the surveillance and tracking capabilities of AlterNet, and he had hoped to locate the original programmers and entice them to rebuild the program.

"And your current programming efforts. Are they progressing?"

"Yes, sir, but not quickly. It's a very complicated program."

Werner nodded again. That was an understatement. A

thought came to him.

"Maybe we're using the wrong logic for this search. Take a backdoor approach. Try locating young men named Afton, say, ages 15 through 40, who have more than one sister. Then think old-fashioned and send real people to question the neighbors. Intimidate them if need be."

This time Edvin nodded. "Actually, sir, I've already initiated that. Our new AlterNet's search capabilities are being tested with just such a search in the St. Louis area. I hope to have final results by the time you land."

Werner sat back in his seat and smiled. He had been correct in selecting and hiring Edvin as his aide. He held no doubt that the man's intellect and proficiency matched his own.

"Very good, Edvin. We shall touch base again then. Come with the driver to meet me."

THREE

Adam Afton sat back in his chair and stared at his screens, shaking his head. Two and a half years earlier, upon fleeing Wallace Chamberlain's goons after Sam Renner had died in his arms, he had laid a complex web of traps and flags across the internet for anything resembling AlterNet. One of those flags had been tripped a day earlier.

Having traced the inquiry backward, he discovered someone was working to resurrect AlterNet. Indeed, much of the database architecture he found was identical to that in their original program. *Rebecca Stiles is back at it*, he thought. He struggled to recall what she might have learned about him while working together. He had been very guarded around her but had been less so around Sam. What might have Sam shared with her?

He had gone to great lengths to erase himself from all computerized records. He had rebuilt those records under a new name, known only to Aric. But now, it appeared these people, whoever they were, were using their rudimentary AlterNet to search for his family. He had intercepted a portion of their data and discovered they were looking for male

Aftons, ages 15 to 40, with more than one sister. And they were focused on the St. Louis area. It seemed clear that Rebecca had learned something about his family.

Earlier that day, he had set his UltraNet program to search the same parameters. His programming was far superior to what he had seen in the new AlterNet, and the search would be far more efficient. In fact, in just a few hours, it was almost complete.

He stood up and paced, his mind reviewing the databases he had altered. Had he missed something? He found himself staring out the window towards the lake behind his East Troy, Wisconsin, lair. The place wouldn't be home for long. He and Rachel, his ex, had finally worked things out. He was going home. Well, he was supposed to be heading home, but if someone was looking for him in St. Louis, was that a good idea? He knew that he knew that he knew that whoever sought to revive AlterNet was not doing so for the benefit of mankind.

One thought kept coming to him. Why were they looking for male Aftons with sisters? The obvious answer was that they couldn't find *him* but had learned he had a brother and sisters. So, if *he* was searching for a man's brother, how would he proceed? If he had the manpower, he would follow up by sending investigators to question those individuals and even the neighbors. Adam had little or no recourse should they follow that route.

Another thought struck him. He hadn't been as thorough as he thought. Hospital records. If they could find Aric, they could find their mother. With her name, they could go directly to hospital records, and their new AlterNet appeared able to perform such a search, even if it took a few days. With the mother's name, they could look for other birth records. He had removed himself from the birth certificate registries, but not from the hospital record of his birth. Fortunately, he knew which hospital system to go to and his birth date. He wouldn't have to hunt and peck through records to find his.

He rushed back to his computer and within minutes was inside the medical center's records system. Calling up the OB records for his birth date, he quickly found his record and altered both his and his mother's names.

He tapped his finger on the desktop. Should he, or shouldn't he? Yes, he should. He called up Aric's birth record and did the same thing. That would slow them down, if not stop those looking for him through Aric. They would be forced to expend manpower and considerable cost to try to track his family.

He stood and started to pace again. He didn't like his options, or rather the lack thereof. He needed to block their search from finding Aric and his sisters. He couldn't "erase" them as he had done for himself. His only option was to intercept the search findings, as well as to penetrate their system for any results they'd already completed. To do so risked their being able to backtrace him, which might be exactly what they were hoping for. Perhaps this was a trap intended to find him. Still, he needed to remove his family from their results.

He rubbed his temples. How could he do this? More importantly, how could he do so without being discovered?

And that problem concerned him. What if Rebecca had also learned of the fourth main man on their team? That man, code-named Seth, would be more than capable of finding someone who didn't want to be found. The guy's work had been compartmentalized, and both Sam and Rebecca were to know nothing about him. However, Adam's work had crisscrossed his, and they had collaborated on several aspects of the code. Plus, being like-minded on many issues, they found it easy to work together.

Adam had once tried to locate the man, but he, too, appeared to have disappeared after the death of Sam Renner. Adam often wondered if Chamberlain had dispatched "Buck" Buckner to deal with him, as he had Sam. But that made no sense. Adam would have discovered a death certificate and everything else pertaining to the guy's life. He had found nothing.

And the total lack of records pointed to his doing just what Adam had done. Plus, the new AlterNet did not appear to be searching for anyone other than Adam. So, Adam could only conclude that Rebecca knew nothing about their fourth coder.

That, however, did not mean the man could not become a potential danger to Adam and his family. If anyone could track down Adam, he could. He knew some of Adam's signature code. He knew how Adam approached searches. He very likely would recognize Adam's hand in the traps and flags Adam had set. Yes, as with eliminating his family from the current search, Adam had no choice here, too. Adam would have to find him first.

"Dr. Wahlburg, please go to L and D. Dr. Wahlburg, please go to L and D."

Caleb awoke from his mental distractions at the mention

of his name over the hospital intercom system. With everyone having cell phones, such announcements were rare. He brushed across the pockets of his slacks and white coat searching for his phone, only to realize he had left it in his locker. Again. He sighed and shook his head. He could hear the taunts and jokes of his staff now.

He rushed out of the cafeteria and hurried toward Labor and Delivery. He was not expecting any of his pregnant patients. Of course, babies came when babies were ready, and that was rarely on a date or at a time determined by him, the mother, or anyone else. He had another hysterectomy scheduled for that afternoon, but that was over an hour away and would be performed in the OR adjacent to L and D.

The automatic doors opened before him, and he scurried to the nurses' station. Their head nurse, Sha'Kyra Taylor, did not look amused. In fact, she had that look of . . .

"Hey, sorry, I left my phone—"

"Not in your locker this time." She extended his phone toward him. "It was at the dictation station."

He grabbed the phone and slipped it into a coat pocket. "Thanks. What's up?" It was at this point that he noticed her wipe tears away from her eyes. The look on her face had nothing to do with his phone.

"I-it's Carrie. She's in exam room one. She hasn't felt her baby move since waking up today. I did a quick ultrasound and couldn't see any movement either. She's asked for you."

"Heartbeat?"

More tears welled up as she shook her head. A year ago, to see this woman shed tears would have been rare. She'd been handling labor and deliveries for almost two decades. She would have told you she had seen it all. Now, a year later, she no longer made that claim.

Caleb raised his hands and rubbed them up and down over his face, before running his right hand through his hair. He took a deep breath and tried to calm the anxiety rising within. He didn't want to face yet another stillbirth, and certainly not with a member of his own nursing staff. But . . .

"I had it again last night. I-I don't know how I can face . . ."

"It? The nightmare?"

Caleb nodded. He had shared the dream with Sha when it first happened, but he hadn't informed her of every occurrence. Where it disrupted his night maybe once a week at first, now it did so two or three times a week. He was physically dragging from sleep deprivation.

The bad dream did more than cause him to lose sleep. More and more it seemed to reflect his real-life practice of obstetrics. And every week he found it more difficult to come to work.

The nurse shook her head slowly. "I'm sorry."

"At least I haven't turned to alcohol. Yet." He gave her a wan grin. Then, he sighed, took a deep breath, and turned toward the exam room. He paused at the door and took several deep breaths before entering.

"Carrie, hi."

"Doctor Wahlburg, I-I-I'm not feeling my baby move. Sha'Kyra wouldn't tell me anything, but from the look on her face, I-I know it's not good." Tears welled up in her eyes and began to run down both cheeks.

Caleb grabbed her hand and gave it a squeeze for encouragement. Still, he didn't feel encouraged himself.

He grabbed the tube of lubricating gel, exposed her gravid belly, and squirted a pile of the gel on top. He took the transducer head of the ultrasound machine and began to scan her abdomen. Nothing. He hadn't doubted his head nurse, but he needed to see for himself. Plus, Carrie would expect him to repeat the procedure. He continued, praying that he was wrong and that miraculously the child inside her would start to move. The little boy didn't.

He looked Carrie in the eyes, trying hard to deter tears from filling his, and said, "I am so, so sorry, Carrie. I don't see any movement and can't detect a heartbeat."

The emotional dam burst, and she began to sob. Caleb took her hand and squeezed it again. Sha'Kyra entered the room, and he turned his head toward her as he shook it. She took a moment to wipe the gel from Carrie's abdomen, cover it with the hospital gown, and then lean over to embrace and comfort her co-worker.

A moment later, Carrie's husband, Brian, entered the room and rushed to her side. "Got here as soon as I could. Is . . . is everything okay?" His tongue stumbled across that last word as if he already knew the answer.

Caleb shook his head. "We'll give you two some time alone. I'm sorry."

He motioned for Sha'Kyra to follow him into the hallway. After closing the door behind them, he said, "We can give her the choice between watching her here overnight or going home. I can't say how long her body will take to start labor."

The nurse nodded. "She knows the drill." She turned toward the nurses' station but stopped and turned back toward him. "Was it the vaccine? We've all been reading the reports."

Caleb shrugged. "Maybe. The hospital refuses to let us test for that, but the literature is filling up with studies and reports of menstrual issues, miscarriages, infertility, and stillbirths because of the COVID jab."

"So, what will it take to find out? We were all forced to accept the jab or lose our jobs. Now? She's one of our own, and I'm . . . well, maybe this job just isn't worth it anymore."

Caleb sighed. He could identify with her feelings. One other nurse from their unit had refused the jab because she was striving for a family and was fired. Three more nurses left after religious exemptions were refused. Six others couldn't take the extra workload and left for quieter pastures. They were severely short-staffed and would likely lose Carrie now, too.

"Sha, we can't afford to lose you, but I understand how you feel."

"I know you do. That recurring nightmare alone speaks to that."

Caleb nodded. That was an understatement. Multiple studies were coming out in various obscure journals because Big Pharma controlled the most prestigious publications. One study revealed a 1200-fold increase in menstrual irregularities. That correlated to a 120,000% increase. Two hospitals in Ontario reported an 800% increase in stillbirths. The hospital in Waterloo, Ontario, had 86 stillbirths over a six-month period when they would normally expect three or four. The incident was even covered in a session of the provincial parliament. Another study revealed a 57-fold increase in miscarriages and a 38-fold increase in stillbirths. PfenRich's data, forced into being released by the FDA via a FOIA suit, showed that in their preliminary study, only 32 of the 270 pregnant women were ever followed up. Of that group, 80% miscarried. And yet, the CDC, FDA, and other governmental agencies that were supposed to safeguard the people sat on such data. They even pushed for vaccinating pregnant women. The level of corruption dismayed him. To be truthful, he no longer considered it simply as corruption but as pure evil.

In this birthing center with 5,000 to 6,000 patients a year, he was seeing more malformations, cardiac defects, preeclampsia, and preterm labor. He saw many more second-trimester abnormalities, abnormal testing results, abnormal appearing placentas, and dead fetuses. Yes, and far too many stillbirths.

He struggled with what he saw. To release and publicize such data might get him promptly dismissed from the medical center. Was he in a position to give that up? What then? Wouldn't withholding that info just make him as complicit as those government agencies? No, he needed to shed light on the problems, not hide them. He would be okay if he lost his job.

And what about the nightmares? Were they the result of post-traumatic stress brought on by what he saw? Would taking a stand against "the jab" finally free him from them? Or would a new version take their place?

PfenRich needed to be held accountable, and he would do all he could to help make that happen.

FOUR

Award day had arrived, and Aric felt a bit awkward. He didn't feel this Award for Courage thing was necessary. In reflection, his actions two winters ago had been a foolhardy, knee-jerk reaction. Yet, he had to admit he would do it all over again if he saw someone flailing in the water and possibly drowning.

He pulled up in front of Jess's home. Chris, her brother, had become one of Aric's closest friends both at the college and in town. The guy was out their front door and at the driver's door of Aric's car before Aric could switch off the engine. Chris stepped back and allowed Aric space to open the door.

"Hey, hero. I —" He stopped short. "Is that what you're wearing? Dude, you're going to be presented an award by the mayor. There are going to be cameras and news people. Is that the best you can offer as a first impression? We need to put our best foot forward here, as representatives of Christ if not for personal satisfaction."

Aric shrugged as he sighed. Jeans and a pullover sweater were the best he had to offer. Oh, and he had a choice of two ties, so he picked the one that worked best with the sweater.

Or so he thought.

"Cut me some slack. My one suit, two sports coats, and dress slacks are at my folks' house in St. Louis. I haven't needed them for college, and my closet in the dorm is the size of a port-a-potty."

Chris nodded. "Okay, okay. Your family is coming, right? Did they bring any of those?"

Aric hesitated in answering. He hadn't even thought of asking his mom to bring his nice clothes.

"They're coming. They couldn't come north yesterday, so they got an early start this morning. I gave them your address, and they should be here any time now."

"So, I'm assuming by your avoiding that question that you didn't arrange for them to bring your suit or anything since you're dressed like that."

Aric shrugged again. "Don't know if my mom will think of it or not. I didn't ask them to."

Chris shook his head. "C'mon, let's get you properly dressed. I've got some slacks and a sports coat that should fit you. And my dad has enough ties to wrap around the world . . . twice. At least the shoes will do."

As they approached the front door, Jess appeared inside the full glass panel of the storm door. Her brow rose, and disbelief flashed across her face. As Chris opened the door, she began to speak. "Is that what—"

"Got it, sis. I've got him covered. C'mon."

He ushered Aric upstairs to his room. Ten minutes later, Aric was spruced up in Chris' clothes and looked sharp. Chris, in turn, had put on some nice slacks and a button-down shirt. Aric acknowledged that his friend didn't require the same level of attire as the award recipient. Yet, Chris looked so much more comfortable than Aric felt. He tugged at the shirt collar and loosened the tie a smidgen. As the two descended the stairs, Jess appeared below and smiled.

"That's so much better. I just heard a car pull up. Did you direct your parents to meet us here, like you said you would?"

Aric nodded. "I did." He peeked out the window. It was his family. He watched as his parents and two unmarried sisters emerged from the vehicle. Gwyneth, his oldest sister, wasn't quite up to traveling with a newborn and had begged off coming for the ceremony. He glanced at Jessica.

"Nervous?"

"Me? Nope."

Aric chuckled. She was. She was doing that thing with her hair that she always did when nervous. This would be her introduction to his family and vice versa. And it would be the first time that the two sets of parents would meet.

He stepped outside and waved. His mom had ducked back into the side door of the minivan and pulled out a suit bag. She knew him all too well. As she straightened up and saw him, she smiled and put the suit back inside the minivan. Moments later, they entered the house.

"Mom, Dad, this is Jess and her brother, Chris. Chris was kind enough to loan me these clothes. Jess, Chris, these are my folks, Alex and Margaret. And these are two of my sisters, Eloise and Mabel."

Jess's parents appeared from around the corner, and the expected round of "Nice to meet yous" followed between Tom and Susan Larson and Aric's folks.

Aric's mom looked at Chris. "Thanks for the clothing loan.

I can only imagine what he would have worn otherwise."

Jess responded, "You don't really want to know" as she smirked at Aric.

Margaret laughed and poked Aric. "Gee, I like her already."

Jess blushed. Small talk ensued for the next ten minutes before Tom spoke up.

"We'd better get going. I realize they can't start without the guest of honor, but we still don't want to be late."

Adam hurried to get ready and leave for Kenosha. He had been so absorbed in his work that he would have missed Aric's big award celebration had he not set an alarm on his system. He hoped the hour's drive to the ceremony would help clear his mind.

He had spent the past week searching for his fellow coder, as well as trying to filter the results of the new AlterNet's search. He had failed so far in the first endeavor, while the second one had ended with "maybe" as the only answer.

He couldn't simply invade their turf and hack their code to his advantage. No, he had made such an attempt and had triggered some kind of "trip wire" that forced him to pull back urgently. At least one of the members of their programming team had experience in securing a network.

After that attempt, he managed to access and download about 75% of their search results before triggering another alert and getting shut out. That time, he made sure to make it appear as if some amateurish kid hacker had accidentally stumbled into their network. Still, as expected, when he tried to obtain the other 25% of their data, they had sealed off that route and secured their system much better.

Aric's name had not appeared in that 75% of the data. But there was always the chance of his being in the remaining 25%. Thus, the "maybe."

As he drove, he wondered what the odds were of Aric being on that list. Here, too, his analytical abilities had stumbled a bit. He had not been able to discern an organized pattern to their searching for men within their parameters. A rational pattern would have made it much easier to determine the odds of Aric being within their data.

Adam realized that trying to mentally calculate those odds was not helping to clear his mind. He chose to simply watch the scenery for several miles. The autumn color was at its peak. He realized he never really paid attention to how pretty the area was with its rolling farmlands and wooded lots. He always seemed to be focused on some problem or trying to analyze some search.

Soon, though, his attention shifted to his old team member. What could he recall about him? While he knew his name, that search had been a wash. What else did he remember? Had a sister two years older than him. Grew up in North Carolina and went to Duke for a year before transferring to MIT. Dad and uncle shared a dental practice. Mom was a medical doctor of some kind. OB/GYN maybe? Wasn't married at the time but had a steady girlfriend. Adam could not recall her name. That would have made a search too easy.

Adam slapped his steering wheel and smiled. The drive *had* cleared his thoughts and allowed him to recall these things. Now he had parameters he could feed his software.

Before he knew it, he had arrived at the Kenosha Yacht Club. The ceremony was to be held on the beach near the north pier lighthouse jetty, with the iconic, red lighthouse in the background. While the light still beamed at night, it was no longer needed by the ships in Lake Michigan. And few people knew that the structure was now privately owned. An artist had purchased it in 2011 to be his studio, and now, his widow still owned it and sponsored an artists-in-residence program throughout the summer.

He parked at the yacht club and made his way to the beach. His family, Aric, and the Larsons were already there. He waved as Mabel spotted him first. She got the first hug.

"Adam, yaay, you made it." His mother gave him a huge smile. He had noticed that she and Jess were deep in conversation as he approached.

"Hi, mom." He gave her a big squeeze, which she held longer than he found comfortable. "Hey, Jess. Good to see you again. You two up to something?" He grinned.

"Umm, mayyybee."

He greeted his dad and other sister, as well as the Larsons, whom he had met when Aric was briefly hospitalized following his "heroic" plunge into the waters just 1,000 feet away.

"Good to see you, son," said his dad.

"Where's the hero?"

His father pointed toward the lighthouse. "There, meeting the mayor and other dignitaries."

Adam laughed. He knew just how much Aric must be enjoying that. Not.

"C'mon. Let's get closer. Looks like they're about to begin."

As a group, they endured the speeches of the police chief, mayor, county administrator, and the area's congressman. Finally, the mayor had Aric step forward and presented him with the plaque and a ceremonial key to the city.

Aric then stepped to the mic. "Thank you, Mr. Mayor. I-I'm not sure I truly deserve this. Christ taught us that there is no greater love than to give one's life for another. I praise Him for keeping both of us from drowning that day." Pointing to the sky, he continued, "He deserves the glory, not me. Again, thank you."

Adam saw Pastor Larson grinning and giving Aric a double thumbs-up. The mayor and other high muckety-mucks, however, looked uncomfortable at the religious tone of Aric's acceptance. Adam wondered whether the mayor would take the award back.

After shaking everyone's hands up front, Aric was "released" to join his family and friends. Jess was the first to give him a hug. Adam hung back to the end of the line.

"Way to go, little brother." He gave Aric his version of a brotherly hug, and whispered, "I need to talk with you alone. Something's up."

To say that he felt uncomfortable was an understatement. Aric stood before maybe a hundred people, including members of the media, city aldermen, first responders, people from the college, friends, and more. Behind them all stood his family along with Jess and her family. So far, it appeared that the two families were hitting it off well. That was more important to him than the award.

He was introduced first to the mayor, followed by the other dignitaries in the front. Their words of congratulation seemed hollow, but he accepted them graciously. He wondered when the speeches would end and breathed a sigh of relief when the mayor finally gave him the award. He was surprised by the ceremonial key to the city. As he understood it, that would entitle him to some free meals and a variety of discounts at stores where he'd likely never shop. He'd heard of the sponsoring restaurants before but had been to only one prior to this. He and Jess would enjoy that part of the award at least.

With the awards in hand, he stepped up to the mic and decided to keep it short while giving credit where credit was due. He smiled when he saw Jess's dad give him the double thumbs up. Finally, the ordeal was over.

He smiled as he watched Jess race over to him and throw her arms around him. "Wow, the key to the city, too," she said.

He laughed. "Yep, looks like a few date nights are in order."

She gave him a sly kiss on the cheek and gave way to the rest of his family. Finally, Adam came up to him, congratulated him, and hugged him, too, which was a bit weird as Adam was not a fan of hugging.

Then he whispered into Aric's ear, "I need to talk with you alone. Something's up."

The words hit him almost as hard as the icy waters of that January plunge.

"Uh, okay, but not right now. Later."

Adam nodded and backed away. As Aric looked over Adam's shoulder, he saw a man who seemed familiar. He couldn't place where or how he knew him, but he was confident they had met before. The guy seemed to want to talk with him. He even stepped toward Aric but hesitated.

Aric's curiosity got the better of him. He looked toward his family and said, "Hey, I'll be back in a moment."

The man saw him approaching and started to walk away, but Aric caught up to him. "Excuse me. I'm Aric Afton, but I guess you know that if you've been here for the ceremony. I know you from somewhere, but I can't place you. How do I know you?"

The man turned squarely toward him. Aric noticed tears in the man's eyes.

"I-I'm Jim Goode. You saved my son's life, in more ways than one, and I'm forever grateful."

Aric remembered now. He had seen the man and his wife at the hospital. And now, he acted on impulse and reached out to hug the man. The action seemed appropriate.

Upon releasing Mr. Goode, he said, "You say your son. Are the rumors I've heard about him true? He's no longer living a trans life."

Mr. Goode nodded. "They are. He's here . . . if you'd like to see him." He pointed to a lone figure standing near the dune grass at the end of the beach.

Aric nodded, and together they walked toward that solitary person. As Aric neared, he could see something of Ashley Love in the man's face, but the haircut was that of a man and he had filled out both in the face and body.

As he came within reach, Aric extended his hand in greeting. "Hi, Sam."

The guy looked down toward his feet for a moment but then looked at Aric and returned the gesture. His handshake was firm but not quite that of a man's grip. Aric figured it would take some time to get that kind of strength back.

"Thank you, Aric. I never got the chance to say that to you. I tried to make your life hell, and yet, you willingly saved my life in that icy water. It took me several months to understand why, but I do now. I was in a really bad place back then, but I'm doing much better now. So, again, thank you."

Aric nodded. "I'm truly glad to hear that."

Sam offered a wan smile. "I liked what you said up front there. I'm learning to trust God now, too."

Mr. Goode nodded. "We're back in church as a family, and we're healing."

"Look, I don't want to hold you up from your friends and family," said Sam. "Maybe our paths will cross again."

"I heard a rumor that you'd be coming back to the college. Is that true?"

Sam shrugged. "To be determined. If so, it will be this next J-term at the earliest."

Aric reflected on the previous J-term when all of this happened. Since then, he had been sensing subtle changes on campus. That Toni didn't flee at seeing him was one of those. But more than that, being called "the guy" now had a different connotation. No longer was it a negative, as in "the guy" who wanted to stir up trouble for the LGBT+ and BLM crowd. No longer the Bible thumper. Now, he was "the guy" who risked his life to save one of their own, even if now that person was no longer part of their lifestyle.

"Well, feel free to stop by anytime. You might be interested to know that Robert—Bobbi, as you knew him—and I are still roommates."

"Who would have guessed? Well, your girlfriend is waving at us, trying to get your attention."

Aric turned to see Jess doing just that. "Yep, gotta go. But I'm serious, feel free to stop by. But be careful not to run into Toni. He has purple hair now and is not happy with you." He smirked.

The wan smile returned to Sam's face as Aric turned and hurried back to his group. Jess gave him a quizzical look. "Who was that?"

"Three guesses."

She shook her head. "No idea."

"Sam Goode and his father."

Her mouth gaped open in surprise.

FIVE

Werner's rounds of meetings with President Sidon, his National Security Adviser, the heads of the CIA, FBI, and NSA, as well the Speaker of the House and Majority Leader of the Senate had gone well. Much coordination was to be done to prepare for the elections coming up. He had left it up to the heads of the three-letter organizations to manage the social media platforms that played so well into their plans, while all parties would work to harmonize the media with their messages.

His three-car motorcade exited the grounds of Camp David where he'd spent the weekend with the Sidons.

"Well, Edvin, what did you think of your first visit to Camp David?"

His aide looked up from his laptop, frowning.

"Did you not enjoy your time there?"

"Sorry, sir, I got distracted." He shook his head, not as a negative gesture but as if trying to clear his mind. "Camp David is beautiful and certainly functions well as a getaway from the White House. I can see why so many presidents have favored it."

"I sense a 'but' coming."

"Yes, sir, in a way. Being so intimate with the Sidons showed me just how frail a man he's become. Without the daily adrenochrome injections, I think he'd be removed quickly from office."

Werner nodded. He, too, had seen just how far 'Po' Sidon had deteriorated. The injections allowed him to function with only minor peeks into his dementia, glimpses that could be passed off as gaffes by the press. Without the injection, the man's dementia became glaring, making him look like a blathering idiot. At his best, years earlier as a senator, he might have blathered, but he had been no idiot.

"True. Fortunately, we have good people running things on his behalf.

The two watched the scenery pass by. Werner had been to Camp David on numerous occasions. When time permitted, he preferred the scenic drive due south along Catoctin Hollow Rd, connecting to Gambrill Park Rd., and then to U.S. 40 and I-70. At that time of year, he made sure they had time for the longer drive.

The fall colors were coming on strong, and a cool front brought that brisk autumn air that folks relished after a long, hot summer. Roadside produce stands promoted their pumpkins and other squash, while those that still had corn pushed the end-of-the-year cobs picked that day.

Soon they entered the interstate on their way back to D.C., and Werner wondered what Edvin's distraction was. It was unlike him to lose focus.

"I'd like to know what distracted you earlier. Is it something I need to be aware of?"

Werner hadn't risen to his position without a certain sense of paranoia. While he remained "off the radar" for 99+% of the world's population, there were those who knew of him, understood what kind of world he sought, and didn't agree with the plans of the WOC.

"I'm not sure yet. Our people working on AlterNet might have stumbled upon something on the dark web regarding our friends in Big Pharma. Since we're headed to meet with the team next, perhaps it would be best to let them tell you firsthand."

The remainder of the hour's trip into DC was spent on their upcoming schedule, but Werner was now the one having trouble focusing. Big Pharma was vital to their depopulation agenda, not to mention an incredible source of wealth. Anything that could upset that cart was critical to him. That had been one of the reasons so many resources and much effort had been utilized to dispel "misinformation" about various toxins and, most importantly, their COVID vaccine program.

The limo pulled into the parking lot of a nondescript building in NW Washington that had once been a Sears store. No signage adorned the face of the structure or announced the current entity within. Only those with technical knowledge of such things would notice that the lines bringing power into the building were large enough to energize a small city. Likewise, the cables connecting the building to the worldwide web consisted not only of a primary bundle of coaxial cables providing a terabyte of data transfer but also over two dozen old T1 copper lines for backup. True, the T1 lines were antiquated by today's standards, but they were reliable and stable.

Inside, they were greeted by the project manager, Randall Granger. He was a man of average stature, mid-forties, overweight, but with a thick shock of dark hair covering his head. His unassuming appearance belied his skill at coding. Plus, he had one other excellent skill—he could manage other coders well.

"Mr. Koch, it is indeed an honor to meet you and have you stop in." The man extended his hand which Werner accepted.

"Mr. Granger, thank you. I'm very much interested in the progress you've made in reproducing the AlterNet program."

Granger nodded. "Yes, sir. This has been a grand undertaking, and we've made great progress considering how short a time we've been working compared to the time taken to produce and refine the original. AlterNet2, as we're calling it, can readily penetrate dozens of databases without detection to produce results from the search parameters we give it. Come this way, and I'll introduce you to the team."

Granger led the way along a hall past windows revealing rows of servers within their refrigerated confine and opened the door to a spacious room occupied by a dozen workstations, by Werner's quick count, and a variety of recreational spaces—a reading nook, foosball, air hockey, board games, and more. Werner had always been a man with a strong work ethic. His personal businesses had been built through hard, focused work, and never required distraction. Yet, he had grown to understand the intricacies of coding and how even a brief period of distraction could clear one's mind and open up new avenues of creativity.

"Allow me to introduce the team."

Granger walked Werner and Edvin around the room and introduced each person, announced their primary role on the team, and allowed them to address the progress they were making. Werner was impressed by their professionalism—direct, succinct, and willing to lay out the pros and cons facing their tasks. Each would have done well in German industry. He suspected they had been coached on what he expected.

"Sir, this is Rebecca Olsen." She extended her hand.

Werner smiled. The woman standing before him held all of the stereotypes one expected from a gifted hacker and coder. Werner was not one to quickly judge someone by appearance, but he would have taken her as being homeless and living under a bridge before being a proficient database designer.

"Yes, Ms. Olsen, our database architect and sole member of the initial AlterNet team. I thank you for assisting us in finding others from your first team."

She nodded and smiled. He found her smile quirky at best.

"You're welcome, Mr. Koch. I'm sorry I had so little to pass on. Wallace Chamberlain was a great fan of compartmentalization."

Werner nodded. "So I understand. How would you rate your current team compared to the first?"

He expected her to be reticent in answering. After all, these were the people she now worked with, and she wouldn't want to rock the boat.

"Equally up to the task. We can't ignore the fact that the first team had almost two decades to develop and refine the program. We've only been at it for under a year. Considering that, I think we're doing very well."

Werner noted no hesitation in her answer that might suggest she was simply being polite. And she made a good point. The original program had started as a PsyOps project during the war in Afghanistan. It started as a program designed to find people and groups open to manipulation by propaganda and grew to a masterpiece of surveillance—both domestic and foreign—that could track down pretty much anyone and also track vehicles in real-time and more.

"Yes. Yes, you are. Speaking of the first team, have we made any progress in trying to identify and locate your old team member, Adam Afton?

Granger smiled and nodded. "Yes, sir, I believe we have. I was going to provide Edvin with the data before you left." He paused and nodded to Rebecca so that she could return to work. He then led Werner and his aide away from her desk. "We were able to identify several dozen males with three sisters, but one stood out . . . for obvious reasons. His name is Aric Afton. However, we could find no record of a brother, just the three sisters."

Werner frowned.

"That was our initial reaction, too, sir. We could not find any birth records for a brother, but curiously, the parents' tax filings from their son's early years showed them taking exemptions for five dependents, not four. Those exemptions continued until Aric Afton was 11 years old. At that time, they began taking only four, which means—"

"Which means a sibling who was roughly ten years older at the time could no longer be claimed as a dependent." Werner smiled. They had a serious lead.

"Well, sir, yes, it could mean that. It could also mean a

sibling who died. However, we've found no death records so far. We also found no birth records for such a sibling . . . or for Aric for that matter. There's always a possibility they were born elsewhere. It will take us weeks to scour all U.S. records."

Werner contemplated that information. The man was correct. Both scenarios were possible, but in his gut, he knew that this young Aric Afton held the key to finding the man who could speed up their software development logarithmically.

They were about to leave when Werner recalled Edvin's comment in the car.

"By the way, Edvin mentioned that one of your searches pointed to a potential threat against Big Pharma."

Granger nodded. "We uncovered nothing specific, but PfenRich Pharmaceuticals seems to be the target. I will keep Edvin updated if we find any details."

"Thank you."

As they walked to the limo, Werner contemplated that last piece of information. PfenRich was the producer of their COVID vaccine and a source of considerable wealth for many influential players in a variety of U.S. government agencies, as well as Werner personally. They were a massive transnational corporation with 10 manufacturing sites and eight research centers within the U.S. alone. How could anyone, or any group, plan an attack on them? A single attack on any single facility would simply be like cutting off the head of the Hydra. Two would grow back in its place.

SIX

The day's festivities had now moved back to the Larson's home where a cookout was planned to honor Aric and his award. Pastor Larson had retreated to the backyard to load up his pellet grill, while the women had congregated in the kitchen. Adam didn't find his dad in either place and presumed he had snuck off somewhere for a brief nap. He was notorious for his afternoon naps.

Adam checked the time. Over a dozen members of Aric's youth group were expected to descend upon the house at any time. He needed to find Aric before that.

Fortuitously, Aric walked out of the kitchen with a can of flavored seltzer water in hand just as Adam rounded the corner in the hallway. Adam almost ran into him.

"Hey, I need to talk with you."

"Pastor Tom wants me to help him out back." Aric took a swig of the water.

Adam nodded. "No problem, but this is urgent and won't take but a minute."

"Okay."

Adam ushered his younger brother out the front door. "I

need to warn you. My software picked up on someone looking for a male with two or more sisters born in or living in St. Louis. I think they're looking for you to try to find me."

Aric furrowed his brow. "That seems like a stretch. Why do you think that?"

Adam could see how he might come to that conclusion. "The people who are searching appear to be rebuilding AlterNet."

Aric stopped mid-drink and said, "Oh."

Adam could envision the "wheels" turning in Aric's mind.

"Okay, sound conclusion, but why not just call you?" asked Aric.

Adam had never told his brother much about AlterNet, just enough to solicit his help in taking down Chamberlain and the child trafficking ring. "Because I can't be found. I no longer exist." He proceeded to tell Aric what he hadn't shared with him during their escapades in Portland and back, as well as what he'd done to erase himself electronically.

Aric smirked. "Cool. So, you don't have to pay taxes? Sweet."

Adam knew he was joking around. Aric was smart enough to understand the ramifications of what he'd just been told.

"Okay, I can see that they'd want you back to work on the new program. And I can see how such a program can't be good for anyone who values freedom. But do you really think we're in danger? I mean, if they can't find any birth record for you or me, why would they continue to bother with us? There must be other males with three sisters that fit the bill. Even with the Afton surname."

Adam shook his head. "That's just it. There aren't. Across

the entire country, there's not one other Afton family that fits the search. Yes, other families meet the parameters, but they'll focus on the Afton name. It's too obvious." Adam felt an urgent need to impress one thing upon his brother. "These people won't stop looking if they think I'm alive, and they'll use any means necessary to get the information they want. Any means. If they follow their usual MO, they'll send out official-looking people first, maybe even FBI agents, to question family members and neighbors. If that doesn't bring results, they'll send out goons who don't care about laws or who they injure."

Aric took a deep breath. "Okay, okay. I got a taste of that two years ago." He paused. "Look, I think it's time you enlisted more people. And you need to bring Rachel and your kids into the loop."

Adam didn't like that idea, particularly about involving his family. They were about to be reunited. Postponing that reunification was one thing. Eliminating it was another.

Aric continued, "As I see it, the people who know you're still alive are right here in this house, along with your family. Oh, and Gwyneth and her husband. Our neighbors back home all know you disappeared and how upset our folks were about it. But they don't know you're alive and well. I understand if you're reluctant. The more people who know a secret, the harder it is to contain, but sometimes you gotta do what you gotta do."

Adam wondered where Aric was going with this. "And what do you have in mind?"

Aric proceeded to tell him his idea. Adam saw some reason in it until Aric got to the part about enlisting everyone's help in propagating the secret. He could certainly plant a fake death certificate somewhere. That was easy. And he agreed that having everyone in on it would be ideal, but . . .

"Think this through a bit more, little brother. How do you think mom's going to react? Not just about trying to be convincing that I'm dead but about learning about what we went through. Plus, do you really think that she's told no one about my coming home with Grace that Thanksgiving after we found her? She's probably told everyone she knows about Grace. And chatty Eloise? Do you honestly think she'll never tell anyone?"

"Well, uh . . . good points."

"And what about Jess? Do you think her folks are going to be wild about their daughter pursuing a relationship with someone who might be or become a target for some truly evil people? Would *she* have seconds thoughts herself?"

Aric looked a bit crestfallen at that idea. "You're right. That thought never crossed my mind."

"But I like your idea about a planted death certificate. Maybe the county where we found the laboratory and children, wherever Camp Douglas is."

Aric nodded. "Oh, and make it a single gunshot wound to the head. With ballistics matching Buckner's gun. You have that data, right?"

"That I do. Nice dramatic touch there, brother. I like it." Adam nodded. Indeed he did. And he knew just how to plant it into the search routines of the new AlterNet. Maybe that would preempt any need to send personnel out asking questions.

George Fleming hadn't always been known by that name. However, he had set out to make right something that had affected his entire family, and a new identity was in order. He glanced in the mirror. His scraggly beard had succumbed to a razor, and his face showed its clean-shaven self for the first time in a decade. His dreadlocks were likewise gone, replaced by a cut any young businessman might sport. In fact, in his new suit, he looked like any other of the thousands of millennial businessmen who walked the streets of New York City. Precisely the look he wanted, and far from the grunge band look of his recent musical past.

He placed his freshly crafted ID into the new wallet he'd purchased the previous week and laid them on the top of the chest holding most of his other clothes. The short-term apartment rental cost him more than he'd anticipated, but its location was perfect. The studio apartment of less than 600 square feet ran $2550 for the month, but it was on the same block as PfenRich Pharmaceuticals' headquarters. Indeed, he could see it from his windows. If his revenge went according to plan, he wouldn't have to leave the apartment to exact it. So, for this endeavor, the expense was worth it.

He sat at the small desk and continued to wind the fine copper wire meticulously around the explosive payload. Who would have thought that a 50-plus-year-old *Popular Science* magazine would provide him with everything he needed to know about the device he now created? Back then, the article touted buying everything necessary at your local hardware store for less than $400. Today, the cost was much higher, but the materials were almost as easily obtained. And, less than an hour's search on the deep web had provided him with refinements he could make to assure him the device would function as expected, with greater range and efficiency.

Adam wasted no time upon returning home. He downloaded a death certificate from Juneau County and determined who had been the medical examiner two years earlier. Like many rural counties, there was no physician as the coroner. The ME was a paramedic certified as a medicolegal death investigator, but forensic autopsies were performed at the University of Wisconsin-Madison.

His fingers flew across the keyboard as he completed his own death certificate. However, he spelled his last name as "Aften." Once completed, he placed it into the county's electronic records in such a way that it fit in with the date he had used. He then hacked into the files of the pathologist and found a report that closely matched the details he wanted. He modified that report and filed it for an appropriate date. He directed the system to forward this to the ME's files and insert itself within the database, where he again massaged the time stamps to make it look two years old.

Satisfied that even the best forensic computer examiner would not see anything but two-year-old reports filed as expected, he stood up and stretched. It was almost one a.m., but he felt energized. He stepped outside into the brisk autumn night air and gazed up toward the heavens. He loved the minimal light pollution in the area. Some nights he could stand and watch as a dozen shooting stars fell to earth over the course of an hour. On particularly spectacular nights, the Milky Way lit up the sky. Tonight, there was just enough of a haze to obscure the galaxy that Earth called home.

Time for part two of his plan.

He returned to the pathology files and found his record. Using a date roughly six months after that of the original filing, he amended the record to add the ballistics that pointed to "Buck" Buckner's handgun. This, too, was forwarded to the ME's database with the appropriate time stamps corrected.

He stood and paced a bit. The final phase of his plan was trickier. The date of this time stamp was critical. He had to assume that the new AlterNet had searched for him. But when? To make the next changes seem to have occurred before that search would be questioned. After all, the earlier search should have turned up his record.

He chose to date the changes to just a week earlier. Calling up the pathology file again, he added more corroborating data about Buckner and changed the spelling of his name to its true spelling, with a note about the misspelling. If all went well, the new AlterNet would now find the report along with a rational explanation about why it hadn't done so before.

He crossed his fingers on his left hand and hit 'Enter' with his right.

SEVEN

Caleb had had enough and finally took to social media to voice his concerns over what he was seeing in his practice. And for the first night in weeks, he did not have the nightmare.

"Well, you look unusually refreshed," said his wife, Ally, as he strode into the kitchen for breakfast.

"I am. No nightmare last night."

She cocked her head and scrutinized him. She had voiced her concern about the toll those dreams had been taking on him.

"What's different?" she asked.

"I laid it all out on social media as we talked about. I'm going to start collecting specific cases and statistics. Maybe write a paper."

"That could be interesting," she replied. "Didn't you recently tell me about some study by a Dr. Thorpe?"

He nodded. "James Thorpe. He's well-known and published in our field of maternal-fetal medicine. I reposted links to his study last night, too."

"Good. People need to wake up."

She had been the one to urge him to go forward with his

numbers. She had told him that she felt almost the same level of distress that he felt at the dramatic rise in miscarriages, stillbirths, menstrual irregularities, and more that he told her about almost nightly. He was glad that she didn't jump into getting the COVID vax. His first wife had died of a pulmonary embolus, a blood clot from her leg that went to her lungs. With all of the bizarre clotting issues being reported by morticians dealing with the vaccinated dead, he didn't want to go through that again.

Both Caleb and Ally had had the virus, at least that's what the test had shown a year earlier. Why would anyone think that a vaccine could provide better immunity than having the infection itself? Made no sense. Both had avoided the vaccine, although it took some manipulation on his behalf to get out of the mandates for healthcare personnel to be vaccinated. He avoided that subject whenever possible. What he did was likely not totally legal, maybe not even partially.

They had talked about the potential ramifications of going public, but neither expected the hospital to do more than slap him on the wrist . . . if anything. The hospital hated anything controversial that could provoke bad press for it, but they continually pushed "trusting the science." Thorpe's paper was hardcore science. How could they argue against it? Plus, Caleb's OB/GYN practice brought in significant capital. He was one of their biggest money makers . . . as far as the administrator and other number crunchers were concerned. To them, dollars spoke louder than patients' well-being.

"I think we should celebrate." With that, she opened the fridge and brought out a pack of cherry-smoked bacon.

He smiled. Breakfast meats in their household were

typically reserved for weekends and holidays. He had expected oatmeal, or a toasted bagel, maybe raisin bran, for breakfast. For bacon, he didn't care if he was a little late getting into the office.

The drive into the office was an easy one. It seemed that the day would be a magnificent one, from a good night's sleep to bacon to the almost traffic-free drive to his office. He parked in his reserved slot and sauntered into the office through their back door.

Unlike the mood at home, the staff here seemed dour. He stood at the unit manager's desk reviewing his appointments and surgery schedule for the day. He had a full day ahead and hoped no emergencies would arise to throw off the day. Was it too much to ask that breaking the "curse" of the nightmare would somehow bleed over into his practice? As he thought that, he realized using the word 'bleed' was inappropriate. A bad pun at its worst. Still . . .

Sha'Kyra walked through the doors to his clinic and headed directly toward him. He groaned at the thought that she bore bad news and that another patient was about to disrupt his schedule before he even started.

"G'mornin', Sha. Lost? L&D is that way." He pointed in the direction of the labor wing. She didn't smile.

She sidled up to the counter and put one elbow on it. "Caleb, Massey was in L&D looking for you. He didn't look or sound very happy."

"Does he ever?"

Greg Massey, the hospital administrator, rarely came looking for anyone in person. His usual modus operandi was to call and request your presence in his office. For the most serious matters, he'd send his secretary to "invite" you to a meeting. Caleb had never been the focus of such urgent meetings. His appointments were scheduled well in advance and centered around equipment or staffing needs, as well as revenues. So, that the man was looking for him in person seemed ominous.

Massey's attitude toward him had always been somewhat stilted. It was almost as if the man was jealous of Caleb's success and ease with other people. Massey was somewhat socially inept and very much a "by the book" kind of guy. He would frequently make snide remarks about Caleb in the presence of others. Caleb tolerated him because the man had succeeded in building the birthing center Caleb had longed for.

"I'm being serious. Anyone who's worked here longer than six months knows how that guy operates. What'd you do?"

He wasn't quite sure but had his suspicions. Could his social media posts already have made waves?

"I posted what we've been seeing since the jab started. The rise in miscarriages and stuff. I also reposted links to Dr. Thorpe's study."

Sha took a deep breath and sighed. "I thought we talked about that."

He nodded. "We did, but I never agreed to stay quiet. I've had enough." He paused to gauge her reaction. "Good news is, I didn't have the nightmare last night."

She muttered something.

"What? Speak up."

"I said it might just be a new nightmare to take its place."

"Caleb, I need to talk with you!"

Caleb hadn't heard the door open, but Massey's voice was

clear and unmistakable.

She whispered, "Been nice workin' with you." She turned around to face the administrator. "Good morning again, Mr. Massey. I was just leaving, unless you need me for something."

The man shook his head. "Not at all. I'll see you around."

Caleb watched her leave the clinic and then faced Massey. "What's up, Greg?"

The man cleared his throat. "Well, I'll get to the point. I received a few calls this morning about some social media posts you made last night."

Caleb instantly didn't like the tone in the man's voice.

"Oh? So, the hospital's monitoring everyone's social media now?"

"No, no. Not from my office. Two of the trustees and a couple of reporters."

"I see." He decided not to volunteer any information and to see where this was headed.

"Seems you're spreading misinformation about the COVID vaccine and its effect on women."

Caleb shook his head. "No." He paused for a second. "No, I'm pretty sure I haven't posted any misinformation about it at all."

Massey retrieved his phone from his pocket and displayed one of Caleb's posts. "This."

"Well, that's not misinformation. That's called truth, Greg. Those are just a small collection of numbers from what I'm seeing in my practice here. And Dr. Thorpe's study is solid science. You know, the stuff you're always preaching about, that the hospital is fond of following."

Massey seemed ruffled at that comment. Caleb hoped he

hadn't come across too strong, but knew he probably had. The guy had thinner skin than an onion and could be just as irritating.

"Greg, I'm going to survey my patient records and pull together some real-life stats for you. After seeing those, then tell me I'm posting misinformation."

Massey shook his head. "No, you won't. Those records are hospital property, and you'll do nothing of the kind."

"Really, Greg? You want to stick your head in the sand and pretend we're not seeing the increases I posted about? What's with you? Do these women and their unborn children mean nothing to you?"

Massey stiffened. "Caleb, I mean it. You're not to use hospital records for any such study, and no more posts like this."

"Or what?"

"Or your position here will be terminated."

Caleb paused. He and Ally had postulated that the hospital might take such a hard stance, but they had discounted that possibility. His clinical and procedural revenues for the hospital were too great. Or so they thought.

But this was the last straw. To be threatened for telling the truth was just too much.

"Wowww. I never thought I'd see the day that Greg Massey caved to politics. That's exactly what this is. And the politicos don't give a feces about women's health, or anyone else's for that matter."

Caleb leaned over the counter and picked up the phone. He pressed a number to speed dial the office manager.

"Hey, Helen. It's me. Cancel all of my appointments and

surgeries for the day. Actually, make that for the rest of the week. After that, the hospital can decide who will cover my appointments."

"Uh? A-all of them?"

"Yep, all of them. I'm going home. Thanks. Oh, and I won't be on call here anymore either. I've been terminated."

Massey's eyes widened, but his mouth gaped open wider. "Wha? Wait, you can't do that."

"I just did. You just said I'm terminated."

"I did not. I said—"

Caleb pulled out his cell phone, called up one of his social media apps, and hurriedly typed a new post: *From what I'm seeing in my practice, the COVID jab is destroying women's fertility and is a clear risk to the developing baby. More to come. Oh, and I've just been terminated from my hospital practice because I'm standing up for your health*. He showed what he'd typed to Massey and hit the post button.

"There. Per your statement of a few minutes ago, I'm terminated. I'll clean out my desk and be gone."

He turned and headed toward his private office. After several steps, he turned back to the hospital administrator to see him standing there looking unsure as to what had just happened. "By the way, Greg, don't forget. I have no non-compete clause in my contract."

As he turned away, a smile crept across his face. Massey had been all too willing to eliminate their standard non-compete clause because he saw only the dollar signs in getting Caleb's practice there. Now, Caleb let that come back to bite him.

And yet, as Caleb entered his office, he began to question

what he'd just done. Had he overreacted? He'd never found Massey a likable sort, and Massey had pushed his hot buttons before. However, the health of the women and babies in his practice was of paramount importance to him. To threaten those lives in any way was a major hot button for him, and Massey had pressed that one hard just then. Yet, who would tend to their health now? Who would stand up for them?

Yep, maybe he had overreacted. His anger had gotten the better of him. Maybe he should have just quietly amassed his practice's stats, continued to post his findings, and called Massey's bluff. Or not. Now he had to deal with it, but how?

EIGHT

Werner dined in his jet as it passed over the French coast on its way to Munich. After the G20 assembly and meetings in the U.S., he looked forward to a few days at their home on his wooded estate sitting on the eastern side of the *Starnberger See*. Starnberg Lake was southwest of Munich and his estate sat just outside the small town of Münsing. The glacier-carved lake was where King Ludwig II of Bavaria was found dead in 1886 and was the headwater for the Würm River.

The *Nördliche Seestraße*, or Nordic Walking trail, passed between their home and the lake. The trail was part of a system of paths and roads that enabled one to walk around the entire lake. Although at 30 miles in length, most people chose to bike the trail if they wished to circumnavigate the lake in a single day. This was a beautiful time of the year for such a trek. If he could convince his wife to join him, he might take on part of that adventure. At his age, the full trip, even on bikes, was a bit daunting.

The chef had done a wonderful job preparing his rouladen with potato dumplings, red cabbage, and gravy. Yes, he could find classic German fare overseas, but there was always something special about it at home, and his chef was able to capture that.

For dessert, the chef had made one of his specialties, sacher torte. Werner often bragged to others about this delicious chocolate cake and for years had tried to wheedle the chef into giving up his secret for making his torte so special. The man would only zip his fingers across his closed lips. However, €500 had persuaded his sous chef into spilling the beans. The chef made his own cherry brandy as part of the filling, but that process remained hidden even from the sous chef. Werner recalled laughing at the revelation. For €500 he had learned, and yet not learned, the secret. He imagined the two men splitting the reward and laughing that they still hadn't given away a "trade secret."

Werner valued mealtimes as a time to focus on the food, company, and conversation. And, although the latter two were rarely included while he dined in the air, his rule to not be disturbed still held force. As the last of his dinnerware was removed from the table, his laptop chimed. He wasn't anticipating any calls. Yet, someone wished to talk with him.

"Ah, Edvin, I didn't expect to hear from you tonight."

His aide had stayed behind in the States to follow up on the progress with AlterNet2, among other matters. He was slated to join Werner at the office in Munich in a week.

"My apologies, sir, if I'm disturbing you."

"Not at all. What do you have for me?"

"Well, sir, nothing new on the software development, but their search routines did come up with something this afternoon that I wanted to pass on to you as soon as I could."

The young man piqued Werner's interest.

"It would appear that Adam Afton is dead."

That was not news that Werner wished to hear. That man was their one best chance at speeding up the development of AlterNet2.

"And we're only learning this now? Is there a flaw in the software that has been searching for him?"

"No, sir. It would appear that the original death certificate misspelled his last name."

His aide went on to explain the mix-up—how the misspelling was just recently corrected, that the forensics pointed to a gun owned and used by Wallace Chamberlain's thug, Buckner, and that the time and place of death fit with what they knew about Buckner's whereabouts before his death.

Werner sat back in his seat feeling a bit defeated. Everything fit—the timing, the means of death, and the error that led to their not finding this earlier. Everything except . . .

"Something isn't right here, Edvin. If this is true, and it all sounds plausible, why have we found nothing else on this man, Adam Afton? No birth certificate, no employment records, no social security number, no tax records. Nothing except the sudden emergence of a death certificate."

"That bothered me at first, too. But, sir, if you think about it, while alive he could cover his tracks and erase himself from these databases. But dead, he no longer could do that. That would be the one record he could never delete."

Edvin had a point. Werner considered that, but his gut told him not to believe it.

"Or, he has learned that we are searching for him and has planted this document to make us believe just what you said.

Did we trigger something when we found Aric Afton and his sisters? Has he been following us all along? He might even be able to track everything we're doing with AlterNet2. That would not be good."

The look of anxiety on Edvin's face matched his own level of concern. To have a mole, so to speak, within their development program held disastrous possibilities. What if he was able to completely wipe out their efforts? Let them get to a point of reasonable functionality and delete it all.

"Edvin, you must alert Herr Granger to the danger. They must refocus their efforts on building up their internal security. We can't afford to have someone penetrate their systems and delete everything."

Edvin nodded. "Understood. Yes, sir, I will do that as soon as we end our call."

"Good. And I think the timing of this, right after finding Aric Afton, is suspicious, too. Get some people out there in St. Louis to check up on this family. Talk with neighbors, friends, coworkers, but be discreet. We do not want to alert the family if at all possible."

"Yes, sir. I'll get on it right away."

Upon disconnecting the call, Werner shook his head. This was not a favorable turn of events. And yet, he felt convinced that this Adam Afton was out there somewhere. However, being out there or not, it seemed evident that he wanted nothing to do with AlterNet2. And then another thought hit him. The man still had the original program, perhaps refined even further. That made him triply dangerous. Werner wanted that program. He needed to double down on finding Adam Afton and the program . . . if it existed.

However, to do that he needed help beyond their current resources. He collected his cell phone and placed a call to a very private number, one that bypassed the White House switchboard. He expected one of two voices to answer and was not disappointed with who did.

"Werner, so soon. It's late in the day, and the president is not at his best."

Werner expected as much. The old man could only tolerate so much of the adrenochrome daily. He likely wouldn't understand what Werner needed, much less be able to remember it to make it happen. But his chief-of-staff would. He explained his need to utilize the FBI, intelligence operatives, and full resources of the U.S. to find one Adam Afton, or whatever name he went by now.

NINE

Anson Hardy had been educated in the public school system of his hometown, had close friends who were teachers, and largely had no complaints about the local unified school district where his five kids attended various levels of education. His oldest, Elizabeth, attended eighth grade in the nearby middle school, while the others, spaced two years apart were in the same elementary school.

His youngest, Jason, attended kindergarten five full days a week, for which he felt grateful. He vaguely recalled his own kindergarten being five half days. With both he and his wife working, he had no idea how they could have managed half days. Few, if any, daycare programs accepted half-day attendees.

He walked toward the kindergarten door to retrieve Jason personally at the end of the day. He appreciated that attention to security as well. The other kids, being older, had been instructed to team up together to come to the car. Jason was typically buckled into his booster seat by the time they arrived.

"Hey, dad. I got a question for you."

"I *have* a question, you mean."

"That's what I said."

Anson chuckled and sighed.

"I told my teacher I was going to marry Annie when we grow up."

That surprised Anson. "You did? You must like Annie."

"Yeah, she shares her lunch with me. Anything she doesn't want, she gives to me."

Anson smiled. "I see. That sounds nice of her. We've talked about sharing a lot, remember?"

Jason nodded. "Yeah. When I said that, Ms. Kittridge told me that I didn't have to marry Annie. I could marry another boy instead."

Anson felt sucker punched. "What?"

"Yeah, she said boys could marry boys and girls could marry girls. Is that right?"

Anger welled up inside the father. Sternly, he replied, "No, Jason, God says boys marry girls, not other boys."

He felt like confronting this Ms. Kittridge right then and there, but his three other children had appeared by the car and were opening the doors. He helped them with seat belts and placed their bags in the back. That teacher would have to wait. He checked his phone for the time. Elizabeth had volleyball for an hour after school, so dad's taxi would have just enough time to get the younger brood home, supplied with a snack, see his wife as her virtual workday ended, and head back to the middle school for Bethy.

Since both he and Hannah worked IT, they were able to work from home and alternate days for school pickups. They loved working virtually. They saved money on gas, as well as wear and tear on the cars. Their days were shorter, having no commute to add to the hours, and they could be more productive. Lunch was easy, too. And the flexibility for dealing with the kids was a game-changer compared to pre-pandemic days.

Sadly, those days were threatened by statements from their companies about returning to in-person office hours. Anson wondered if he would have to return to freelance work. In ways, it had been more lucrative, but the job security wasn't there. Still, one of them would have to sacrifice the guaranteed paycheck to have the flexibility needed for the kids.

At home, he glanced at the time again, kissed his wife goodbye, and headed off to retrieve their eldest. Expecting to wait ten or fifteen minutes as usual, he was surprised to see her sitting in front of the school . . . in her gym clothing at that. As he got closer, he noted that she seemed distressed and had been crying.

He pulled up and proceeded to open his door to get out, but she ran to the car and jumped in before he could pass by the headlight on his side. He returned to his seat.

"Sweetie, what's wrong?"

She didn't answer, and that got him worried. She'd never hesitated to talk with him before.

"Can we talk?" he asked.

Tears welled up again. "I-I need to talk with mom. It's . . . it's, well, a girl thing."

"Okay. Let's get home then."

He was a bit heavy on the accelerator until he saw another car pulled over by a police officer and noted his speed. He eased off the pedal, but they still made it home in record time.

Bethy ran inside and straight to her room. He found Hannah in the kitchen adding something to the slow cooker.

"Hey. You might want to go see our eldest. Something happened at school, but she wouldn't talk with me on the way home. Said it's a girl thing."

Hannah furrowed her brow. "Can't be her period. That ended a week ago. Hmmm." She stirred the pot, which Anson hoped would not be foretelling of what would happen next. "I'll go talk with her now," she said as she placed the lid back on the cooker.

The clock on the microwave said it was too early for a beer, but what did it know? He grabbed a cold one, popped its tab, and took a long, cold drink. He sat down at the kitchen table and waited for Hannah. He nursed that brew for 20 minutes before she reappeared. She went straight to the cabinet, retrieved a wine glass, filled it with Cabernet from a previously opened bottle, and sat next to him.

If she was already having wine, he knew he didn't want to hear what she had to say. So, he thought he could put it off by telling her about Jason's conversation with his teacher.

"Do you know Ms. Kittridge? I haven't met her yet."

"She's new. She took over for Susan Harris when she went out on maternity leave."

"Okay." He proceeded to tell her what happened with Jason. "I'm not happy with this woman. Telling a kindergartner he can marry someone of his own gender. She needs to go."

Hannah took a deep breath, followed by two more swigs of wine. "It gets worse."

"Huh?" He'd been reading about school systems

promoting the LGBT+ agenda, but those were flaky east and west coast school districts, not their district in the Midwest.

"There's a boy who identifies as a girl, who has been accepted on the girls' volleyball team. The school is allowing him, uh, her, uh, whatever, to change in the girls' locker room, and they're forcing the girls to accept it. All of the girls are upset and refuse to undress in front of him, and they don't want him undressing in front of them. When they complained, the coach told them they had to accept him. They have no choice."

That was it. Two of his kids hit with that nonsense on the same day. That did not bode well.

"When's the next school board meeting? I'm gonna be there."

TEN

Adam sat at his computer consoles and worked through the results of his new search for the fourth man. He had been introduced to Adam as Seth. Chamberlain had had a distorted appreciation for the Bible and had given each of them "code names" to be used in all communications. Adam was, unsurprisingly, Adam, while Rebecca was Eve. Sam had been Able, which would have been fitting if Buckner had been Cain, but Buckner was just Buckner. If there had been another Cain, Adam knew nothing about him.

Of course, in working together, real names came out. Chamberlain had lost the battle to keep everyone's real names buried amongst the team. That's how Adam knew Rebecca's true name, and vice versa. That reality was also responsible for Chamberlain's insistence on compartmentalizing the work.

At this point in time, however, the name Simon Sŏk had been effectively buried and forgotten by the man himself. Adam could find no trace of him, whether within the U.S., Korea, or anywhere else in the world.

His latest search involved the parameters he had recalled

two days earlier while driving to Kenosha, as well as a variety of misspellings of the name. Using the parameters alone had drawn a blank . . . unless he had become a she. He shook his head and thought, *No way, not gonna happen.* Several women turned up as Simone Sŏk in the search using those parameters, but no males.

As he reviewed the data, another memory surfaced. The man was a serious lover of weird music styles. He had preferred to call his tastes eclectic. True to that love, though, the man was a talented guitarist and more than proficient on the keyboard. Adam had once been invited to one of Simon's gigs and had heard him play firsthand. How had he forgotten that night until now?

As he added those new details to his search, an alert sounded from his system. He scrolled through to find the alert notice. He loved Ring doorbells. He found close to a dozen along the street where his parents lived and set up intercepts on each. Over the past two days, only two of them had rung. Each alert showed only a delivery by UPS. He expected the same for this alert.

However, he was dismayed to see two men in dark suits standing at the door to the home of one of their parents' immediate neighbors. One man held a credentials packet in his hand, although Adam couldn't see what those credentials were.

Adam knew that both the man and his wife worked outside the home, so whoever these guys were, they were going to be out of luck at that house. The doorbell's camera showed them leaving and walking across the street to another house. That neighbor had no Wi-Fi security cams nor a smart doorbell. Adam was able to keep the camera on long enough to see the woman of the house answer the door and begin to talk with the men. He wished he could see the creds that the man had shown her.

Old Mrs. Campbell had been widowed five years earlier and was lonely. His mom had befriended her and often took her baked treats when she made them for the family or others. If anyone among the neighbors could confirm Adam's existence, she could. Fortunately, she knew nothing of consequence about Adam's family or his current whereabouts. At least, he didn't think she did.

He pounded the desktop in frustration. His death certificate ploy had seemed perfect.

Now, whoever was behind the resurrection of AlterNet would know that he was alive and well, even if they wouldn't be able to track him down. On the positive side, ever since his cooperative efforts with The Remnant, he had used Mike Jurgesmeyer's unique software to completely delete all traces of a phone call or text between him and his family, or with anyone else for that matter. On the negative side, Mrs. Campbell knew where Aric attended college.

Adam needed to warn his brother. He grabbed his phone but then thought better of that. If they had an active tap on Aric's phone, they could capture the call and record it before he could permanently delete it. That was the one major weakness in Jurgesmeyer's program—it only worked upon completion of the call or text.

No, he needed to warn him indirectly. And then he would need pay-as-you-go phones—burners to use Hollywood parlance—for both of them.

Aric finished his morning routine at the dorm with time to spare, so he decided to text Jess and see if she could meet him before class outside the admin building.

Ready to head out. Meet me at the admin building?

He walked as slowly as he could toward the elevators, hoping she would reply promptly. With no response prior to exiting the lift on the ground floor, he eased toward the main doors, again hoping for her answer.

Her text finally appeared as he exited the building.

I'll try. Will need to push Chris along. He's dawdling.

He nodded in understanding. They shared the car, and his class started 15 minutes after hers, so he hesitated to arrive on campus any earlier than necessary for her to rush to class.

As he looked up from his phone, he noted a man he'd not seen before dressed in running gear who was bent over making it appear as if he was tying a shoe. But the laces were already tied. The guy wasn't a student. Too old. Maybe an alumnus. They had access to the athletic center just like the students.

He continued toward the admin building but glanced back twice. The man's gaze seemed to follow him. After Adam's caution two days earlier, maybe he was being paranoid.

Up ahead was something else out of place—a white van with government plates. It sat in a "No Parking - Loading Zone" area of the main drive. The only thing loaded or unloaded there was foodstuffs for the cafeterias. What would a government van be doing there? As he neared it, he noticed that it was idling, and a man sat in the driver's seat. Even more unusual.

As he closed in on the van, about to pass by it on the passenger side, he heard footsteps behind him. The man in running clothes appeared to be closing in on him. His heart accelerated. Was this about to be a scene straight out of the movies? Was he about to get shoved into the van and taken away?

"Hey, Aric!"

The three guys from the football team that he'd gotten to know during his very first J-term were heading toward him. He waved!

Mitch Johnson, one of the starting ends on the team, feigned drowning and yelled, "Save me, my hero, save me!" in the best falsetto he could manage. His friends, Zach and Dan, laughed and all three rushed up to Aric with paper and pens in hand.

"Autograph?"

"Can I get your autograph?"

Aric laughed but obliged each one of them.

Dan looked at his. "Hey, that says 'Captain America.' "

"Mine says 'Chris Pratt.' "

Mitch laughed as he looked at his paper. "Gee, you sure don't look like Taylor Swift."

As they busted his chops over his big award, Aric noted the van slowly pull away. No big deal there. But when he saw the van stop and let the man in the running gear enter the passenger door, he took notice.

He needed to get hold of Adam. But how? If they—whoever 'they' were—were onto Aric, he didn't want to risk making a phone call. Those were too easily traced, and a tapped phone meant recorded conversations. He could no longer risk driving to Adam's place either. He could turn off the location on his phone but that wouldn't stop them from tracking him. That just made it a bit harder to do.

He thought about using Jess or Chris as a go-between, but he didn't want them involved. Besides, if these people had done their homework on Aric, they'd already know about Jess. They'd be watching her, maybe her whole family, just as closely.

Yes, he really needed to connect with Adam. He just had to figure out the best way to do that.

ELEVEN

Adam hopped into his Audi and began the trek toward the college. He had the perfect person to act as his middleman. Ryan Krueger had been a Portland, Oregon, police officer who'd been fed to the political lions. Like Daniel, however, he came out of that debacle unscathed. Mostly. He had to leave Portland and returning home to SE Wisconsin seemed like the wisest choice. Adam had been instrumental in getting him a coveted position on the campus police.

As he drove, he told his car to dial the officer's cell phone.

"Adam, to what do I owe this honor?"

"Hey, Ryan. How are Sarah and the boys?"

"Doing great. We owe you the world. That house and property you got us couldn't have been more perfect. And this job, well, it's a piece of cake compared to PPD."

Adam nodded. His thoughts returned to Sam Renner and the memory of the man dying in his arms. He had owed it to Sam to pass on his estate to his half-brother. Not to mention that Ryan had saved Aric by helping to pull him from that icy water. He should have gotten the same award as his brother.

"I'm heading your way. Can we meet someplace for lunch?

Someplace out of the way."

"I know just the spot."

Less than an hour later, Adam pulled into the parking lot of a place called The Beer Gardens. Located in a lower-class neighborhood behind some light industry, it didn't appear to be the kind of place where Adam would run into anyone he knew. Of course, why would he expect to run into anyone he knew when he didn't live here?

He spotted Ryan as soon as he entered through the plate-glass door. The man's campus police uniform stood out from the potpourri of flannels that seemed to make up the majority of folks' wardrobes there. The "atmosphere" was one of a typical tavern, with a long bar filling half the room and high-top tables for four lining the opposite wall. The place appeared to have started with an addition to an old house, followed by multiple add-ons over time, which led to a maze of small seating areas.

After shaking hands, Adam said, "Smells great."

Ryan took a sip of coffee, and then replied, "I learned of this place from Professor Cully. He seems to have a knack for finding hole-in-the-wall joints. Not much to look at, but the food's good." He laughed.

Adam's idea of culinary adventure was switching from an all-meat pizza to a deluxe with all the veggies included. So, the standard pub fare on the menu was perfect for him.

"Aric told me that Cully once took him to a place that served all sorts of game meat."

Ryan nodded. "Oh yeah. He had me go there once, too. Another fine dining, Kenosha establishment. I figure the next time I go should be on a Wednesday, and I can order a camel burger." He laughed, but Adam didn't get it. "A camel burger? On hump day?" He shook his head. "Nevermind. Dad joke."

With their orders in, Adam got down to business. He spoke in tones that would not be overheard.

"I know that you know little to nothing about me, and for your sake, that's probably a good thing. But I think some of my past is trying to catch up with me, and it's putting Aric in danger."

Ryan gave him a quizzical look. Adam wondered what the man was thinking, but he had a pretty good idea what it might be.

"To put your mind at ease, I was not wrapped up in anything illegal." He paused. Maybe that wasn't totally true. "Look, what I'm about to tell you has to remain confidential. I mean, completely confidential. Not even to other law enforcement types."

Ryan hesitated but nodded.

Adam continued, "Like Sam, I'm an IT guy. We developed a software program for the military that later fell into the hands of some unsavory characters, even though some of those characters once wore stars on their shoulders. Once we realized what the program was being used for, we started to collect evidence against our bosses. Well, our main boss primarily. That's what led to Sam being murdered. I've sort of been in hiding ever since."

Adam paused as their food arrived. He took a bite of his burger. *Pretty good*, he thought.

"Sounds a bit dramatic." Ryan paused. "I know you told me that Sam died in your arms, but you never elaborated. Am I to believe that he was killed because he knew too much about someone or certain people?"

Adam nodded. "That's exactly why. He had come to my apartment even though we had agreed never to meet at either of our homes. He was followed, and a sniper round through my front window killed him. I got away only because I had prepared an escape route in case they ever came for me."

Ryan took a deep breath. Anger crossed his face as he came to terms with how his brother was killed.

"Did you ever hear about a major child trafficking ring in central Wisconsin that was taken down by the FBI a couple of years ago?"

He hesitated but slowly shook his head negatively. "There's something vaguely familiar about that, but we only moved back here nine months ago, so I'm not sure."

"What about a dozen or so children's bodies being found in an old Civilian Conservation Corps camp at French's Dome near Mt. Hood?"

"Oh yeah, that was all over the Portland news. We were supposedly on high alert but never told for what."

"Aric and I uncovered those graves and alerted the authorities. We did so anonymously, and no one except he and I knew that until now. I'm taking you into our confidence. All of this has to remain confidential, even if I have to get you to swear on Sam's grave."

Ryan nodded and crossed his heart. "Man, if you two were behind uncovering that, you both deserve medals."

Adam shrugged. "Yeah, well, that led us to central Wisconsin where we uncovered another, still active, node of that trafficking ring. I know we did some significant damage to that group, but they had nodes, probably still have nodes, where they imprison children all over the country."

He finished the last of his double-bacon burger and fries and cleared his palate with the iced tea he'd ordered.

"So, you're saying you have enemies and maybe they're on to you?"

Adam thought about how to answer. "Well, yes and no. Our names were kept out of the FBI files, so that group doesn't know who we are or what role we played in that. Yes, if they caught wind of who we are, we'd both likely become targets. But their retaliation would more likely be a sniper's bullet that we'd never see coming. No, someone is trying to recreate the software that Sam and I developed and not for honorable purposes. You see, in order to hide, I've erased my identity. I no longer exist in any electronic database. I was very thorough. But they discovered and recruited another member of the team, and she gave them my name. She also knew a little bit about my family. When they couldn't find me, they started searching for my family. I think they've found Aric, and now they want to use him to get to me."

"So, just tell them you aren't available or don't want the job."

Adam shook his head. "They don't work that way. They'll use any means to get me to comply. They have no reservations about killing my family members one by one until I agree."

"You know that for sure? I mean, this is the United States. Stuff like that is for the movies."

Adam sighed. "Don't I wish. Look around, Ryan. Is this the same country you grew up in? You dealt with Antifa in Portland. Child trafficking is big business. The left keeps agitating to remove police through funding cuts, all the while crime rates explode. You were on the front lines. Why is it impossible to think they'd do that to my family? How many people with evidence on the Clintons are no longer with us? I'd tell you more about the program itself because then you'd understand, but you're better off not knowing. You know, the whole plausible deniability thing."

Ryan finished his coffee and put his hand over the cup as the waitress came by to top him off. Adam did the same with his iced tea.

Ryan gave Adam a steely look. "When you asked me to keep an eye on your brother, you mentioned shenanigans, not cold-blooded killers."

"I know. A year and a half ago, how was I to know this would happen? I thought I was in the clear, and Aric, too, by extension."

The waitress came by with the bill, which Adam quickly snatched. "On me. Least I can do for taking your time and hearing me out."

Ryan scooted his chair back and stood up. Adam paid the tab, and together they walked outside.

Ryan stopped next to a pickup that Adam assumed to be his. "Earlier on the phone, I told you we owed you the world for what you've done for us. I meant that. I will keep a closer eye on Aric, but understand that I can't cross the line into anything illegal."

Adam nodded. "Would never expect you to. Thank you." He held up one index finger. "One more thing. Give me a sec." He raced to his car, opened the passenger door, and retrieved a small box, which he took back to Ryan. "Would you give this to Aric? It's a phone he can use to contact me. Tell him not to use my other number and to erase it from his phone. The new number's written down inside. You can use it, too. Only you two and my dad will have this number. I need to keep that circle small. Okay?"

Ryan took the box and gave him a thumbs-up. "Got it. I'll keep in touch, but hopefully, only with good news."

"Thanks." They shook hands, and Adam turned toward his car. After a step, he turned back and said, "Let's do this again sometime. Next time we can do the camel on hump day."

Caleb walked into the kitchen at home, where he found his wife preparing lunch. She turned to him and smiled.

"It's been nice having you at home these last couple of days. Just wish it wasn't under the circumstances that led to it. Anyway, thought you'd be hungry."

She handed him a plate with a grilled cheese sandwich and homemade macaroni salad. He smiled at seeing the sandwich. Although her kids got your typical grilled cheese with white bread and American cheese, she had made his favorite— homemade sourdough bread, two kinds of cheese, and the bread slathered with mayonnaise instead of butter for grilling. He grabbed the carafe of filtered water from the fridge and poured a glass. He held the carafe up to her.

"Water?"

She shook her head. "No thanks. I still have some tea."

They sat down at the kitchen table, said grace, and began to eat. After a few bites, he sighed. "Sooo goood. Thanks."

She smiled. "I knew you'd like it."

After taking a drink, he said, "I talked with Ted." Edward

"Ted" Ngo was a good friend and lawyer, although they had never needed his services before. "He said that based on my contract, the hospital has no recourse against me. They might try to sue me for breach of contract, but such a suit would not succeed."

"Maybe. But defending yourself will cost some big bucks." She looked worried.

"I hear you. Fortunately, I've invested well, and even with this lousy market we're in, we can afford it. And when they lose, they'll have to reimburse all our costs. I'd insist on that."

"Still . . ."

He placed his hand over hers. "You know, don't worry about that. We once talked about creating a stand-alone birthing center. I've dusted off those old plans."

Indeed he had, but not without reservations. Did he truly want to stay in medicine? The profession had changed so much since corporate America took it over. The bottom line had become more important than patient care. And then, this whole COVID debacle, where good science and logic had been thrown out the window, now threatened the health of those he had committed to helping to the point where he had no remedies, just frustration.

"Yes, but that was before the hospital enticed you to come on staff. They built a new birthing center and brought in new doctors to help you. Do you think you can get state approval? You will still require a certificate of need."

He nodded as he chewed, but it was halfhearted. "That will be our biggest hurdle, proving the need." Indeed, he saw that as an almost insurmountable problem, or as he preferred to think of it, a God-sized problem. "One way or the other, God will provide." Yes, he had his faith to stand on. Or so he kept trying to convince himself. Maybe God was telling him to take a different path, to brush off old talents.

Of one thing he was certain, he wouldn't be offered a position with either of the other two hospital systems in town. They had been the most draconian in terms of requiring COVID vaccines, which had put them in worse staffing positions. One hospital had lost almost 20% of its staff. He had only had to work around a 10% loss in staff, and that was a major challenge. Of course, as he had witnessed just three days earlier, the jab itself would soon be taking its toll on their staffing. Staffing issues aside, they would not take his social media posts lightly either.

While he had focused on the obstetric and gynecologic ramifications of the mRNA vaccine, other studies had shown its effect on the heart and other major organs. One study revealed a 100% rate of myocarditis in vaccine recipients—100%. Of course, there were varying degrees of heart inflammation, so only the worst cases led to obvious consequences. Yet, younger, previously healthy people were dying of sudden deaths in which such myocarditis was the leading cause. Insurance authorities in the state of Indiana had led the way in exposing the 40% increase in excess deaths in that state since the beginning of the jab. More recent stats now showed that this increase in deaths occurred most in 18 to 65-year-olds with a high preponderance in employees of major corporations that had required the mRNA vaccine.

After cleaning up from lunch, which for him meant putting dishes in the dishwasher, he walked out to the mailbox to claim that day's mail. His heart skipped a beat as he found a large packet from Massey and the hospital. He calmed down as he recognized that it couldn't be a lawsuit. Local law enforcement would have served him with such documents if that were the case.

Back inside the house, he opened the other mail first. He wanted to be able to focus on the hospital's correspondence.

He took a deep breath and sliced open the large envelope. Inside, he found a formal letter of termination, along with a statement showing that he had seven days to complete all outstanding patient records. He sighed. He dreaded going back to the hospital for that, worried about the reception he might get. Yet, his dedication to patient care would push him to complete the records so as to prevent any gaps in care for the women he had treated. His anxiety eased as he realized he held the moral high ground and could walk into that building with his head held high.

The doorbell rang. As he passed the front windows, he noticed a postal truck in the driveway. Sure enough, a different postal carrier stood at the door.

"Good afternoon. I have a registered, certified letter for Dr. Caleb Wahlburg. I need a signature."

"Uh, that's me." Caleb signed for the letter, which the carrier then turned over to him.

"Have a nice day."

Somehow those words rang hollow. Since when was any day nice after receiving an unexpected, registered letter? He looked at the return address, and his heart sank. He tore open the envelope and found himself needing the closest chair to sit down.

The letter was from ACOG, the American College of

Obstetrics and Gynecology. The letter informed him that he was accused of professional misconduct and the spreading of misinformation to the detriment of the public. As such, they would be investigating the complaint. If found to be valid, they would require him to undergo social media training and re-education. Failure to do so would lead to his clinical board certification being revoked.

He bowed his head in silent prayer, but no answer was forthcoming.

TWELVE

Aric couldn't concentrate in class. The thought of being snatched brought up too many mental images of Hollywood kidnappings. And to think that whoever those guys were, they were willing to do it in broad daylight in front of dozens of witnesses. He looked to the front of the class and tried to focus on the professor but found it difficult.

His mind kept drifting back to that morning, and it bothered him that he hadn't paid attention to the details. He wouldn't be able to provide any sort of description. Certainly not any real details. And he hadn't even caught part of the license plate of the van, other than it had been a government tag. Or was it?

Here he was majoring in criminology, and he couldn't even be a good witness. The experience put the whole witness reliability issue into perspective.

But then, maybe he was just being paranoid. He didn't know everyone on campus, so just because he'd never seen the jogger before shouldn't imply the guy was watching him. On the other hand, the more he mentally perseverated on it, he was sure it was a government vehicle. Nobody with the government would kidnap an American on American soil, would they? This time he didn't want to use Hollywood plots as examples. They had government agencies kidnapping anybody anywhere. Warrants were an afterthought for Hollywood.

Still, why did his thoughts keep rebounding back to TV shows and movies he'd seen? He should know better.

Before he knew it, the professor was announcing the end of the class. He collected his books and the few scribbles of notes he'd managed to make, stuffed them into his backpack, and filtered out the door with the rest of his classmates. His gut growled with hunger, and he needed to get back to the dorm for lunch and an afternoon of studying. Maybe within the security of his dorm room, he'd be able to focus on the materials he should have picked up during class.

As he walked down the hallway toward the doors, another thought hit him. He hadn't seen or talked with Lynch Cully for quite some time. Maybe he was in his office on the second floor.

Lynch, with his breadth of experience and expertise in criminal forensics, was Aric's mentor and role model. More than that, he had become a friend, someone Aric knew he could call on and trust if a problem came up. He was the reason that Aric chose criminology and came to the college with its fledgling program. He could have stayed at home in St. Louis and attended one of the top criminology programs in the country.

He knocked on the closed office door.

"Come in."

Aric eased open the door and poked his head into the

office. "Hi. Do you have a minute to talk?"

"Hey, Aric. I was thinking about you earlier. C'mon in."

Aric entered the room and sat on one of the chairs facing his friend's desk. He placed his backpack on the floor next to him.

"What's up?"

Lynch was one of less than a handful of people who knew about Aric's and Adam's roles in taking down the child trafficking ring in central Wisconsin, but he didn't know about all of their exploits that year. He also knew something about Adam's role with the Remnant. It had been Lynch's friends Mike Jurgesmeyer and Mike Southwick who had started that whole thing. So, while Lynch knew a bit about Adam's IT expertise, he knew very few of the details and nothing about Adam's UltraNet software. As such, Aric was going to have to be careful how he approached the subject of their possibly being in danger.

"I need your advice. Um, Adam and I, well, we might be in trouble."

He half expected Lynch to say "Again?" but he didn't. A serious look came across his face.

"Go on."

"Adam's previous job in Washington was highly classified, but then he learned that his boss was a pedophile and that led to, well, all that stuff at Camp Douglas that you already know about."

Lynch nodded. "Let me guess. The people behind all that stuff, as you put it, have learned about you two, and Adam's gotten wind of it."

Maybe getting Lynch involved wasn't such a good idea.

The man was very perceptive and able to read between the lines. Aric struggled with how to proceed. He waggled his head back and forth.

"Not exactly. At least, he doesn't think it's them. What you might not realize is that Adam has largely been in hiding ever since. I know, he visits here and seems pretty open about it. But he goes home rarely, and although he and his wife have reconciled, and he's been hoping to move back with his family, now that this has come up, he's afraid of putting them in jeopardy."

"That's gotta be hard."

Aric nodded. "It is."

"So, who does he think is after him?"

"It goes back to the classified stuff, which I don't really know a lot about. It involved a software program. It was through that program that Adam learned about his boss." Aric hesitated. The next part was more sensitive, and perhaps incriminating. "More than that, he learned that his boss and those connected to him used that program to spy on people, blackmail them, and more. Adam destroyed the program so it couldn't be used illegally anymore to infringe on people's freedoms and such."

Lynch sat back in his chair, looking pensive. After a moment, he said, "Two questions. Was the program government property? And if not, who owned it? Adam could be liable for felony property damage."

Fortunately for Aric, the first was a simple question. The second was a bit murkier. "No, it was not government property. As for your second question, as far as I know, the company he worked for owned all rights to it, and Wallace

Chamberlain fully owned the company. With his death, that company went defunct. I don't know anything about his estate and whether or not rights to the program were passed on. That said, Adam has said some things to me that lead me to think the program was off-the-books. He didn't know that until he started collecting evidence against Chamberlain. I've been told that only one or two people outside the company knew about it."

The fingers on Lynch's right hand softly tapped the desktop. Aric had learned that this meant the man was thinking.

"So, back to my other question. You answered who, but what leads you to think they're after you."

Aric proceeded to tell Lynch about Adam's getting "a tip" that someone was trying to resurrect the program and wanted Adam's programming skills. Since they couldn't find Adam, they were looking for Aric as a means to get to Adam. He then described his unusual situation earlier that morning. At the mention of government plates on the van, Lynch seemed more concerned.

"Am I correct in reading between the lines that these are people who won't take no for an answer?"

Aric nodded. Lynch stood and walked to one of his three bookcases. He ran his finger along the titles until he found what he was looking for and pulled that book out.

"You know I've been studying the Book of Revelation. We've talked a bit about it before."

Aric nodded again.

"Well, I'm fully convinced we're well into the timeline described in that apocalyptic book. The tribulation is going on all around us. Wildfires across the globe are destroying millions of acres of woodlands each year. Drought is burning up grasslands across the globe. Famine has already hit much of Africa and the Middle East. What everyone wants to call climate change fits well with God's judgments, just as they've done throughout history. The whole COVID thing fits right in with the pestilence judgments, and lockdowns have led to famine in India, China, and elsewhere. And now, we have the beasts of chapter 13."

Aric furrowed his brow. "Huh? I was always taught that those were the Antichrist and his False Prophet. Some world dictator and his right-hand guy that come on the scene during seven years of extreme tribulation."

Lynch nodded. "I know. Most Christians in this country believe that, but nowhere in the Bible is a seven-year period described. Three-and-a-half, but not seven. Even the three-and-a-half can't be taken literally. And nowhere is an Antichrist, capital A, mentioned. All reference to antichrist is always to the *spirit of* antichrist, little A."

"So, who do you say the beasts are?"

"To understand the two beasts, we have to go back to the book of Daniel, chapter 7. The beasts in Revelation have the same traits as those in Daniel. The beast from the sea has the traits of the governments that were yet to come, while the beast from the land speaks words against God and wears down the saints. I believe that what we call the Deep State today is the beast from the sea. It is the epitome of secular humanism which is definitely the spirit of antichrist. The corporate world—Big Pharma, Big Ag, social media, mainstream media, and the like—are the beast from the land.

They do the bidding of and promote the first beast."

Lynch paused. Aric knew he did so to let it sink in. It made sense. Where the government could not legally censor those who spoke against it, it had social media do so. When critics of the COVID jab spoke out, the mainstream media and social media shut them down. When the government couldn't mandate the vaccine, the corporate world enforced and promoted the need, threatening people with the loss of their livelihoods. Throughout it all, these people pushed what the government wanted the people to hear and believe.

Another thought struck him. "Does that mean that these vaccine passports we keep hearing about could be the mark of the beast?"

Lynch nodded. "The World Health Organization is pushing for digital identity certificates that will, at first, restrict travel during a pandemic. If they succeed in getting those in place, they will supersede the laws of all countries and in fact, make the WHO a global government in and of itself. They will be able to mandate lockdowns, business restrictions, and more, all in the name of fighting a pandemic."

Aric saw where this was going. "They create and declare a pandemic and then control everything. You'll need a vaccine passport just to shop for food or clothing."

Lynch said, "Yep. And just watch. Although technically they require senate approval in this country for such a treaty, they're making the changes provisional so they can sidestep that formal approval. Most people understand that the Senate must approve all treaties, but they forget that it takes a two-thirds vote to do so. In reality, only six percent of our international treaties have full, formal Senate ratification. In today's divided society, that ratification will never happen, so the current administration will approve the provisional status of the changes and let them supersede our sovereignty."

George rested his hands from the tedious construction of the wire coil he wrapped so meticulously around the explosive core of his device. He flexed and extended his fingers numerous times and stretched his fingers by steepling them together and pressing. Despite all of his years working at keyboards, he'd never found that work as hard on his fingers as this task was. Or perhaps, the tension lay in knowing that he was working with enough C4 to take out his tiny apartment and two or three others adjacent to it.

He decided to take a break and stood and stretched. He walked over to the small refrigerator and retrieved a beer. With that in hand, he walked to the chest of drawers and looked longingly at the young woman in the picture that sat on top. *Oh, my Bella!* he thought.

Isabella Giordano had been the love of his life. She had come to the states as an exchange student at his high school, where they dated in his senior year. They kept in touch while he studied software design and engineering at MIT and she studied fashion design in New York City. When she returned to Italy to work in the Milan fashion studios, he visited several times, even meeting her family. That's when he knew that she was serious about him. When he landed his big job in Washington, she returned to NYC which allowed them to see each other regularly . . . until the pandemic hit. Wedding plans had to go on hold.

He had managed to avoid the vaccine when it was released after zero animal studies and a single human study that abandoned not only the gold standard of being double-blinded with a placebo control group but by having no control group at all. Just weeks after starting the study, PfenRich gave everyone in their "control" group the vaccine. Any hope of discovering adverse reactions that might occur a month after the jab was long gone. And yet, even with serious side effects affecting over 20% of their study participants, they pushed through the emergency use authorization for it.

Bella had not been able to avoid the vaccine. Her corporate overseers had made it a requirement of employment. They had also insisted on the booster despite early data showing the vaccine did not work and might actually be the cause of variants of the virus developing. A week after the booster, her roommate found her dead in bed one morning. The coroner declared it a case of cardiac arrest without implicating the vaccine.

But George knew otherwise. He blamed PfenRich. But since they had not yet married, he had no recourse. He had no standing for any legal action that might be allowed under EUA laws. He had lost his soul mate, and he had decided that PfenRich would pay dearly. They were not going to get away with it. He had found a partner to make his revenge complete.

He took his beer and climbed the ten flights of steps to the roof. Someone else was up there. The door had been propped open. Yet, when he stepped out into the cool afternoon air, he saw no one else.

He walked to the side of the building facing the PfenRich headquarters. The wind was coming from that direction, from the Hudson River to their west. He would need a slight breeze from the east, or no breeze at all, for his plan to work.

While up there he took the time to look around. He would need one more item to complete his device. Plus, he needed to get helium. Those tanks he would need to hide on the roof somewhere so that they would be available at the right time.

And that time was soon.

Lynch handed the book he was holding to Aric. "This goes into more detail about the symbols and stuff in Revelation. I think you'll find it interesting."

Aric looked at the book—a study guide not by a theologian or well-known pastor but by some medical doctor he'd never heard of. Well, if Lynch found it thought-provoking, he'd make a point of reading it.

"You said it was a government van that the guy got into?"

"Yeah. You had a funny look on your face when I mentioned that."

Lynch smirked. "Gotta work on my poker face."

Aric wasn't sure what to make of Lynch's reaction.

"Is that significant?"

"Maybe. I know you've heard about the FBI raid on President Graham's Florida home two months ago."

Aric nodded. "You'd have to live in a vacuum not to have. The media keeps making him out to be a danger to democracy. The irony of that is clear to anyone who can think."

"True. The result is that we have to be worried that the federal bureaucracy has been weaponized to the point of coming after regular citizens, too."

Aric didn't like the sound of that with regard to Adam and himself. "But we're seeing that already. The FBI raided a pro-life guy's house and took him away in cuffs for defending his young son from an aggressive pro-abortion activist who was pushing the boy. And parents protesting at school board meetings are being labeled as terrorists by the head of the FBI. Doesn't that point to the FBI being weaponized already?"

Lynch nodded. "I should have phrased that differently. Yes, exactly. And my worry is that the FBI itself might be involved in helping these people find Adam, which means you need to be especially alert, too."

Great, thought Aric. Now, even the police would be suspect, acting in cooperation with the FBI or, maybe, Homeland Security.

"And if the FBI and other law enforcement and intelligence organizations are involved, that means only one thing—the beast is roaring. The Deep State must want that program as a surveillance tool, and that really makes it dangerous for you two."

Aric sighed. All he wanted was to attend college in peace. Was that too much to ask?

"Thanks for your time, Lynch."

"My door's always open to you, Aric. By the way, let me know when you've finished that book. We'll get you over to the house for dinner and discuss it."

He'd never turn down a home-cooked meal from Lynch's wife, Amy. "Sounds like a plan. I'll let you know."

Aric walked to the building's exit and hesitated. What was his best bet on getting back to the dorm unnoticed? He could take a path worn into the grass behind the building, past another dorm, and into a back door of his dorm. Or maybe his best route was to hide in plain sight. It was the lunch hour, and dozens of students currently walked to and from classes on the main walkway along Campus Drive.

He chose the grass trail behind the buildings. Anyone intent on taking him would be instantly obvious since they, too, couldn't hide in the crowd. Plus, they'd have to somehow get him to Campus Drive to get away.

He disliked that his mind instantly returned to the idea of being kidnapped. If the FBI was involved, they could simply "arrest" him for some trumped-up reason, take him away in one of their trademarked black sedans, and waterboard him at some urgently created black ops site before he was missed.

He shuddered. That thought was not reassuring. And neither was his imagination.

As he passed the first dorm, it appeared he was in the clear. He'd passed only one other student, a guy he knew from his freshman English class.

He walked through the grassy gap between dorms and saw a campus police officer coming his way. At that moment, his heart began to race. He debated making a run for the dorm but that would make him stand out and appear guilty of something. He had nothing to be guilty of. He stayed on course and hoped that the officer was back there for some other reason.

Ten yards from the door, he heard a voice behind him. "Aric Afton!"

Aric's heart skipped a beat. Should he run for the door?

"Aric, it's Ryan Krueger."

Aric stopped and took a deep breath in relief. He turned to

face the officer who had pulled him out of the water those many months earlier.

"Officer Krueger, wow, glad it's you."

The man gave him a puzzled look. "Umm, why?"

Now Aric chastised himself. If he were in the officer's shoes, he'd be asking the same question.

The man looked around. "Are you back here because someone is watching you? Have you had a run-in with someone?"

Now it was Aric's turn to wonder why. "W-why would you ask that?"

"Look, I just had lunch with your brother. He explained some of what's going on and asked me to keep an eye on you."

Aric felt relief. He explained what had happened earlier that morning, as well as the concern that the FBI might be involved. He didn't mention Lynch.

"Okay. Adding the FBI to the list might be over the top, but in today's political world, maybe not. You still have my number, right?" Aric nodded. "Good. You can call me anytime. I'm not on duty 24-7, but I'm also not far away. And if anyone else suspicious shows up, let me know."

"Gladly. Thanks."

The man reached into his coat pocket and pulled out a small box. He handed it to Aric. "For you, from Adam. Don't use his old phone. In fact, he asked that you erase that number from your phone ASAP. You can call me on this, too. I have both of your numbers, just in case. Oh, and your dad will have both numbers according to Adam."

"Thanks. Um, can I ask just what Adam told you?"

"Just enough to know you both might be in trouble with

some unsavory types, guys with connections that, well, shouldn't be part of our government. I'm on your side."

That made Aric feel a lot better. He turned toward the door.

"Oh, and remember, God's got your back."

THIRTEEN

Adam was a bit surprised when the new pay-as-you-go phone suddenly chimed a notification as he drove back toward his home. *So soon*, he thought.

The info center on his dash announced that it was Ryan. He had the car read the text to him.

Aric being watched. Might be FBI. A government
van was involved. Was able to slip him the phone.

He rarely used that feature in his car and thought the monotone male voice sounded like archaic technology. He decided he would upgrade the voice to something female, maybe Australian, at his soonest opportunity. He loved that Aussie accent.

Ryan's mention of the FBI upset him. The use of what was supposed to be an apolitical, non-biased law enforcement agency—the best in the world by some accounts—had started even while President Graham was in office. Back then, however, its target *was* President Graham. Now, anyone labeled conservative was considered a terrorist by this "esteemed" agency. Adam wasn't that old, but already he wondered what had happened to the America of his youth.

He finished the trip and pulled into the driveway of his house. Before climbing out of the car, he twisted and turned in his seat to survey the area around him. No unusual or unexpected vehicles, only those of his neighbors. He exited the Audi and hurried into the house.

He lamented that this would once again become an integral part of his lifestyle—looking over his shoulder everywhere he went. He thought he'd left that behind in Washington, DC, with his old job.

He grabbed a bottle of water from the fridge and moved into his office. After sitting down at his console, he called up a couple of windows to see what had transpired in his absence. He smiled. His ploy had worked.

While he had no way yet of getting into the new AlterNet software to directly alter it, he knew what techniques they were likely to use to penetrate secure databases without detection. He picked the top two and used them to set up alerts in over a dozen major databases that they would need to access almost daily if they wanted to develop a thorough profile of an individual. He had developed a few "proprietary" techniques to access those databases, and these had been successful in placing the alerts where he needed them.

As he sat there, he accessed two of those databases and discovered that his flags had indeed been tripped. *That's gonna set 'em back*, he thought. Maybe, if he created enough problems for them, they'd get so frustrated they'd give up on AlterNet. *Naw*, he thought as he shook his head. These people were not going to give up. But at least he could have fun making life difficult for them.

The last few days at his lakeside estate had been as refreshing as he had hoped. His wife was delighted to have their chef, Elisha, back, as he traveled with Werner more and more these days. To friends and colleagues, even to her, he stated that he enjoyed the taste of home that Elisha delivered. In truth, he admitted only to himself that having their personal chef with him provided a level of trust in his meal preparation that he no longer had with other chefs. Being paranoid over a possible poisoning was not becoming to a man of his stature. His trust in Elisha avoided that.

As he lay on his belly with only a towel over his buttocks, the masterful hands of his masseuse worked the tension out of his upper back and neck muscles. She came to their home twice a week, whether at their lakeside estate or their villa on a wooded lot just outside Baldham, east of Munich. His family home in Daglfing, built before WWII, had been much loved, but as his wealth and status rose, he found he needed more privacy, and the new villa afforded him such. Sentiment aside, housing prices in Munich were among the highest in the world, so rather than sell the family home, their youngest son and his family now occupied it.

He closed his eyes as the masseuse worked down along his spine. Her fingers kneaded his para-spinal muscles and worked out to his flanks. He could feel the tension release. Unlike the dozens of prostitutes who descended upon Davos at €700 per hour whenever they met there, she was a highly accredited therapeutic masseuse. Nothing sexual. For Werner, political power was a stronger drug than sex.

As she turned her efforts to his right shoulder, his cell phone rang—Edvin. He lifted his head from the head cradle.

"Klara, would you give me a moment in private, *bitte*?"

She offered a curt bow of her head and replied, "Of course, Herr Koch." A moment later, he remained alone in the room.

"Yes, Edvin?"

"Sir, just a quick update as you requested. Is now a good time?"

"Yes, go ahead."

"On the search for Adam Afton, we have confirmed with several neighbors that the Afton family we identified in St. Louis have or did have an older son named Adam. We're getting contradictory reports."

Werner turned over and sat up on the massage table. "Contradictory?"

"Yes, sir. Evidently, Adam disappeared several years ago. The family was quite upset, having not heard from or seen him for months. Some neighbors say they heard he had died. A few say he's alive and well, but they've not actually seen him. Their youngest child is Aric Afton, Aric with an A. He's currently in college in Wisconsin, so we have a team observing him now."

Werner nodded. "Good. Have they found anything to suggest he's in contact with his brother?" Werner continued to operate on the assumption that the older son was alive. He felt convinced of that.

"No, sir. We're still arranging to monitor his phone calls, and so far, his only contacts on campus appear to be with other students or faculty."

"Well then, keep watching. His brother is likely to contact

him sooner or later."

"Yes, sir. As for AlterNet2, some unexpected glitches have come up. Where they once could search secure databases undetected, their searches are now suddenly triggering intrusion alerts in a variety of those databases. They are working to identify the problem."

"That's not what I hoped to hear. Is it something they've changed? Is it outside interference?"

The suddenness of this issue struck Werner, as did its timing. If Adam Afton knew of their search for him, could he have somehow caused the problem? If so, he was a programming genius far ahead of those working on AlterNet2 now. And that was all the more reason they needed to find him and to bring him back onto the team—whether of his own accord or shanghaied and chained to a workstation.

"They still don't know, sir. I will alert you as soon as they inform me of the cause."

"*Sehr gut.*" Werner wanted to get back to his massage. "Keep me informed."

"Yes, sir. One more thing, sir."

"Yes?"

"The threats to PfenRich, sir."

Werner once again appreciated his aide's thoroughness. He hadn't thought much about this issue since arriving home.

"Yes, yes, what do you have?"

"Well, sir, I wish we had more. We still don't know exactly what form this threat might take. We've monitored and checked fertilizer sales, explosive transactions, area gun sales, and anything else that comes to mind. We're monitoring employee communications in case it's some kind of inside job."

"But do you know what to look for? Do we know who? What did this tip come from?"

Werner was more than upset. He liked to think the elite of the world had the ear of the world, as well as ears on the world. U.S., British, German, French, and other intelligence communities across the globe fed information to the WOC all the time. Little escaped them, and few events happened without their hand in it, to further their cause. Big Pharma was critical to their endeavors to reduce the overpopulation of the world, and PfenRich, with its COVID vaccine, was at the top of the list.

"Sir, we're looking at disgruntled employees. We're checking any and everyone who might have lost loved ones because of their products, but with the growing number of deaths from the vaccine, that list is growing daily and exponentially. But we do now believe it's a valid threat. Personally, I don't have the expertise to explain it, but our people monitoring the deep web came across it and vouch for its accuracy."

"Just what did they find?"

"As best I can explain it, sir, someone was researching PfenRich's headquarter building. Location, size, architectural layout, mechanicals, and more. It was more than a casual inspection. Whoever it was, was looking for very specific details."

Werner shook his head. He didn't like the sound of that. "Do we know where the search originated?"

"Whoever was looking was very good at hiding his trail, but he was online long enough that they believe the trail led back to the U.S. Where in the U.S.? They couldn't say."

Werner was not happy. He demanded perfection of those who worked for him and his organization, but he also recognized that some things, like art, took time to perfect.

"Keep me posted, Edvin." He hung up and then sighed. He shouldn't take it out on his aide. The man performed well, but he certainly couldn't do everything. He could only work with the information given to him.

"I'm done, Klara," he yelled out, and then repositioned himself on the table. He did his best to cover his backside.

The masseuse returned to the room and covered him with a sheet appropriately. He felt her fingers begin to work his neck again.

"Herr Koch, maybe you should turn off your phone during our sessions. You are so tense, again. I will need to start over."

Tense wasn't exactly the word he would use to describe how he felt.

FOURTEEN

Aric didn't much feel like eating breakfast, which was not his norm. However, it wasn't some stomach bug or upper respiratory illness that had pushed his appetite aside. His nerves were getting the better of him, and he didn't understand why. He'd been kidnapped and forced to participate in a riot in Portland. He'd helped uncover a powerful child trafficking ring. He had faced off against fellow students who tried to "cancel" Lynch on campus, while also agitating for LGBT+ and black rights—rights that had the potential to cancel *him*. He'd spoken up for free speech at that time, but free speech still seemed to come with a cost for anyone with even the slightest rightward lean.

As he picked at his scrambled eggs and bacon, he realized the difference. In those past events, his focus had been on, first, his brother and, second, Lynch. Even when he jumped into the icy waters, his focus had been on someone else. Now, he recognized that he was being self-focused. He worried about something happening to him.

He ate maybe half of his eggs but managed to finish off the bacon. If he'd left bacon on his plate, he figured someone would recommend counseling. Back in his room, he prepared for the day and then hurried downstairs.

As he emerged into the light of day, he breathed a sigh of relief to find Jess and Chris waiting for him. *Safety escorts*, he thought, as he grinned at the thought of Jess being his bodyguard.

"Hey, you two."

" 'Bout time. I was beginning to think you decided to sleep in and skip class," said Chris.

He ushered them to the side, away from the more trafficked part of the walkway, and glanced about. The coast seemed clear.

"I'm glad you two are here. I think I'm being watched." He informed them of Adam's concerns, without revealing too much, and of the men with the government van the day before. "We can still talk and text like normal but just don't mention Adam. Oh, and ask your folks to do the same. Okay?"

"Sure. We'll keep our eyes open, too."

"And take photos if we can."

"Oooh, we're gonna spy on the spies," joked Chris. "Sounds fun."

Aric shook his head. "Don't underestimate these people. These are not nice guys in white helping mankind. They'll do whatever they think they need to do to get what they want."

"Which is Adam," said Jess.

"Which is Adam," replied Aric in agreement. "Hey, we need to get to class."

The trio started walking toward their respective classroom buildings when Jess pointed to a white van ahead of them. Aric felt sure it was the same van.

"That's it. I'm pretty sure it's the same one from yesterday. Ignore it. Don't let on that we've spotted them."

As they neared it, Chris pulled out his phone and pretended to be texting. Aric saw that he was actually setting up his camera app. He wanted to stop Chris, but they were too close now. He didn't want to call attention to themselves. Just as Chris tilted the phone to capture a shot of the back of the van, movement in front of the van made Aric jump.

The two men he had seen yesterday were preoccupied. Officer Krueger was talking with them so that their backs were toward the sidewalk. Chris managed to get a couple of photos of them from the side before Aric saw the campus policeman signal with his eyes for them to get lost.

"Get outta here," he whispered to the others.

The three split up and hurried toward their classes.

Caleb's week was moving from bad to worse. Had it only been just three days since he'd been terminated for his free speech rights on social media? And now, he found himself in his friend's legal office.

"Dr. Wahlburg, you can come on back now."

As he stood, he said, "Thanks." A moment later, he sat in Ted's inner office facing the man sitting across the table. "Nice office."

The solid, live-edged walnut table had a river of dark green, whorled epoxy running through it and sat eight. To his right and left were bookcases filled with hardbound books of Wisconsin state statutes, case law, and more. Behind Ted, a solid mahogany executive desk faced them. The office invoked a sense of stability and legal prowess. It was meant to impress, and Caleb was suitably so.

He nodded his head towards the bookcase to his right. "So, you've read all of these, right? Cover to cover?"

Ted laughed. "Have you read your old medical textbooks cover to cover?"

Caleb grinned. "Actually, yeah, at some point in time. And some parts multiple times."

"Same answer here. Goes with the profession." He leaned over the table toward Caleb. "So, what can I do for you?"

To be honest, Caleb wasn't sure. Was his case one of wrongful termination? The infringement of First Amendment rights? An invasion of his privacy? All of the above? Well, maybe not the privacy thing. Posting anything on social media made it a public discourse. Of course, using it to fire someone must cross some kind of line.

"I'm just wondering whether or not I have any legal recourse against the hospital for my termination."

The lawyer nodded. "Okay. So, tell me what happened."

Caleb recounted his encounter with the administrator, Greg Massey. He showed Ted the termination letter he'd received the day before. He then showed him copies of the social media posts he'd made that led to the confrontation.

"I assume you have documentation to support all the statements you made on social media."

Caleb nodded. "Everything I said there is backed up by medical studies, and I have copies of those papers."

"Tell me again the sequence of things when Massey confronted you near your office."

Caleb did so and noticed the slight frown on his friend's

face as he spoke.

After a moment of reflection, Ted spoke. "I wish you had quietly posted another comment and let Massey terminate you. Your typing another post and thrusting it into his face, whether out of anger, frustration, or any other emotion could come across as arrogant to many on a jury. Likewise, your calling the office manager and canceling all your appointments *before* being formally terminated. It's like you invited the administrator to fire you and provoked him. That won't sit well with a jury either."

Caleb acknowledged he had let his emotions get the better of him. Ted made some excellent points.

"What about my free speech rights? Can they legally terminate me for posting what I posted?"

"No. And that's where we can get them. Whether the administrator himself followed your posts, a hospital trustee, or even a member of the public, they have no right to threaten or ultimately terminate your position based upon your free speech. That you have documentation to support your online statements is great. We need that. So, here's my next question. What exactly do you want to get from them?"

Caleb thought about that. He and Ally had discussed this. A previous career and an inheritance had set him up for financial security, as long as they stayed somewhat frugal in their spending. They couldn't take long lavish vacations, as they had on occasion while he was in practice, but the house was paid for, the cars as well, and the basic necessities of life would be no problem to obtain.

"We've talked about this. I don't want to simply retire at this point. Having a professional position is important to me, and I still have a good fifteen to twenty years of practice ahead of me. With this mark on my record, I'm going to have a hard time getting a new position at a hospital." He paused. "Years ago, Ally and I had talked of creating and investing in a stand-alone birthing center. We had financing set up. All we required was state approval. Then the hospital stepped in, offered to build a new birthing center, and offered me the opportunity to direct it. I took it. Now, we still have those plans, but we will require a certificate of need before the state would let us continue, and I've checked, financing would be based upon state approval as well."

"And if you can't get state approval? After all, the hospital built the new birthing center you wanted. Has the population of the area grown enough to justify another one?"

That was the question keeping Caleb up at night. How could they justify another center? It wasn't just population growth that mattered; it was the ages of the people in that increased population. Yes, the area's population was growing solidly, thanks to high taxes just across the border in Illinois. But that growth wasn't in couples having children. Like the rest of the country, the overall population was aging. The birth rate continued to slowly drop.

"If state approval appears doubtful, then I'd want to sue for potential lost income."

"So, 20 years at what? What did you make last year?"

The average income for an OB/GYN doctor was just over $300,000. He had made more as the unit's director and primary physician.

"My 1040 showed a gross income of $375,000."

Ted did the calculation on his phone. "So, we're talking

seven and a half million, plus legal fees."

"Sounds about right."

"You might not get close to that, but that will certainly get their legal team's attention." Ted sat back and smiled. "It would certainly get *my* attention."

They talked some more about the pros and cons. Ted pointed out that suing the hospital could come back to bite him, as other facilities would be less likely to forgive and forget his termination if he had a reputation as a litigant. Caleb offered up some stats that made state approval of a new birthing center less likely and reinforced his need to sue. Finally, the decision was left to Caleb.

"Give me a few days to discuss this with Ally and digest it all. I'll get back to you."

They shook hands. "I'm here for you, buddy. Ready and willing, so let me know. I think you have a good case."

Caleb spent the time driving home to think about what Ted had said. He pulled into the garage and parked before walking back down the drive to retrieve their mail. As he thumbed through the short stack of envelopes, the last one hit him like a hammer. The return address read "Wisconsin Board of Registration for the Healing Arts."

He stopped in his tracks and with his heart racing, tore open the envelope and pulled out the letter. While much of the content became blurred, several things stood out—"received a complaint about professional standards," "spreading misinformation harmful to your patients," and "will be investigated." But what got him hyperventilating was the threat to "revoke your medical license to practice in the State of Wisconsin."

FIFTEEN

Adam often wondered why no groove had developed in his floor between the chair at his computers and the back windows overlooking the lake. He paced between them often enough. He found himself doing the same now as he pondered a new dilemma.

He had evidence that the current meltdown in the stock markets was not just the result of bad policy by the current Sidon administration, but of collusion between the Federal Reserve, the IMF, several "too-big-to-fail" banks, and numerous other international players. The problem was that the source of his information was so specific that revealing it would point to that source and likely lead to his death. Adam couldn't be responsible for that.

Besides, the chances of his revelation making a difference were nil. The mainstream media would never cover it. The alternative media *would* cover it, but he knew the power brokers would simply label it a "conspiracy theory" to debunk it. Although the CIA has been, fairly or unfairly, credited for popularizing the term to disparage those critical of the Warren Report on President Kennedy's assassination, the term could be traced back to the 19th century. Today, it was used as a pejorative for anyone critical of various political activities. Adam, after reviewing numerous "conspiracy theories" from the past 60 years, believed "spoiler alerts" to be a more appropriate phrase.

No, this information would be data he would have to sit on.

As he sat back down in his chair thinking about it, the name Kennedy struck him. Ellen. No, Eloise. Nope, Elena. Elena Kennedy. That was the name of the fourth man's girlfriend. He'd only met her once or twice and never expected to recall her name after ten-plus years.

He quickly turned to his keyboard and began typing. First, her name. Then he added an age range. Caucasian or maybe Hispanic. He added both to the search parameters with a Boolean "OR". He thought back to those couple of times he'd seen her and decided on a height range gauged by his own. Five-foot-six to five-foot-nine. Brunette. He was horrible at guessing weights and would never risk insulting a woman by doing so, but he went out on a limb and added a range: 135 to 160. Nope, he decided to play it safe and changed the lower weight to 125. What else?

He couldn't recall any other details, like where she worked or whether she was a professional. They did talk about music, but he could not remember any mention of a favorite band or genre of music. He quieted his mind. He knew that if he strove too hard to remember, it was a guarantee that he wouldn't.

He finalized his search by prioritizing certain databases and sat back to review what he'd entered. Satisfied, he hit the enter key to start the search.

He wanted to sit there and watch the results come in, but that could be like watching a slowly leaking faucet drip. He decided to take the time to fix and eat lunch before checking on the progress.

He walked into the kitchen and peeked into the fridge. Leftover pizza from five nights earlier called his name, but he had promised his mom he would start eating better. There were also leftovers from Aric's celebration four nights earlier at the Larson's home. One shelf was dedicated to beer and mineral water. Another was dedicated to condiments, various sauces, preserves, and the like. Two were barren. He discovered a sheaf of Romaine in the vegetable drawer, but it had compost written all over it. *Sorry, Mom*, he thought as he pulled out the pizza. It was, after all, the oldest. He needed to go to the grocery if he was to fulfill that promise.

He warmed the pizza on a plate in the microwave, grabbed a beer, and sat down to watch the ducks on the lake as he ate. He never got tired of watching them go butt and tail straight up before disappearing underwater to snatch a small fish. Then, with their heads in the air again, they would juggle that meal into just the right position to slide down their gullets. He had yet to see one lose a fish.

He also thought about Aric. Was he truly being watched, or was it his imagination? He couldn't risk contacting him, even on the new phone, until he was sure Aric was in his room. He also didn't want to put Ryan in an awkward position or become a nuisance by contacting him too much. He had earlier decided to let Ryan be the one to contact him whenever the man thought it necessary. He would stick to that decision.

He returned his plate to the sink, only to discover every

plate he owned already sitting in it. *I guess I'll kill some more time*, he thought. His dishwasher was broken. He needed a new one, but with it just being him living there alone, he procrastinated in buying one. Still, he'd have to buckle down and get one if he wanted to sell the place. Fifteen minutes later, the dishes, glassware, and utensils sat on the drying rack.

With nothing else to help him kill time, he sauntered back to his computer. Almost an hour had been spent on the search so far, and Adam gave out a groan when he saw the pending results that had accumulated already. Almost five hundred Elena Kennedys had been identified so far. Only some of them matched all of his criteria. After all, some databases such as Facebook and Instagram didn't include things like height and weight. Once the primary search finished, he would have the program try to identify each woman, cross reference them, cull duplicates, and the like. With a little luck, he might have only 10% of the original list remaining. Those he would have to research himself.

That task could be daunting. But if it led him to "Seth," then the time would be well spent.

SIXTEEN

Aric's afternoon class had been engrossing, but not necessarily for the right reasons. He had anticipated his ethics course to be interesting and offer open discussion. Instead, the professor seemed more prone to indoctrinate and avoid discussion. After six weeks of classes, he saw little that truly qualified as moral principles. The secular humanistic approach to the class showed that everything was based upon relativism. Your morality might not be someone else's morality, with all of it based upon your life experience and subculture.

Aric once or twice attempted to bring up absolute morality, as based upon the Bible. He knew better than to mention the word "Bible." That was considered a trigger word by far too many. And yet, throughout history, the absolutes of the Bible had been the basis of ethics. What so many today ridiculed as "Thou shalt nots . . ." were the core of western common law. You shall not murder. Don't steal, bear false witness against someone, or commit adultery. In today's relativistic society, too many prosecutors looked the other way if someone who was caught stealing or looting was considered part of a persecuted class. Adultery no longer bore a societal stigma. Lying about a political opponent was just part of politics. Even murderers were given leniency and sometimes released to kill again.

Today's class discussed worldview, but it offered only one of what Aric considered the six major views—secularism. Aric had tried to inject the idea that five others existed: Christianity, Islam, Marxism, New Age Mysticism, and Postmodernism. Some believed in only three worldviews—theism, pantheism, and naturalism, but to him, Christianity and Islam were so markedly different, they defined separate views within the theistic collective. Likewise, Marxism, secular humanism, and Postmodernism were distinct enough to be able to split naturalism into three. New Age Mysticism well represented today's pantheistic religions and groups. But his attempts to introduce any level of discussion to include these were shot down.

Even those students whom he knew claimed to be Christians did not come to his aid for whatever reasons. Aric had recently read that only something like four percent of American adults held a Biblical Christian worldview. Why should he expect their children to be different? Most American Christians were treading on spiritual thin ice by holding onto a syncretic worldview that took a pinch of Christianity, a dash of humanism, and a shot of mysticism and blended them into a personal worldview that looked nothing like Christianity.

Christ told a story of those who would stand before Him in judgment saying they had eaten and drank in His presence, and He had taught in their streets, and yet He cast them into utter darkness saying He did not know them. By embracing such a mishmash of ideas, were many of today's "Christians" risking hearing Him say that come Judgment Day?

Aric's thoughts were so consumed by the class session he hadn't paid attention to those around him as he walked back toward the dorm. Halfway there, he stopped in his tracks as his mind registered that the white van now sat directly in front of his dorm. He glanced about but did not see either of the two men he had noticed previously.

With his spidey senses tingling, he slowly approached the main doors of the dorm. Just then Mitch walked out.

"Hey, Aric. On my way to football practice and passed two men outside your dorm room. I asked who they were looking for, and they sorta shrugged. One guy said they were just testing the Wi-Fi. I peeked out the elevator door before it closed, and they used a key to enter your room. Looked pretty suspicious, but they did have a key. Might want to call security before going in."

Aric took a deep breath. "Thanks, Mitch. I will."

Aric made a beeline to one of the study rooms off the main lobby. Sitting out of sight there, he texted Ryan and told him what he'd just been told and where he was. "Sit tight," came the reply.

Maybe five minutes later, the door opened, and Ryan walked in. "C'mon. Let's see what's going on."

As they left the study room, Aric glanced out the main doors and pointed. "The white van is gone. It was there when I came in."

When Anson had mentioned to his wife about going to the

next school board meeting, he hadn't been expecting the meeting to be just three nights later. The day after the incidents, he had gone to both schools to discuss each situation with the respective principal. Jason's principal had listened patiently but said little. Anson had been led to believe that his concerns would be discussed with Ms. Kittridge. However, as of this morning, it appeared that she hadn't and that the district was not interested in the concerns of their parents. The previous day, Jason had brought home an announcement that the school would be hosting a drag queen story hour in the kindergarten the following week.

At Bethy's middle school, a line of parents had formed outside the main doors, and the police department's school liaison officer stood guard. Anson recognized most of the parents, as their daughters were also involved in the sports program. As he walked toward the officer, they acknowledged him with nods of their heads.

He also knew the officer. They had gone through school together. The man nodded to Anson as he approached.

"Anson."

"Craig. I'm hoping to see the principal, Mr. Kiplinger. I'm guessing now's not a good time."

The officer nodded. "Take a number. If this is about the girl's locker room situation, all of these parents are here about that, and Kiplinger's not willing to see any of them. I suggest you take it to the school board."

"Guess we will. Thanks, Craig. Sorry you're put in this situation. Must be hard, having a daughter who's just two years older than my Bethy. What if this was the high school's locker room?"

The man frowned. "Not sure what I'd do, to be honest. But right now, I have a job to do, so here I am."

"So you are. You get to be the face of the school to all these upset parents. Not a good place to be. If this stuff keeps getting worse, someday you're going to have to choose—your job or being in the right. See you around."

With that, he turned around and returned to his car. Several other parents followed him.

"Anson!"

He turned to see three others walking to catch up with him. Upon reaching him, they discussed putting up a united front at the school board meeting. That's when Anson learned that it was tonight.

All day he'd had a hard time concentrating on work. Between text messages, phone calls, and emails from other concerned parents he was surprised he got any work done at all. In addition to that, though, he hadn't had time to prepare what *he* was going to say.

After an early dinner, he was lost in thought when Hannah reminded him of the time. He had a few written notes to take with him but still was unsure how to say what he wanted to convey to the board. All he knew was that he needed to get across the concerns of a father's heart.

Upon arrival at the school district's educational support building, which held the board's meeting room, he found the parking lot nearly packed. He found a parking slot at the far end and then headed toward the main door. There he found over a dozen people milling around, apparently unable to find room inside. He felt disappointed in thinking he'd be unable to witness the proceedings.

Yet, as he tried to peer around people to see inside, several people recognized him and pushed him forward. A moment later, he found himself inside and standing in a line that had formed behind a microphone that had been set up in the middle of the room for the public comment session. The meeting had already started.

Erin Standish, whose daughter was also on the volleyball team, stood in front of him. She turned and whispered, "There weren't any awards or appointments, so we're already into the superintendent's report. Glad you made it."

He nodded, not that he had any inkling of the agenda's order. He looked down the line of people in front of him. Most were parents of girls in the sports program. If the messages he'd been receiving all day were any indication, the board was in for an earful.

The superintendent droned on for another ten minutes, and then the board president announced the opening of the "public concerns and comments" segment of the meeting. The first person in line, another father of one of Bethy's teammates, stepped up to the microphone.

"I'm Roger Deare and I'm here to voice my concern and to protest the use of the girls' locker room at Marston Middle School by a boy. Our 14-year-old daughter on the volleyball team is being told that she has to undress, shower, and dress in front of a confused boy who thinks he should be a girl. And she is expected to accept his undressing in front of her."

That brought a loud round of applause and shouts of agreement.

"Order, please," said the board president. If the board had been alerted to the potential protests at tonight's meeting, they didn't appear so. Most looked surprised at the outburst. A few squirmed uncomfortably in their seats.

"As parents—"

The microphone cut off.

The president spoke up. "Let me remind you that each individual has two minutes to speak. If you go over the two-minute mark, the mic will be shut off."

That led to shouts of protests. Several parents stood and shook their fists at the board. After the room settled down, the president asked for the next speaker.

A mom from the team stepped up to the mic. "My name is Shannon Waring. As a woman, I do not expect men in any women's restroom, and I certainly do not want boys in my daughter's dressing rooms. It's inappropriate. In Virginia, such a situation led to a male student wearing a skirt raping a younger girl in a girls' restroom. The board's only action was to transfer that student to another school where he sexually molested another female student in a restroom. Is that what you're telling us you want here?"

Again, thunderous applause erupted. Again, as the mom tried to continue, she was cut off.

The same thing happened with the subsequent three speakers. But to Anson, it appeared that the mic was being turned off sooner and sooner with each one. When it became Erin's time to comment, he used the timer on his phone to check. Her comments were cut off at one minute and twenty seconds. He wondered if he would get to speak at all.

He stepped up to the microphone. With his phone timer started, he spoke. "My name is Anson Hardy. I, too, have a daughter on the volleyball team, but I want to speak to a different issue. Three days ago, my kindergartner was told by his new teacher that he might grow up to marry another boy. Are you now endorsing the grooming of kids as young as five to accept the gay lifestyle?"

Now the members of the board all squirmed in their chairs as the parents in the room stood and began shouting. No one had expected this bombshell.

Anson tried to speak but found his mic already cut off. He held up his phone to show the timer, and began to yell, "Hey, I still have over a minute! Don't turn off my mic!"

Others around him picked up on his demand.

"I still have over a minute!" he shouted.

Off to his side, he noticed several police officers moving into the room. Three positioned themselves between the crowd and the board members. Others began to clear the room. His old classmate and one other officer moved toward him.

"Anson, we need you to leave," said Craig.

Anson protested. "This is a public forum. We're all taxpayers and have a right to speak. They told us we have two minutes, which is ridiculous to begin with, but they aren't even giving us that."

Across the room, a new chant began. "Recall the board! Recall the board!" Others yelled, "We'll remember this on election day!"

"C'mon, Anson. Move!"

Anson's anger continued to rise. "So, I guess you've made your choice, eh, Craig? Forget morality and do the job."

"Anson."

"Cuff me and drag me out then."

He placed his hands behind his back . . . and they obliged him. Each officer put an arm under his and proceeded to drag him outside. The cell phones flashed as photos and videos were recorded on dozens of the devices.

Once outside, Anson stood to his feet. Craig looked at him and shook his head. "We should arrest you for—"

"For what, Craig? Not resisting arrest because, one, you never said I was under arrest, and two, I didn't resist you. Not for disturbing the peace either because all I was asking for was what they promised us, two minutes to speak. You didn't hear me chanting or see me shaking fists. It's all on video, Craig. You're already being seen as the face of the school and now, you're locking up parents. You're going to become a pariah in your own neighborhood if you take me in."

Anson could see Craig's mental wheels turning. A moment later, he whirled Anson around and unlocked the cuffs. "Don't cause any more trouble."

"*I* didn't start any here. It's the school board who's causing trouble."

With that, he turned and started walking toward his car. His anger began to subside, but his heart still raced. He'd never been in trouble with the police before. He'd always sought out a peaceful life for himself and his family.

Halfway to his car, Erin and a few other parents caught up with him.

"Anson, that was brilliant."

He didn't follow. "What was brilliant?"

"Getting them to cuff you and drag you out. Those images and videos will be on every conservative news site by morning, along with the story of your kids' encounters at their schools. You'll be viral before noon."

Anson took a deep breath. He didn't want to go viral, to become a spokesman for their cause. Yet, what was more important than his family and a moral upbringing for their kids? He had a more immediate concern, though. How was Hannah going to take it?

SEVENTEEN

A week had passed since Aric saw the white van outside his dorm. When Officer Krueger joined him in going into his dorm room, they found nothing obviously amiss. Everything looked just as it had after lunch when Aric had left for his afternoon class. He found nothing missing from his closet, desk, chest, or bookshelves. But someone had been there. Aric had left a few old-fashioned tells—techniques he'd read about in spy novels as a younger teen—on his closet door, one drawer to his desk, and one drawer in his chest. All three had been "broken," which he pointed out to the officer. The man had agreed that while one such tell failing on its own was a possibility, all three being broken was not.

The campus policeman agreed to take a statement from Mitch and file a report on the situation, but they both recognized that little was likely to come of it. He also promised to investigate how someone had gotten hold of a key to the room. Entering the room without permission could be a misdemeanor, even for law enforcement officers without a warrant. The college itself could file trespassing charges against the two men if they had entered the dorm without permission, and it appeared that the college had not granted such a right.

The week had passed, and Officer Krueger had nothing to report. The college had three magnetic key card imprinters. Each kept a log of the keys created, along with each key's location. None had been used to make a key to his room or a dorm master. Curiously, at the time in question, the security camera system for all of the campus developed a glitch, so that images of the men could not be obtained from security video logs.

That last item alone made Aric cautious all week. He used his room for sleeping and studying, as usual, but made zero phone calls or texts from his room. It was probably overkill, but before entering his room, he not only turned off his phone but also removed its battery. As for the burner phone supplied by Adam, he had already decided upon receiving it to remove its battery and only re-install it as needed . . . and only in locations well away from the dorm. In hindsight, that had been a good move.

He'd once read about cell "sniffers"—devices capable of capturing cell phone numbers, but more importantly, the phone's IMSI (International Mobile Subscriber Identity) number. Whether a pay-as-you-go phone or not, with the IMSI someone could track the calls made, isolate where the call was made, and where the call went. Yes, such a device might "find" every phone in the dorm, but it wouldn't take long to check every one of them and isolate any phones not tied to a specific person with an account with a U.S. carrier.

As he walked toward his morning class, he saw Officer Krueger ahead of him. As soon as the man saw him, he headed toward Aric.

"Good morning, Aric."

"Good morning, sir."

The officer laughed. "You don't need to call me sir. Ryan's fine."

Aric shook his head. "Maybe in private. Out here, it'll be sir and Officer Krueger. Do other students address you on a first-name basis?"

The man nodded. "Actually, yes. Either way, I just wanted to check with you. Any other problems?"

"No, sir. You—"

"Now you're making me feel old." The man grinned.

"Sorry, *sir.*" This time Aric emphasized the word and returned the grin. "You could do me a favor, and let the appropriate parties know that I will be contacting them sparingly and that their device has no power in between contacts. Maybe you could be an intermediary if needed for emergencies."

"Okay, I catch your drift. Sure, I could do that. I'll let them know."

Aric leaned toward him a bit and whispered, "I think there's a cell sniffer in the dorm."

That made the officer's brow rise.

"But if we were to track it down and disable it, then they'd know we're on to them, and it would really look suspicious."

The man nodded. "Well, have a good day." He raised his fingers to his brow, as if tipping a hat, as he said it. Then, as Aric walked on, he heard the officer say in a loud voice, "And Afton, don't forget to move your car. It'll get a ticket if you don't."

Aric resisted smiling and put on a frown as if he'd been chastised. *Nice touch*, he thought. Made it seem as if the officer had approached him about a parking infraction, but Aric knew that his car was legally parked. Yet, as he walked away, he recognized that the statement meant something more. Aric had not yet inspected his car. What if a tracking device had been placed on it?

George recalculated his need for helium. He had purchased an eight-foot diameter weather balloon to deliver the payload. He had two helium calculators at his disposal. The first, for determining one's helium needs to fill party balloons, told him he would need 267 cubic feet of helium to fill the balloon. The second, a balloon performance calculator, told him what he would need to lift the weight of the balloon and its cargo. He wouldn't require any lift, other than to hold the package up and allow it to drift in the breeze toward the PfenRich building. That computation told him he would only need 255 cubic feet.

He had several other concerns, mainly moving the tank. He wouldn't be able to transport it on the subway, so the tank would need to be small enough to fit into a cab or Uber. The size would also come into play in getting the tank to the roof, and then hiding it. The extra-large or jumbo tank would provide the cubic feet of gas he required, but it weighed nearly 200 pounds and was five feet tall. How would he get that to the apartment, much less manage to get that up the final two stories of steps to the roof?

He searched for nearby helium rental locations and found

the Balloon Shop NYC about two-and-a-half miles from the apartment. They also offered a variety of rental tanks. Their large tank held almost what he needed—242 cubic feet and weighed only 45 pounds at 50 inches in height. Now that was doable. They also offered a mini tank from which he could get another 25 cubic feet.

When he looked at the price he almost choked. He knew helium was in short supply and that costs had gone up considerably over the past six months, but he hadn't planned on spending over $500 on gas. Then there was the deposit on the tanks, too. He had no plans to return them so that cash would be gone as well.

Still, he'd come this far. He wasn't going to stop now.

EIGHTEEN

Caleb had been an "older" student in med school, having decided a bit later in life to pursue that calling. As such, he had always considered himself more mature and able to deal with people. The result? In the course of almost 20 years as a practicing obstetrician, Caleb had been served only once with a lawsuit. Even then, however, that suit was dismissed before he'd had the first meeting with his insurance company-appointed attorney. Other than a meeting with an estate lawyer to set up their family revocable living trust, he'd never spent time in a legal office. Now, he was meeting with Ted for the second time in a week.

Ted had retreated to his inner office to make a couple of phone calls. Caleb had the choice of sitting at the ellipsoidal conference table and twiddling his thumbs or pacing. He chose the latter, stopping periodically for a sip of water from the complementary bottle. It had warmed to room temperature long ago.

After 20-plus minutes that seemed like an eternity, Ted reentered the room. He pointed to Caleb's chair and said, "Have a seat."

Caleb obliged his friend. "So, what did they say?"

Ted frowned. "A lot less than I'd hoped." He had taken the time to call both the state Board of Registration for the Healing Arts and ACOG. "In a nutshell, ACOG told me they had received a letter from the state stating they were starting an investigation into complaints alleging professional misconduct and the spreading of misinformation that could potentially be harmful to patients. So, it would seem that this state investigation will be crucial to the outcome they decide."

He paused. Caleb didn't need to let that revelation soak in. He felt as if he was drowning in it.

"As for the state, they wouldn't divulge who made the complaints, but the gal I talked with let something slip that, to me anyway, implied that it was the hospital administration, not one or more individuals."

To Caleb, that made sense. The hospital grapevine's tendrils still reached him, and he'd already heard from Sha'Kyra that Greg Massey was fit to be tied. He'd made demands of two of the remaining OB docs, telling them that they would not only need to fill the void left by him but would also need to start dealing with transwomen and their hormone needs. The older of the two had told Massey that, unlike Supreme Court justices, he knew how to define a woman and that it was women he had dedicated his career to helping, not deluded men. Rather than comply, he announced his immediate retirement.

So now, their expensive birthing center was down two doctors and ten nurses, maybe soon-to-be eleven or twelve, if Sha left. They couldn't keep up with the "normal" pregnancies, much less the patients with complications—the wave of stillbirths, miscarriages, and bleeding irregularities—that Caleb had spoken out about.

Perceptions were growing in the town that if you went to that hospital, you'd lose your baby. It was just a perception, but perceptions were critical for any business. Caleb had seen it at every medical center he'd ever been affiliated with. A few people with a bad experience, who went about vocalizing about that experience could create the illusion of serious problems at the hospital. Of course, there were also those who'd had outstanding care, but somehow their stories always got buried under the avalanche of those about bad care. What was the old saying? If ten people had great care, only one would talk about it, but regarding bad care, twelve of the ten would broadcast it to the world.

Plus, Massey was something of a control freak, a micromanager, with thin skin. He would be the sort who would take Caleb's actions personally. Yeah, Caleb could see him retaliating through the state board.

"I took a look at the studies you dropped off earlier. I don't understand *all* of the medical stuff, but the stats sure seem straightforward."

Caleb nodded. "They are. And they're well-done studies. The CDC, FDA, and NIH have the propensity to design studies to support their desired outcomes and to ignore or belittle the studies that don't. Real science aims to find the truth. That's what I was pointing out on social media. And, curiously, these government websites often cite studies that don't even support their claims. They cite a large number of studies hoping to impress the average website visitor with the sheer number, knowing that most people won't go any further.

Then, for those who do go to the citations, the abstracts are ambivalent, so it makes it seem that the study supports them. But when you finally read the full study, you discover that the data actually goes against their claims."

"So much for their claims of following the science."

"Exactly."

"Okay, so we're going ahead with the lawsuit. It might be weeks or months before we get on the docket, but the discovery period should be fruitful, particularly if we find emails or other documentation showing ill will toward you by the administration. And if we can prove animosity, that will go a long way in mitigating your attitude toward Massey when he approached you about being terminated. If we can show that as the proverbial straw breaking the camel's back, the jury should be sympathetic toward you."

"And the science aspect of it?"

"Well, that will be more important with the state's investigation. Science is always iffy stuff with jurors. The defense will have its experts, and we'll have ours. It becomes something of a he said, she said situation. But there are no jurors with the state investigation. The investigators will have their own biases, and if they don't accept your science as valid, well, you're out of luck. Plus, in this day and age, they might have marching orders to ignore any and everything you present. You could just be a scapegoat for them. You represent all the science that challenges them and the public health edicts they made. Those studies basically prove they were wrong, so you also challenge the power they hold. They don't like being shown to be wrong, and you become the face of that challenge."

Caleb closed his eyes for a moment. While he didn't like that prospect—that of being a scapegoat—he had a feeling, a premonition, that that was exactly what he now faced.

NINETEEN

Anson sat at his desk facing his boss on a Zoom call. The call had started as expected . . . poorly.

The past week had been both fascinating and a nightmare. As predicted, his story as a concerned father of two kids being groomed by a leftist school system had become a national story on conservative news sites. He had had interviews with *The Epoch Times*, Newsmax, OANN, Fox News, and more. The story trended on social media for days.

On the more positive side, friends at their church had raised the tuition monies needed to pull all five of their kids from the public school system and put them into a private, classical Christian school. At first, they protested leaving their friends at school, but now, just a week later, they all loved Tall Oaks Academy. They had been welcomed with open arms. The atmosphere was one of learning, and the smaller class size made the children feel like part of the group right from day one. Plus, both he and Hannah already noticed a difference in their behaviors . . . for the better.

"Anson, I'm seeing your productivity declining, and the team is getting behind."

Anson nodded. The man was right, but his boss had no idea what kind of time demands had been placed on him. "I know, Jim. It should be short-term. Really. This stuff hit me out of the blue. I didn't ask for it, and I didn't expect it."

"I understand that, but the higher-ups are concerned. One, about the team getting behind without you. This is an important project. Also, though, they've started getting some blowback about your working for the company."

While Anson had been told to expect some level of celebrity, having his job questioned hit him hard. That somebody would take the time and make the effort to hunt down his employer and complain was hard to fathom. Had they nothing better to do?

"You mean, somebody's complaining that my concern for my family makes me unfit to work there?"

Jim waggled his head back and forth. "When you put it that way, it sounds nasty. My superiors are framing it against the company's DEI policy."

Anson had to think how best to phrase his next statements.

"So, you're saying the company's stand is that kindergartners should be taught to accept a sexual lifestyle that we, as their parents, don't want them to learn about until they're much older. Is that what I'm hearing? What about women's rights? Do they now accept that girls should be forced to compete in sports with boys who have a physical advantage no matter what their hormone levels are? How does that fit into the DEI policy?"

Anson felt his anger rising again, as it had at the school board meeting. He needed to reign it in before he lost his job.

"Anson, look, I understand where you're coming from. I'm on your side. I've told them that you're critical to the project and that this will all blow over. Don't blow it on your end. And should the call come to let you go, it won't be from me. Ball's in your court now."

Anson nodded. "Thanks, Jim, for being upfront. I'll double my efforts to get things done."

"Good. Don't makes us all look bad. I'll be in touch."

Anson closed his laptop. "Don't make us all look bad," he muttered. "He means don't make *me* look bad."

Was this God's way of telling him to move on? Was it the handwriting on the wall? He thought about how the change in his kids' lives had turned out so positive. Maybe he needed something new, too.

Before sinking his teeth back into the project, he did two things. He fired off emails to the last headhunter he had worked with as well as a friend at Titus Talents, a recruiting company that had started locally and expanded nationally. Then he did a quick web search on his name. He had found that to be the easiest way to keep up with reports on him and his story. He smiled at finding nothing new over the past 24 hours. Maybe his story was no longer trending. That was good news with respect to his job.

But then he saw a new story pop up on *The Gateway Pundit.* He went to the story's web page and what he read made his gut twist. A whistleblower in Washington, DC, had reported by name that he, Erin, and the other parents who had spoken at the school board meeting, had been placed on the FBI's list of domestic terrorists.

TWENTY

Werner's stay at their country retreat ended abruptly. Certain events in the U.S. necessitated his return to that country. He hoped the trip would be a brief one as he had to return to his own business affairs soon. However, while there he planned on making the most of the trip. At his request, he had set up meetings with various world leaders in the business realm. Their activities had become fodder for the alternative press—buying up farmland in the nation's great plains and Midwest, funding election initiatives, supporting like-minded district attorneys, and such. He wished to encourage them and invite some of them to speak at the upcoming World Order Council meeting less than three months away.

His first stop was New York City. Edvin had arranged for a helicopter service to take him upon landing and clearing customs at Republic Airport in Farmingdale, New York, east of the city. Having no commercial airline traffic, it catered to those traveling by private jet to the Hamptons and other Long Island destinations of the rich and famous. The helicopter delivered him to the West 30th Street Heliport 15 minutes later.

Edvin greeted him as he exited the aircraft.

"Good morning, sir. I'm glad you caught me before I took off for Munich. We would have crisscrossed over the Atlantic somewhere." He took his boss' bags and escorted him to the private car he had arranged for the short stay.

"*Guten morgen*, Edvin. Before we go to the hotel, are we set to meet with Herr Bouras?"

Edvin nodded. "Yes, sir. He will meet with us as soon as we get there. The PfenRich headquarters is roughly 15 minutes from here, depending on traffic."

"Good."

They entered the back of the car and were soon enmeshed in city traffic.

"We may have caught a break in the plot against PfenRich."

"Oh?" Werner was pleased. He'd heard nothing encouraging to date.

Edvin nodded again. "Yes, sir. Their security and the consultants they hired spoke of monitoring sales of ammonium-based fertilizers and gas tank sales of hydrogen and oxygen."

That sounded run of the mill to Werner. The security wonks seemed concentrated on explosives.

"So, if they're concerned about an explosive attack, have they beefed up perimeter barriers around their facilities? An explosive attack would have to penetrate such a barrier to reach the buildings and have an effect."

"Yes, sir. They have. They are taking this seriously."

"And the break you mentioned?"

"Per the consultants, I tasked our new AlterNet2 program

with searching for such things within a 150-mile radius of a PfenRich facility, both scientific and production. They found a pattern of fertilizer sales around Hartford Connecticut, well within the radius for the headquarters building and their southern New York production plant."

Werner thought about that. "It also puts their facility north of Boston within easy reach. Why the 150-mile radius? Someone intent on doing this could just as well move it from Ohio or Missouri."

Edvin was about to reply when they pulled up to the PfenRich building. Security escorted them from the car to the lobby where the CEO Constantine Bouras, MD, met them.

"Welcome, Herr Koch and Herr Bergstedt. Come, let us go up to our board room to discuss things."

Security followed them to the elevators and one guard escorted them to the executive suites. Once there, he stayed on duty in the hallway.

"May we offer you something to drink?"

"Thank you. Coffee, black, for me," replied Werner.

"Water is fine for me. Thank you," said Edvin.

Another man joined them, and introductions were made. Marshall Tucker was head of security. They discussed the situation and reasonings for expecting a bomb. Werner noticed Edvin lost in thought. As Werner's aide, he had not been an active participant in the discussion. And yet, Werner had come to value his insight.

"Edvin, do you have something to contribute?"

The younger man looked up at the group. "Perhaps. Two things are bothering me. Mr. Tucker has shown us all of the preparations made at the company's various facilities. It would seem that something like a car bomb, or a van loaded with explosives, would have no chance of doing any real damage. We've only seen photos. The perpetrator will be seeing this in real-time. Why would he, or they, continue along this route? Surely, they must see that their efforts won't work. There must be a different method of delivery."

Werner considered that. His aide made a good point. He could see Tucker's mind contemplating this as well.

"Our facilities are not along water routes, so an air delivery is the only other possibility. A drone comes to mind. It's the only thing that could provide pinpoint delivery of an explosive package."

Edvin shrugged. "I was mulling that over, too. How much explosive would be required to inflict significant damage? You asked me to look into fertilizer sales, but it would take a van's worth of the stuff to inflict real damage. How is a drone going to carry that much? Which means we need to look at other explosives.

Tucker spoke up. "In the military, we used C-4 for lots of demolition. But for major damage, the explosion had to be well-focused. Even then, it takes roughly ten pounds of the stuff to take down an 8-inch square steel beam. With a drone, they still would have to know the layout of the building and where a strike from outside would inflict serious damage. They might be able to take out a few offices and the people inside but nothing critical like a lab."

Werner looked at Edvin again. "You said two things were bothering you."

"Yes, sir." He looked at the CEO. "Sir, you've spent a great effort working to safeguard *all* of your facilities. But what if we could narrow it down?"

The CEO looked at him quizzically. "Okay. What are your thoughts?"

"What's your company doing today that is causing the most anger against you?"

"Our mRNA vaccine for COVID. It continues to stir up a hornet's nest of controversy."

Edvin nodded. "I would agree. Whether or not it's causing the deaths that so many seem to attribute to it, a growing number of people strongly believe it's responsible."

Werner saw where this was going. "So, if someone who has lost a loved one is set on revenge, where are they most likely to do so?"

"Precisely, sir."

"We've not said where the mRNA vaccine is being produced."

"Haven't you, sir? Your corporate website states that both mRNA, gene therapy, and vaccine research and production are done at your Research Triangle facility outside Raleigh, North Carolina."

The CEO seemed defensive. "But that's not where—"

"Sir, whether or not that's where it's made, that's where an angry family member is likely to target. That, and right here, corporate headquarters. The only other concern is whether or not this person, or these people, can hack into your secure electronic files. And if that's the case, they could inflict major damage without needing a drone, van, explosives, or anything else."

Tucker nodded. "I see your point. But if they could hack our systems, which I truly doubt they could, they would already have done so."

Werner said, "Possibly. That would depend on what they want. Maybe they're in there right now ferreting out the information they need to go public with damaging claims. Maybe they want airtight evidence of something else. Your corporation has a lot of files they would need to scrutinize."

Tucker stood up and walked away from the table. He pulled out his cell phone and made some urgent calls. He sounded upset and his instructions came across as quite firm. Werner had a pretty good idea that he was talking to the head of their cybersecurity, followed by his chiefs of security in North Carolina and here.

As the man returned to the table, Edvin again spoke up. "One other thing comes to mind right now. You have a big event coming up soon, don't you?"

CEO Bouras smiled, and replied, "Why, yes, we do. You might have noticed the large sculpture gracing the front grounds now. It's new. The four sets of forearms and hands reaching up represent the white, black, Asian, and red, or indigenous, races. They unite holding a great torch. At dusk, a brilliant spotlight shoots up from the ground, through the torch, and into space representing man's reach into the heavens. The light illuminates the red glass of the torch and shoots red beams of light toward the four cardinal points of the compass. I was here for the first tests. It's beautiful."

Tucker replied, "The event is the dedication of the sculpture. It's scheduled for dusk next Monday."

Bouras nodded. "Just as the sculpture shows our dedication to our DEI policies, we had wanted to dedicate it last month on the autumnal equinox, a day when the universe shows equity between day and night, but supply chain issues didn't allow it to be completed in time."

"So, what better time to organize an attack."

The CEO's smile disappeared.

Tucker sighed. "You have another good point. We should have hired you instead of those consultants."

Edvin smiled. "You couldn't afford me." Werner resisted grinning.

Their time was up. Werner needed to get to his hotel and freshen up before an afternoon meeting with two mainstream media CEOs. Then, dinner at Per Se, with its Napa Valley-themed fare. As one of a handful of Michelin three-star restaurants in the city, even Werner had to call in some chips to get reservations on short notice. After that, he would be leaving for Vail for more meetings.

As they headed toward The Plaza on 5th Avenue at Central Park, he scrutinized Edvin. The young man had impressed both the PfenRich execs and Werner. He made a decision.

"Edvin, you did an excellent job back there. I was impressed."

"Thank you, sir."

"I want to stay on here and continue to head up things here and in Washington."

His aide furrowed his brow. "But, sir, Vail. Won't you need me there?"

Werner shook his head. "I can manage there by myself. I think you'll be of much greater service to us here. I'm giving you full autonomy to act as you see fit. I expect only to be briefed as necessary on major developments."

"Thank you, sir. Thank you for your confidence in me."

Werner nodded. "You've earned it." Edvin started to say something, but Werner held up a finger to stop him. "Don't say anything about not disappointing me. I know full well how difficult these two tasks are. Almost nine million people live in this city with over one-and-a-half million just here in Manhattan. How do you find one man, or even a small group, planning an alleged attack against a company here when we have so little to work with? If corporate, local, state, and federal authorities are unable to stop such an attack, I do not expect you to do so. That said, you've already given them something to work with."

"Yes, sir."

"As for our errant programmer, locating him is much more important to our long-range goals. If PfenRich goes under, it will be disappointing, but there are other pharmaceutical firms we can use to fill the gap. But we need AlterNet2 to be the best it can be. Find Adam Afton."

TWENTY-ONE

Edvin both relished and dreaded the position he had been given. He wanted nothing more than to excel, to show off his capabilities. Yet, he feared disappointing Werner Koch. Not just because the man could make or break his career, but because he had become like the father who never seemed to be there when Edvin needed him. He hated to admit to daddy issues, but . . . his father had been in military intelligence and never seemed to be home.

He sat in a side cubicle at the AlterNet2 offices. He had taken the time to analyze the latest batch of search findings. Nothing stood out.

Needing a caffeine boost, he stepped into the small kitchen and prepared a cup of Starbucks® Pike Place Roast. All of their seasonal flavors were being advertised again, but Edvin preferred their original when he couldn't get his favorite organic German coffee—Denns Biomarkt. As the water percolated through the K-Pod, he overheard two of the programmers discussing a recent, local criminal case. They mentioned GPS.

He stepped around the corner to face them. "Hey, what is

this about GPS?"

Rebecca sipped her coffee and said, "A recent case where the guy's GPS in his car was the evidence that got him convicted."

Granger nodded. "There've been a fair number of cases like that."

"And you have used this in our search for Adam Afton?"

Granger shook his head. "We have no car to track."

"But you do. The brother."

Granger rushed away to his workstation. Edvin began to wonder if these so-called elites of programming knew what they were doing. But then, perhaps he was being too hard on them. They were programmers, not detectives.

Thirty-five minutes later, Granger and the one they called Scratch, approached him in the cubicle.

"You look hopeful. Do you have something for us?"

Granger nodded. "We sure do. We have downloaded Aric Afton's GPS data. It will take us a little time to analyze it, but we have it." They turned away to their stations.

Edvin made a call. He needed only mention Werner to have his call put right through.

"Director, this is Edvin Bergstedt, calling on behalf of Werner Koch. Mr. Koch will require some assets shortly. We might have a location for the person of interest he discussed with you."

"Very good. Please tell Herr Koch we will give him whatever help we can."

"Thank you, Director."

As he hung up, the lights in the facility flashed. A moment later, they went out altogether and a disharmonious racket of beeping followed. The programming team scurried to their stations.

Edvin stood and walked over to Granger. "What is this?"

"We were alerted several days ago that planned maintenance of the power lines in this area would take place today. We were told that it was unlikely to disrupt service, but it apparently has. The beeping you hear is from all of our UPS backups firing. They're alerting us to the loss of power. But we're good. These systems can keep us running for six to eight hours on batteries. If the power isn't restored within say, three hours, then we'll systematically shut down units so that nothing crashes."

Edvin frowned. "I was told that you were self-reliant on green energy."

"We're working on it. In case you didn't notice, it's heavily overcast today, so our solar panels aren't producing at peak. We need more battery backup, and that's on order. We also have a small wind turbine, but local ordinances prohibit a structure that tall here. We're trying to get that waived. Perhaps, Herr Koch could help with that."

Edvin took a deep breath. It became obvious to him that he needed to spend more time here. How did the English idiom go? To ride roughshod over this operation?

Just as suddenly as the power disappeared, it returned, and the beeping stopped. That's when it hit Edvin . . . their power.

He placed an urgent call to Marshall Tucker at PfenRich headquarters.

"Hello, Herr Bergstedt. How may I help you and Herr Koch today?"

"No, sir, it is how I may help you. Your power grids at the headquarters and North Carolina plant. Are they secure?"

"Why, yes, sir. As secure as we can make them. Why?"

Maybe he was wrong, but he pursued his thoughts. "You mentioned that an explosion might take out an office or two, which would be minimal damage."

"Well, yes. Except to those in the offices."

"What if the attack was to cut your power?"

"Again, there would be minimal damage. All of our most critical systems are on backup batteries, and each facility has its own backup power generators that click on within microseconds of a power outage."

Edvin nodded. He suspected as much. "And if the attack took out the backup generators?"

"They are redundant. There are units on the ground outside the buildings, and our headquarters has two units on the roof, primarily for the HVAC systems. You know these executive types; don't like being uncomfortable in their offices." He laughed.

Edvin didn't. "And if drones took out both?"

"Hmmm. Well, again, our critical systems have extra backup precautions, but I see your point. Disruption of power on that scale could certainly inflict some damage on the company, temporarily. I'll make sure the generators have extra security and order a full, off-site system backup of our data."

"I think that would be wise."

"Agreed. I will keep you and Herr Koch updated."

TWENTY-TWO

Adam had spent the better part of the week refining his search for Elena Kennedy. The final result totaled 75 women, and so far, he had eliminated 15 of them. It was slow going as he manually looked for information within their social media profiles, online white pages, tax records, state DMV records, and more that he could use to better profile them and build their life history. He had thought that by looking for photos of them he could visually rule out many of them quickly. However, his memory of her was cloudy enough that such an approach didn't help. Plus, it had been over a decade since he'd seen her. She no doubt would have changed. Perhaps a new hairstyle if nothing else. His best bet continued to be trying to locate those who had lived in the DC area ten-plus years earlier when he had met her.

As he worked to develop a timeline for one more Elena, his burner phone beeped. He jumped to get it. He hadn't heard from Aric since that first day after the phone had been delivered to him by Ryan. He was glad to see the message was from his brother and not Ryan.

Update: Two men seen entering my room last week. Clear that they went through my stuff but nothing there to find. Gov't van nowhere to be seen. Suspect a cell sniffer in my room or dorm, but unable to locate it. This phone will be used only in isolated areas. Battery removed otherwise. Also, found AirTag tracker attached to my car. Moved it to Mitch's sister's car. Her visit's over and she's heading back to Minnesota. Haha

Adam smiled. Minnesota. Good play. He wrote back:

Glad to hear from you. Hope they think they tagged wrong car, but funny anyway. I don't expect regular contact. Ryan helping to keep me updated, too. Heard about the men from him. Nothing suspicious on my end. Would like to see you but we can't risk visiting right now. Starting to feel antsy, like when Buckner would get too close. Spidey sense. Might have to change location.

Aric replied:

Hear there's a vacancy at Hotel CD. Lol

Adam laughed. He had recalled historical references to a POW camp during the Viet Name conflict being called the Hanoi Hilton. So, Hotel CD had become their private code word for the "prison" that once held children at Camp Douglas.

Might call for a reservation.

Aric replied with a thumb up and "gotta go."

As Adam thought about it, he knew Aric to be joking, but maybe that wasn't such a bad idea. Unless the FBI had emptied the place of everything, the old lab had working plumbing, an electrical generator, and best yet was very isolated. Still, he shivered at the thought of returning there. What they found there was every parent's nightmare. Adam didn't want to relive it, even if his daughter, Grace, had never been there. He couldn't help but imagine that she might have been.

Setting the current Elena aside, he focused his efforts on finding out more about the current status of Hotel CD. The facility was on its own wells—two of them—and septic system. He suspected the electrical generator to still be there as it was a large Generac Power System integrated into the building and potentially needed by a future tenant. His main concern was security. He could find no contracts for security services at the place. Still, he might have to head there and place a camera somewhere near it to make sure no one checked on the place on any regular basis.

He walked to the kitchen, made himself a cup of coffee in his Keurig, and returned to work. There was something about this Elena that looked familiar. He did some digging and found a social media post of her at a music gig in an eastern Maryland tavern. That, too, looked familiar. The post was on someone's "deleted" account on Facebook. Few things online were ever truly deleted, despite privacy and other laws dictating such. You just needed to know where to search.

He looked into the person holding the defunct account.

That woman had died over a year ago, a cardiac event roughly a month after her COVID booster. Adam could read between the lines—one of the nearly 34,000 deaths following the vaccine, as reported on VAERS, the Vaccine Adverse Event Reporting System, at the CDC. He could not find anything on VAERS that he could connect to her death specifically, but that wasn't surprising. Studies continued to show that as few as 1% of adverse events were ever reported to the system.

His gut told him to follow this lead. Perhaps a name change. What he found looked quite familiar. He set his program to further investigate what he suspected.

However, as UltraNet went to work, another one of his many online tripwires sounded. He backtracked the alert to find the new AlterNet had stumbled onto something he'd never thought to fix. Someone had tapped into Aric's car's GPS data.

How could he have been so forgetful? Basic CSI stuff. He always disabled the GPS in his own cars but hadn't thought about Aric's vehicle. Now, whoever had Aric's GPS data would find his occasional trips to East Troy and Adam's place. Adam doubted that the name on the property deed would fool anyone. He needed to clear out. Now!

As Aric headed back to the dorm after the morning class, he decided to make a detour into the library. Amongst the stacks, he could always find an isolated study nook and Wi-Fi was available throughout the building, even in the remotest corners of the basement. And with his minor paranoia, he believed this to be a location where he could safely text his brother. Not that he had anything earth-shattering to report. He didn't like the feeling of separation from Adam.

With lunchtime nearing, he didn't expect many people within the library. That, however, was a two-edged sword. The fewer the people, the less likely he would encounter someone in the stacks. However, in terms of the risk of cell sniffing, the fewer the phones, the more his phone would stand out. He took heart in the belief that no one unusual appeared to watch or follow him into the building. Still, he took care to check the area before settling into a study carrel deep inside.

As soon as the phone logged on, he received a notification of a text. That surprised him. He read:

Bugging out of here. Your car GPS has been hacked. They will see your trips to East Troy and identify this place. Don't know how much time I have, so am leaving ASAP. Likely you will be questioned. You will need some reason for being here. Remember, place is listed as owned by Robert Holmes. Will contact you once I've landed somewhere. Sorry you're wrapped up in this. Again. Love you, bro.

Aric sat back in the straight-backed chair and took it all in. His car's GPS. He had read about criminal convictions being won on such data. Why hadn't he thought about that? *I'm learning forensic criminology firsthand. Who needs college?* he thought.

Love you back, big bro. Soon.

As usual, his pragmatism kicked in. As Adam had stated, he was going to need a reason for those trips. But first things first. He logged his laptop into the network and researched disabling his car's GPS. He could use his phone for mapping and directions. He didn't want some other invasion of his privacy mapping his every whereabouts. As expected, a dozen YouTube videos on how to do so popped right up. He took some notes on his phone and determined to take on that task as soon as he could.

Next, an excuse. He knew how Adam operated. Upon leaving, his brother would make sure the place looked uninhabited. But would that be enough to thwart anyone who investigated the property? Aric pondered what *he* would do. He would want the house to look like a seasonal cottage, used only for brief periods during the year. He would have the place winterized, with the heat turned down but not off, and the water turned off so the pipes wouldn't freeze.

Under such circumstances, what would Aric's reason be for going there? Visiting a friend? Checking on it for a friend?

He shook his head. That wouldn't hold up. He could hear the interrogation now. What friend? Robert Holmes. How are you friends with Robert Holmes? Yeah, how indeed. Aric was from out of state. Was this Robert Holmes from St. Louis? If so, where does he live? What does he do? How old is he? Is he white, black, Martian? Being from St. Louis, does he prefer Bud Light over Miller Light? Aric knew nothing of the backstory Adam might have created for this guy if he was backstopped at all.

If he had thought that creating a plausible story would be easy, he was wrong. But then a thought came to him. He shook his head. No, no. Jess would not like this idea one iota. Not at all. Plus, he would want her father's blessing on the idea. After all, he would be part of the storyline, too.

TWENTY-THREE

George spent the morning researching his route between the balloon shop where he planned to get the helium and the apartment. New York was known for its extensive surveillance system consisting of over 15,200 cameras. While many argued that the placement of these cameras was racially motivated, with many more placed in areas where non-whites lived, George was simply concerned with avoiding as many as possible.

Amnesty International, using over 5,500 volunteers from around the world to analyze Google Street View images, mapped out all of the cameras and published that data as an interactive map online. From that map, George determined he could easily move between the two locations while avoiding publicly owned cameras.

The privately owned cameras were another story. In many areas, the private cameras outnumbered the public ones 20:1. Owned by businesses that typically cooperated with police, they provided a nearly complete net of facial recognition over the city. Indeed, city leaders bragged about being able to follow anyone within the city using their FRT, facial recognition technology.

In reflecting upon that, George shook his head. Nothing like bragging on FRT and then ordering everyone to wear masks. And with the ever-increasing crime rates in the city, just who were they following? Clearly, it wasn't the criminals.

Still, he would have to devise some other way to reduce the risk of being followed on camera. Or would he?

He returned to the balloon store's website on his laptop and looked through their offerings. His idea might just work . . . if he could avoid being stopped by a police officer asking for a vendor's license.

George placed his order with the store and then pulled out his phone to call up his Uber app. Thirty minutes until arrival? Nope. He chose not to wait and hurried down to the street, where he flagged down a taxi.

Opening the back door, he leaned in. "Hey, I need to pick up two helium tanks and some more balloons for a party. Any problem with that in your cab?" His voice seemed muffled by the mask he wore, but the driver did not seem to have a problem understanding him.

"No problem at all, sir." The response held a thick Indian accent.

George climbed in and gave the driver the address. The man shot out into traffic, and they were on their way . . . a car length at a time. Soon, however, the driver found the timing of the lights and within 40 minutes they had arrived at the destination. He could have walked there in that time, but this was New York City, and he didn't want to walk those streets with cash in his pocket. And he didn't want to walk back with the tanks.

"Keep the meter running. This shouldn't take long."

And it didn't. He paid cash, and in return for not having to give a bank 3%, they threw in a dolly to carry both tanks. As he emerged from the store, the cabbie exited his vehicle and moved to the trunk.

"That go in here, please."

George nodded and again they fought the traffic. George gave the man an address two blocks from the apartment.

"Must be big party," said the driver.

George didn't want to stand out, although having the tanks likely eliminated that hope.

"Big retirement party. We have something like 400 balloons to fill," he lied.

"Ah, yes. Big, big party."

A short while later, the cab pulled to the curb at the address George had given him. He paid the tab, again with cash, along with a more-than-appropriate tip. He wheeled everything into the lobby and waited for the taxi to leave. He donned a lightweight windbreaker over his sweatshirt and added a Yankees cap. Then he inflated a dozen of the balloons he had purchased, tied them onto the tallest tank, and added a sign that said, "$15."

Nothing like hiding in plain sight. He looked like any other grifter trying to make some extra dollars on the side on the streets of the city.

Standing outside, within ten minutes, he'd sold three balloons. From there, he moved about a hundred feet closer to his apartment and stopped. Again, it didn't take long to sell a few balloons. He inflated the remaining dozen and tied them to the tank. He moved to the next block. He saw one police officer, whom he avoided, and slowly worked his way back to the main door of the apartment building. By that point, he'd sold 20 of the 24 balloons and wondered why he hadn't purchased more and worked his way back from the store. He could have paid for both tanks and avoided the extra taxi fee.

Ducking inside, he made a beeline to the elevator. A family with two kids joined him for the ride up, so he gave them the extra balloons. The parents gave him a funny look, but the children didn't care that one said "Congrats!" and another said, "Happy 40th!" He shrugged and smiled.

"Hey. At their age, a balloon is a balloon."

They pushed the button for the fourth floor, so he selected the third. Standing in the hall, he then hit the "Up" button again and waited. With an empty carriage, he ascended to the tenth floor where his apartment sat.

So far, so good. He moved to his worktable where he began to review his checklist. He was ready to go. All he needed now was satisfactory weather, and the forecast for the big sculpture dedication seemed to favor him.

Adam had wasted no time packing up and clearing out his house. He followed a routine that he had learned all too well in evading Buck Buckner and Wallace Chamberlain. He had minimized his computer resources to two powerful laptops and three ancillary monitors. They were powered down and inside his car within minutes of making the decision to leave. Clothing, too, was minimal and quickly packed.

More problematic were the foodstuffs in the kitchen. The freezer's contents were hastily packed into his cooler, with the fridge contents following into whatever space remained. The items in cabinets were packed into used grocery bags that awaited recycling. He passed through all the cabinets a second time and nodded. Nothing more than one would expect in a cabin closed down for the season. All of these items were packed into his car—all six bags. He also grabbed one set of dishes and some cutlery.

He took a couple of old sheets and spread them across the couch and chair in the main room overlooking the lake. He threw another over the small dining table and its four chairs. He had a floor lamp on a timer already and decided to leave that as is. A touch of looking lived in. However, he wiped it clean of fingerprints. He did the same for all of the surfaces he might have touched, as well as those of rooms he hadn't used. He stripped the bed and cleaned the bathroom, taking care to empty hair traps. He wanted no DNA or fingerprint remnants to help anyone in finding him. He wasn't concerned that they might find a match in any databases, they wouldn't, but he didn't want to give them a basis for future comparison.

Finally, about 90 minutes later, he decided he was ready for the last tasks. He turned down the thermostat and shut off the water for winter. He took the remaining grocery bags— with potential fingerprints—and stuffed them into the kitchen trash which now held all the trash from the cabin. This he dumped into a large, black plastic trash bag. In hindsight, he also wiped clean any cans and containers he had chosen to leave behind in the cabinets. He also collected the trash from the can outside and tipped the can over to look like raccoons had gotten to it—which they had on a few occasions. The trash would find its way into the dumpster behind his favorite pizzeria.

He didn't have to concern himself with neighbors. The nearest house was a hundred yards away. He could not recall ever seeing them, and the best they might recall is seeing his light on—the light with the timer.

He took one final pass through the cabin, and satisfied that his bases were covered, he climbed into the car. All told, it had taken him just over two hours to clear out. During that time, someone could have come looking for him. He was losing his touch. He'd gotten used to settling in.

Minutes later, having tossed the trash, he had a choice—to pick up the interstate or to wend his way westward across rural Wisconsin. The former would take him southwest into Beloit before picking up I-90 west. The latter was a straight shot west to I-90 although it would likely take longer as he passed through numerous small towns along the way. He chose the latter. It was a nice day for a drive in the country, and he had no place special to be. Well, Hotel CD would never be special in his mind. Yet, it seemed to be the best option.

TWENTY-FOUR

His phone hadn't stopped ringing all morning. He had been shocked at how fast his school board photos had gone video, but this? Being named a domestic terrorist? That news spread at warp speed.

The first call, which woke him up, had not been his boss. The man had told him that he wouldn't be the one calling for his dismissal, and he was correct. The CEO himself called and wanted to see Anson in his office as soon as possible. When the man was reminded that Anson worked remotely—1,200 miles away—he hemmed and hawed, apologized for not being able to meet with Anson face-to-face, and then terminated him. He had no desire to hear Anson's side of the story or to see a video of what actually had happened that led to Anson becoming a "deadly threat to democracy," as one MSNBC pundit proclaimed. At least he had the decency to give Anson his contractual separation package. That would help cushion the financial blow of losing his income for a few weeks, and Anson wouldn't have to fight for it.

Then, after a very silent breakfast and getting the kids to school, he returned home to a barrage of calls. Even conservative outlets he'd never heard of were after him for his reaction to the FBI's pronouncement.

Hannah found him sitting at his laptop. She had work to do and a deadline to meet, but she took the time to stand behind him and massage his neck and shoulders.

"Look on the bright side. We were just talking about one of us moving into contract work to be free to deal with the kids." She offered him a wan smile. "Word's getting around that my company will be calling at least half of us back into the office beginning with the new year. I might be one of those people."

He lifted his hand to his shoulder and placed it on top of hers. "I know. At least your office is in commuting range. I'll reach out to the headhunters tomorrow."

"So, what are you going to do now?"

He had been contemplating just that. "Well, it's not like I can add domestic terrorist to my CV."

She buffed him on the side of his head.

"Seriously, I need to clear my name. I need to get the word out about what really happened at that board meeting. I mean, think about it, all of this just because I insisted on getting my two minutes to speak as a concerned parent? I never shook a fist, threatened anyone, or assaulted a board member. Push come to shove, we might have to sue the FBI to get them to issue a retraction. I don't know. I do know we're not financially in a position to hire a lawyer. I'm just grateful the kids' tuitions are covered."

As Hannah left him to begin work at her desk, Anson began to filter through the voicemails on his phone. Newsmax. OANN. *The Gateway Pundit.* Newsmax again. Several smaller outlets he'd never heard of. Fox News, twice. Having been on some of these outlets already, he wondered if they had a full-time position open. It seemed like he was "on air" with them enough to qualify.

Then came a call he hadn't expected. The voicemail said, *"Mr. Hardy, my name is Denton Pierce, and I'm a lead attorney with the Midwest Justice and Freedom Defense Alliance. We've been following your situation and now believe you might require our services. You can contact me at this number. I look forward to hearing from you."*

He finished listing the voicemail requests with callback numbers and sat back. The Midwest Justice and Freedom Defense Alliance. The name was familiar. Where had he heard that before? Sounded like a legal firm. He looked toward the heavens and wondered if God was answering a need.

He arose and walked to Hannah's desk in a corner of what had been their dining room. He watched from the side as a Zoom meeting seemed about to end. He didn't want to get in the picture. After clicking off, she looked up at him.

"What?"

He replayed the one voicemail. "I've heard that name before, but where?"

She nodded. "That's the group that defended that Christian baker somewhere in Colorado who was fined thousands of dollars for refusing to make a cake celebrating a same-sex wedding."

That was it. "Oh yeah. And didn't they also defend a woman who designs websites for something similar?"

"I think so. Shouldn't be hard to look 'em up online."

"I know, but I wanted you to hear the message. We might

just have the legal thing being handed to us."

She smiled and said, "Thank you, Lord."

He moved to the back of the house where he wouldn't disturb his wife and placed the call.

"MJFDA. How can I direct your call?"

"Hi. My name's Anson Hardy, and I'm returning a call from Denton Pierce."

"Yes, Mr. Hardy. He told me to expect your call. One moment."

A minute later, the voice from the message came on the line. "Mr. Hardy, this is Denton Pierce. Thank you for returning my call."

"Um, yes, sir. Thanks for calling earlier."

"I called because we suspect that you might be in need of some legal assistance. Several of us here have been following your situation. We've seen multiple videos from the school board meeting, and frankly, to read what the FBI has labeled you good folks has us riled up. Can you tell me what's been going on at your end?"

Anson did just that, informing the attorney about all the media requests and his recent termination.

"Sir, I suggest that you not engage in any more media interviews without a legal representative present, whether that's us or someone else you choose. As for the firing, the state where your company is based is an at-will state, and I doubt they relinquished that right in your contract. Also, you live in an at-will state, so you can't fall back on state law. As such, as long as they've met any termination requirements, they can fire you as they wish."

Anson had suspected as much. He'd never had to deal with

being terminated as he was, but he had a basic understanding of at-will employment.

"They have. I was told I would receive my separation package."

"Good."

Next came the $64,000 question. "So, if I contract you to represent me, what will that cost us?"

"Not a thing. We're funded by donations, and many of our donors are quite generous."

Anson breathed a sigh of relief. "So, how do we go about this?"

"One of our associates from either Milwaukee or Madison will be in touch within the next 48 hours. He or she will go through the paperwork we need to do, and once it's official, that attorney will also be available for media interviews. If you're going to do a national network, such as Fox News, then I might be with you personally. Our goal is to make this as easy as possible for you while we clear your name. If we have to sue for damages, we'll take that step, too. But, under the circumstances, I don't think we'll need to do that."

Anson was about to hang up when he heard Hannah yell from the front. "Anson! You better come see this!"

"Mr. Pierce, a moment please. My wife's yelling for me."

He stood and, with phone in hand, raced to the front. Looking out the window, he saw two local news vans parked in the street opposite their home. More concerning, however, was a band of protesters marching along the sidewalk.

"Mr. Pierce, you might want to get someone here sooner, not later."

TWENTY-FIVE

Adam hadn't forgotten how to get to Hotel CD, as much as he often wanted to. The images of ragged children in cages, with gaunt faces void of emotion, having no hope, still haunted him whenever he allowed them in. Keeping busy was his primary means of battling those demons.

He often wondered why Aric hadn't been affected as he had. He had concluded that it was because Aric had no children. More specifically, he didn't have a daughter who could have occupied one of those cages had there not been a fluke, what some might call a lucky coincidence. He couldn't identify with parents who had lost children.

Of course, Aric didn't believe in coincidence. Everything had a God-granted reason. His little brother often told him that he, Adam, was the reason Grace had been spared. If Aric was with him now, he'd be preaching about thanking God instead of wallowing in despair about what might have been.

He pulled up to the gates near dusk. The place had changed only in that it looked weedier and more unkempt than before. There were no signs of life, and from the amount of debris that had blown up against the gate, no one had opened them for a long time. That was a good sign.

He glanced about to make sure no one had crept up behind him and proceeded to pick the lock. Cheap lock. Piece of cake. He removed the chain, opened up one side, and pulled his car inside the lot. He replaced the chain and lock, kicked much of the debris back against the gate, and then drove around to the back where he recalled a ramp descending to the lower level. He would have to work on opening the metal roller overhead garage door so he could fully park inside. He preferred to stay completely hidden while there.

The man door next to the garage had an electronic lock, but there appeared to be no power to it. He returned to his car, grabbed some equipment from the trunk, and returned to the lock. First, he powdered the keys and was rewarded with enough of it sticking to residual fingertip oils on the keys that he could determine the four digits used in the combination. The powder's distribution was fairly even, so he deduced that no digit was used twice. That gave him confidence that only a four-digit code was used and not a five or six-digit sequence.

He loosened the outer cover, found two terminals, and with a small battery pack, powered the lock. The digital screen alerted him to having entered the wrong code. He cleared the screen and began to consider various four-digit codes. With 210 possibilities, he might have to resort to recording those that were tried and failed, but people had certain habits when devising codes. Rarely were they purely random. Sometimes it would be lowest to highest numbers, or vice versa, but many people thought they were too sophisticated for such simplicity. So, maybe they'd try the first two lowest, move to the highest, and then back to one in the middle.

Since this was supposed to be a secure lab, he reasoned the security chief would consider himself smarter than the average intruder and use some logical pattern. He noticed one possibility as soon as he could determine the digits. The highest digit was the product of the two lowest while subtracting the lowest led to the other middle one. Thus, he pressed 2, 3, 6, and 4 and opened it on his second try.

He smiled. So far, between the cheap lock on the gate and this electronic lock, his entry to the facility had been easy-peasy.

As Adam entered the basement, he felt a shiver engulf his body. His first visit there had revealed the children in cages being held there. At first glance, he thought they were still there. After blinking his eyes, he could see that, now, the space was cleaned out except for accumulated dust, webs, and a smell of mildew. Using his phone's flashlight, he inspected the garage door. He would need power to open it.

After more hunting, he found a side room holding the generator. He was in luck on two counts. It was safely vented to the outside, and it had half a tank of fuel. After several attempts, the generator caught and suddenly the place was bathed in light.

He panicked. Had he just turned on every light in the facility? Had he just broadcast a beacon to the local authorities of his illegal entry? Had he powered up a security system that now alerted the traffickers that the facility had been breached? He ran from one end of the basement to the other until he found the service panel. Forcing the door open, he sighed in relief to find that only the breakers to the basement were on. He continued his search to include the main floor until he found the security system's panel and satisfied himself that the system was turned off. To be sure, though, he ran out through the basement man door, up the ramp, and around the entire perimeter of the building. No security lights. Nothing was visible from the main floor.

He returned to the basement and raised the garage door. After moving his vehicle inside, he closed the door and sat back inside his car. He had nowhere else to sit. He would have to finish searching both levels and hope to find a chair, maybe a table. Otherwise, his car would become his home until he found something. He shook his head. That just didn't seem right—to be inside a building, with power, and still have to live in the car.

Oh well. It was what it was.

He retrieved some of the bags of foodstuffs and found some chips and other items he could use to fashion dinner—one that a six-year-old would love. While his mother would cringe at the thought of it, the junk food would suffice to keep his gut from grumbling.

Somewhat satisfied, he returned to his search. He found a storage room in the basement that still held a folding leg table and a couple of folding chairs. They weren't exactly comfortable, but at least he wouldn't get claustrophobic from sitting in the car for hours. Upstairs, he found what must have been an office. There were half a dozen empty filing cabinets, for which he had no use.

What he could use, however, was the old couch. If he could manage to slide it to the service elevator, he could get it downstairs to use as a bed. Using it in place was not a consideration, thanks to the large windows looking out across the front parking lot. One night? Sure, but tomorrow he'd have to see about moving it.

He laid down to test it out and was asleep before he took three breaths.

In a panic, he found himself in one of the cages. Light from a distant source provided just enough illumination to turn the bars into shadows he couldn't break. His heart raced, and he felt oxygen starved as he hyperventilated. And next to him in the adjacent cage was Grace. Her body was emaciated and barely covered with rags, her face devoid of hope. There was no light, no life in her eyes. Rats encircled her dirty, shoeless feet.

He grabbed for her, but the bars held him back. He rattled the cage, but the door wouldn't budge. Suddenly a burst of demonic laughter rose from within the room. He fought the cage, and fought, and fought, but it wouldn't budge. He couldn't free her.

Adam awoke in a sweat. He jumped to his feet and paced until his heart rate calmed. Maybe he didn't want that couch downstairs. He raced to the stairwell and descended to the basement. He was exhausted, but going back to that couch was not an option. Maybe it had been a mistake coming to Hotel CD. He could live in his car anywhere.

He cleared the back seat, placing the food on top of the table. With the cooler uncovered, he lifted it out, too, and reached inside for a cold beer. He needed it.

With the back seat emptied, he laid down. Again, he fell into an agitated sleep. The dream returned, but the distant light seemed brighter. As that light shone onto Grace, her eyes began to brighten. Imperceptible at first, but he could see a difference. As the demons shrieked, he tried and tried again to get to her, to release her from that cage.

And again, he awoke in a sweat. The first beer had worked through him, so he calmed himself by finding a bathroom and relieving himself. Afterward, he returned to the car. He tried to stay awake by starting to set up his computers, but soon he could barely keep his eyes open. Again, he found himself supine on the back seat.

For a third time, the dream came back. But the differences were marked this time. The light was so bright he could barely look into it, and this time a figure stood there. As he looked, he realized that the figure *was* the source of the light. And as that light shone onto Grace, her skin became radiant, her eyes began to shine, and she stood wearing a white gown. Her cage fell to its sides all around her, and she walked to join the figure. In a flash, Adam knew that the figure was Christ, but Adam was still in *his* cage, fighting, as he awoke.

TWENTY-SIX

Edvin waited for a reply. Granger and Matt, one of the other members of the team, had reconstructed the travels of Aric Afton's car over the previous four months. Early on, as expected of a college student, he had traveled mostly around his family's home in St. Louis. AlterNet2 had already found payroll records for two part-time jobs over the previous summer, and his travel logs jived with that.

Two weeks before school, he had headed north. Most of that time was spent in Kenosha. However, in the period between his going north and this day, he had traveled to a location in East Troy, WI, no less than six times. What, or more importantly *who*, was there?

A call to the director had solicited the bureau's help. Edvin expected a return call at any time.

"Edvin, we have the data on that property." Granger approached him at his desk.

Edvin scooted his chair back from the desk and swiveled toward the team leader.

"Place is owned by a Robert Holmes. He's owned it for the past two years. Age 68. Widower. Retired civil servant. Tax records confirm that. Utility usage points to the possibility that this is a summer place. Haven't found other property for him, yet, but if he's a snowbird . . . um, that's someone who moves to a warmer climate for the winter—"

Edvin frowned. "Yes, yes. I know what snowbird means. Go on." Europe had its versions of snowbirds, too. Most went to places like Mallorca, southern Italy, or the Canary Islands. The wealthier ones would head to Thailand or the southern U.S.

"Sorry. Well, we might have to search the entire southern tier of the U.S. for another residence. Even then, he might go to Mexico, Costa Rico, the Caribbean, or any number of tropical places. We aren't yet at a point of being able to penetrate many of these international databases."

"So, do you find any connection between this Robert Holmes and Aric Afton?"

"Nothing so far."

"Keep at it."

"Yes, sir."

As the programmer walked away, Edvin stood and began to pace. How far should he go with this investigation? While he expected a report shortly from the director, he now realized that might not get him any closer to his goal. If there was a senior citizen named Robert Holmes living there, then clearly that was not Adam Afton. If the place appeared to be a seasonal home, that, too, did not support any connection to Afton. Still, why would Aric Afton go there so many times? Was Afton living there with the Holmes man?

His phone rang with his expected call. "Hello, Director. Thank you for your quick response."

"You're welcome, Herr Bergstedt. Anything for Herr Koch. We didn't have any agents who were close enough to check this promptly, so we asked the local police to do a check. The home appears to be closed for the winter. We couldn't ask them to enter the home. They'd expect a search warrant. However, the officer was able to peek in windows and reported furniture being covered and no linens on the one bed he could see. No trash in the collection cans, which appear to have been toppled by animals in search of scraps."

"I see. Well, again, thank you, Director, for your assistance. I will inform Herr Koch of your cooperation."

Edvin sat back at the desk and eased back into the chair. He rubbed both temples with his fingertips as he pondered his next move. The only way to get a definitive answer would be to question the college student directly. However, that would give them away. He had gone to great lengths to make sure the young man was unaware of his being observed. To now have agents approach him and ask why he made trips to a certain location, would open up a Pandora's Box of trouble. How did they know he had been there? Had they searched his GPS records without a warrant? Even if they created and backdated a warrant, what would they use as probable cause? What judge's name would they use on the warrant, and how would they get it into that judge's files? AlterNet2 was progressing well in terms of collecting data, but placing data into databases was well beyond their scope at present.

No, the only way to interrogate Aric Afton would be illegal. In essence, kidnapping. What would Werner do? He suspected he knew the answer to that question but was he prepared to take that next step?

*   *   *

George needed to find a spot on the roof where he could both secure and hide the tanks. Being Saturday, many, if not most, of the occupants of the building would not be working. He figured he should get up early and "beat the crowd" to the roof, although admittedly he had no idea how many people frequented the roof.

As he walked along the hallway to the elevator, he could hear Saturday morning cartoons playing behind a few of the doors. He couldn't imagine living with a kid or kids in the confines of these temporary apartments, but then, affordable housing was tight, and people had to do what they had to do. He felt a pinch of remorse that what he "had to do" had the potential to disrupt their lives as well.

He took the lift to the top, where it ended on the twentieth floor. There was the equivalent of two more floors for which he had only stairs to reach the roof. That could be laborious with two helium tanks, which was why he wanted to secure them ahead of time.

He didn't have to think much about his egress. He'd have only one way to leave and that was down the emergency stairwell. Of course, there was the off-chance that the range of his device wouldn't affect the building, and in some ways, he hoped that to be the case so that the people here wouldn't have their lives upended. In that case, he would still use the emergency stairs as they would be much faster.

At the top of the stairs, he found the door to the roof propped partially open just as he had every other time he'd visited the roof. This time, however, he discovered a young woman looking out over the skyline with a cup of coffee, with a straw, in hand. She turned toward him at the noise of the door opening.

"Hi," she said, looking a bit uncertain at his arrival. "I try to get up here before anyone else." She kept her eyes on him.

He nodded. "Hi. Me, too." He didn't want her to feel threatened, so he kept his distance as he, too, eased toward the edge to look out over the city. "I'm Mike. Twelfth floor," he lied. She seemed to be more at ease that he wasn't some kind of nut job or assailant.

"I'm Cassandra. Eighth floor. Nice to meet you." She took a sip of coffee through the straw.

That's when he noticed the deformity of her face. He thought her to be an attractive lady, maybe a few years younger than himself, but one side of her face sagged, and she struggled to keep the coffee from dribbling out of her mouth on that side. Now he understood the need for the straw.

He resisted pointing, but said, "Bell's Palsy? Sorry."

She nodded. "Yeah. Surprised you know about it. It seems I have to explain it to everyone new I meet."

"What happened?" he asked, although he had a pretty good guess. Over 3,700 Bell's Palsy cases following the COVID jabs were recorded in the Vaccine Adverse Events Reporting System, and it held an even higher incidence than myocarditis, despite myocarditis making the news with all the young people and athletes dying from cardiac arrests.

She shrugged. "Most people tell me I'm crazy, and my doctor tells me I'm wrong, but a week after my COVID booster, I woke up like this. That was three months ago."

"I believe you. Six months ago, my fiancée was found dead

in her bed by her roommate a week after a COVID jab. Her autopsy showed heart damage. They called it a sudden death by cardiac arrest. She was only 28." He couldn't avoid the tears that welled up in his eyes. He never could when talking about Bella.

The sadness on her face reflected how he felt. She moved closer. "I-I'm so sorry. Here I am worried about my face maybe drooping for the rest of my life, and you . . . you . . ."

"Hey, you couldn't have known."

She turned and pointed toward the PfenRich building. "It's their fault. Those greedy people only care about their wealth, not us."

He could hear the animosity in her voice. He felt a sudden sense of camaraderie with this woman. She understood. She was living with the results of their greed, too. For a fleeting moment he wanted to assure her that they would get what was coming to them, but he resisted the temptation. No one else could know what he was about to do.

TWENTY-SEVEN

Aric welcomed Saturday mornings. Even with the day being dedicated to studying, mostly, he didn't have to rush to get ready for a morning class. Unlike his roommate, who could sleep in until noon, he still awoke early. It was the ability to take the day on a leisurely basis that he relished.

Unable to make a morning cup of coffee in his room because he would awaken Robert, he headed down to the cafeteria. He picked up a stack of pancakes, some sausage *and* bacon, a four-ounce cup of yogurt, an apple for later, and his coffee *grande,* as he jokingly liked to call it, although it was half the size of the Starbucks equivalent. He found several of the football team members sitting together. For them, most Saturday mornings held yet another round of practice.

"Hey, Aric. Come join us!" yelled Zach from across the room.

Aric placed his tray on the table and slid into the chair next to the guy.

"Dude, you gotta hear this. Mitch was just telling us this story about his sister."

Mitch nodded. "Yeah, I was just telling them. You know my

sister was just here for a visit. Well, she headed home a few days ago, and she notices this car following her. I mean, like, right from the parking lot, onto the interstate."

Aric tried not to choke on his food, while still looking interested in the story.

"Well, after some time and noticing it still hanging back there, she's starting to get a bit worried. So, she pulls into the first rest stop, and it follows her in. Whoever was in the car kept their distance and she didn't get a good look at them, but it was clear there was a passenger as well as the driver. Anyway, she sees a highway patrol car there, so, she goes up to the officer and explains what's going on. As the officer approaches the car, they pull out and drive away. Not fast. Nothing suspicious, except they'd followed her for, like, eighty miles by that time."

Dan nodded. "What happens next is what's freaky."

"Yeah. Thirty miles down the road, the same car picks up her tail and follows her all the way to Brainerd. That's 500 miles, eight hours on the road. As she gets to the city limits, she dials 911 on her cell and explains what's going on. She gives them a detailed description of the car and even a partial license plate number. Like a mile from our house, the cops pull these guys over and talk with them. Then they call her back and tell her everything is okay, and she won't be bothered anymore. And she wasn't. No explanation but also no sign of the car since then. Talk about freaking her out. She signed up for tae kwon do lessons the next day. Good thing I wasn't with her."

Zach started laughing. "Yeah, yeah, yeah. She would have to have protected little brother," he said in his best whiny voice.

Mitch punched him in the arm. "Not funny, man. She was scared."

Aric felt awful. He hadn't thought his action through. He thought it would be funny to lead whoever on a wild goose chase, but he hadn't considered her side of things.

And yet, as much as he wanted to, he couldn't apologize to Mitch. Not that he was scared of the beating he might get—deserved as it might be—or of alienating a good friend—which he didn't want to do. No, he knew that Mitch would want to know *why* an Apple AirTag tracking device had been placed on Aric's car to begin with, and Aric couldn't give him that answer.

He said a silent prayer asking for forgiveness and promising he'd make it up to Mitch's sister somehow.

The players all left for practice, leaving Aric at the table alone. He checked the time. He needed to talk with Jess and figured she was probably up by now. He dialed her number.

She answered with her most flirtatious voice. "Hey, lover boy."

Aric cringed. If only she knew what he was considering, she might have reconsidered that greeting. Still, he smiled. It *was* sexy.

"G'morning. Hey, I need to talk with you, like, this morning, and your parents, too."

"Oh?"

"NOTP." Nothing on the phone.

"Oh." She sounded disappointed. "Well, everyone's up. Dad's finishing up his sermon for tomorrow. Mom's baking something for the youth group bake sale."

"Okay. Need to shave and shower first, so give me an hour."

True to his word, an hour later he showed up on their doorstep. Pastor Tom answered the door.

"Good morning, Aric. C'mon in. Jess is in the kitchen with her mom. I'll join you in a minute.

He walked into the kitchen to find Jess making brownies with her mom.

"Ooooh, looks good. G'morning, Mrs. Larson, um, Sue."

She gave Aric "the look," as Jess called it. She insisted on Aric's calling her by her first name, as any other adult in the church would. Aric was still getting used to that.

"You can have one, just one."

Jess handed him a brownie on a paper napkin. "Yummmm," he mumbled as he took his first bite. A minute later, as Jess's dad entered the kitchen, he shoved the last bite into his mouth.

"So, Jess says you need to talk with us all. Oh, Chris can't be here. He had another commitment."

Aric nodded as he swallowed. "Actually, might be best if he's not here." That brought him a look from Jess.

"Oh?" replied her father. "You Afton boys sure keep us in surprises."

Aric shrugged. "Just don't want to give him any more fodder for teasing Jess."

"Curiouser and curiouser. Have a seat." Tom pointed to the chairs at the table.

Aric proceeded to tell them about being watched, his concern about his cell phone being tapped, and that his car's GPS log had been downloaded by someone. He decided to keep the AirTag on his car out of it. That would remain between him and Adam . . . and him and God.

"So, can I ask how you know your car's GPS log has been copied?"

Aric shrugged. "Honestly, I wouldn't have a clue about that, but Adam's an IT wizard. Ever since our, well, our last escapade two years ago he's done things to make sure I'm safe. He told me it was hacked. How he knew, I couldn't tell you. But he was sure enough about it that he's moved out of his house to avoid being found by these people."

He then told them a bit more about Adam's precarious position and the enemies he'd made. He told them the house in East Troy was owned under a fictitious name, Robert Holmes.

"So, here's my predicament. If they have my GPS log, then they'll see the various trips I took to his house. That's why he left. But it also means they might come to ask me why I went there. And I'm worried about Jess being dragged into this. Sorry. But if they can access this kind of information, they'll likely know about our relationship. People might come to ask her, and you, questions. We suspect they'll frame it in a way to seem legit. You know, like they're doing a security background check for a job or something."

No one said anything. He felt sure that they didn't like the idea of Jess getting involved. If he was a parent, he wouldn't.

"I know God hates lying. And I'm not asking you to lie about knowing Adam. I need to help protect him just like he's helped to protect me. I'm asking for your wisdom and insight on how to proceed. If they ask if you know where he is, you can honestly say no. I don't even know for sure where he is."

Pastor Tom nodded and took a breath. "Wow. I can't say I've ever run into something like this in counseling sessions as a pastor. What do you have in mind?"

"Well . . . my first thought would be to say that Robert Holmes was a friend of my parents from the past, which is kinda true. Then, when they discovered he had a place near here, they suggested I visit and befriend him since his wife died a few years ago. And that's what I did. I went out there to reconnect for my parents, liked the quietness of the lakeside property, and returned a bunch of times simply to get away from the campus for a few hours."

"Sounds like a good story to me," said Sue.

Aric nodded. "I think so, too, but as I thought about it, it sounds too convenient. These people will be suspicious. They're trying to get to Adam. They'll want confirmation and details and that's where things trip up. I can give them an age and a few details, things Adam planted in support of creating Robert Holmes. But how do I describe him? What kind of car did he drive? What did you do there? Stuff like that. And if they question Jess or you or Chris and you have a story that doesn't completely match mine, then that'll really get them suspicious and angry. For all our sakes, I don't want them angry."

"So, we work out a common story and get our details straight," said Jess.

Tom shook his head. "No, Aric has a point. What if you feel pressured and say something wrong or different? When people try to do stuff like this, it always backfires. That's why telling the truth is always the best way." He looked Aric squarely in the face. "You said you didn't want to give Chris fodder for teasing Jess, not that she doesn't hold her own." Jess grinned. "What did you mean by that?"

Aric explained how Adam had planned to leave the cabin looking like a summer place. "If he makes Robert Holmes look like a snowbird, that makes him hard to pin down. He could spend the winter anywhere warm. The problem then arises that these people might wonder if my most recent trips there occurred after the guy left to go south. I figured I could counter that by saying he asked me to keep an eye on the place every few weeks and gave me a key to make sure the water lines and stuff are okay."

"Again, sounds very reasonable," said Sue. "I guess I don't see how this is a problem, or how Jess might be involved."

Aric hesitated. "I'm worried they might keep pushing, that they might not believe the story."

"Good point," said Tom. "And . . ."

"Um, well, I figured I might need a really good, plausible backup story. Umm . . ."

"And . . ." said Tom again.

"Well, sir, Jess and I *are* in a relationship, and we *are* college students, and you *are* a local pastor . . ." He looked about at the three of them.

"And . . ."

Aric finished his thought, and Jess turned crimson.

TWENTY-EIGHT

Adam awoke in the chilled, dark basement. His night had been one of torment, and now, in that windowless space, he had no idea whether he'd slept at all. Was it early morning? Noon? Afternoon? He'd lost all track of time.

He fumbled around in the back seat of his car trying to find his phone. The area was pitch-black with near-total darkness, something he hadn't anticipated. He made a mental note to purchase some kind of lighting, but then questioned the wisdom of that. Could he risk allowing the generator to run for extended periods?

He opened the car door, and the interior light flashed on. He sighed and shook his head in disbelief that he hadn't thought of that moments ago. That's how disoriented those dreams had left him.

With that, he eased out of the back seat, turned, and searched for his phone. Nada. Then he recalled leaving it on the folding table. He walked to the table and found it just where he'd left it. Upon picking it up, the screen activated, and he saw that it was well after ten a.m. He hadn't slept that late in years. But then, he'd never had a dream like the ones he'd encountered that night.

He closed the car door and utilized the phone for light. He pulled a can of flavored seltzer water from the cooler and popped the top. He realized he would need to use the hamburger and the handful of other frozen items he'd pulled from the freezer or else they'd go bad quickly. For now, they remained frozen, but he would need to buy ice daily, and did he really want to do that? The cost of the ice would quickly overshadow the cost of the frozen goods.

He rummaged through the grocery bags and found his one remaining, overripe banana. He devoured that within a minute. He then searched for and found his box of crunchy raisin bran cereal. He retrieved the set of dishware he'd brought and placed the bowl on the table. Before dumping some of the cereal in it, however, he checked the remaining milk. Phew! *That's gone*, he thought. He ended up eating several handfuls of the cereal dry.

As he ate, he sat there and looked about. How in the world had he ever thought he could make this place a suitable hideout? Why had he come there? Clearly, he had no desire to reminisce. So, why? And look how his first night had been rewarded . . . with horrible nightmares.

At that thought, the nightmares began to replay in his mind. He closed his eyes and tried to banish them from his mind, but the darkness added to the realism of the replays. In the end, Grace had been saved by the figure of light, but not him. Why? Why hadn't he been rescued, too?

And the figure of light. He remembered having the distinct thought that the being was Christ. Was that correct? Or was he simply acting upon childhood teachings and guessing that it was Christ?

Growing up, the whole family had gone to church. As Adam grew older, though, attending church became just another check box, something to do on Sundays. Something had clicked there for Aric and his sisters, but he had lost interest and strayed away as often as he could. As soon as he left for college, he left the church behind. And he'd felt vindicated in his beliefs in college where none of his professors or friends thought of the Bible as anything more than a collection of myths.

Had they all been wrong?

Again, the thought of Grace being saved but not him plagued him.

He needed to make himself busy, to drown out the thoughts with activity. His first action, after reactivating the generator, was to completely search every nook and cranny of the facility. He found a second folding table in one of the labs. In another storage room, he found an old microwave. It worked, but he suspected he'd be able to do little more than heat food up and make popcorn with it. In fact, from the smell on the inside, it appeared that the latter had been its primary function.

He moved both to the basement where he cleaned them. On one table he set up a makeshift café with the foodstuffs he had salvaged from his home. On the other, he set up his computers. Although he got everything up and running, his satellite service appeared blocked by being in the basement. He placed his transceiver outside along the retaining wall near the ramp, but his coaxial cable was a good 20 feet short. He would have to correct that if he hoped to get any real work accomplished. He prepared a list of items to buy.

As he reviewed the list, he decided now was as good a time as any to go shopping. He opened the garage door and backed his car out onto the ramp. Back inside, he closed the overhead roller door, opened the man door to let some light inside, and then powered down the generator. He had already equipped the man door with a battery on the lock, so he'd be able to get back inside without a hassle.

Camp Douglas offered little in the way of shopping. The farmers' co-op might have some things he could use, but not most of it. Besides, they likely knew everyone who shopped there and would notice a stranger. He wanted to avoid questions. And, other than a couple of taverns and a Quiznos, there wasn't even food available.

He needed a Menards or Home Depot. According to his map app, he was right between two Menards—Baraboo to the south or Onalaska to the west—with each being about 45 minutes away. The Home Depot in Wisconsin Dells was closer, so off to the Dells he went. He would also grab a big meal and fill up the car and a gas can with diesel while there.

Three hours later, he returned to the old lab. He again double-checked being alone before picking the lock on the gate. Upon closing it, he replaced the lock with his own. Once inside, he unloaded the car and set up his purchases. Now he had a couple of lamps, as well as battery-powered lanterns for when the generator was off. He had the equipment to finish his computer installation and within 30 minutes, his system was up and running and connected to the web via satellite. He also had additional battery backup units for the system.

One additional task awaited him. He went back outside

and placed a battery-powered, Wi-Fi motion detector on the front corner of the building, aimed at the gates. It wasn't so sensitive as to pick up small animals, and the fencing around the property prevented deer from getting inside. His concern was someone snooping around, particularly some sheriff's deputy or teens looking for a secluded place to hook up. He didn't think his running the generator could be noticed from outside, but he didn't want to be surprised by an unwanted visitor.

Lastly, he unpacked more food—items more in line with his situation. He also had a hotplate for heating food and cooking simple things like the hamburger he needed to use. That would be tomorrow.

It was dark outside now, and he was exhausted, but he had one last thing to do. He had told himself the night before that he wouldn't, but now he found himself pushing and dragging that couch out of the office, down the hall, and into the service elevator. The effort took enough out of him that he wanted to lie down on it in the elevator, but it was standing up on one end in order to fit inside. After 40 minutes of labor, he finally had the couch positioned where he wanted it. He stood back and looked about his new little domain. It would work, but he hoped he wouldn't have to hide here long.

With everything powered down, he took a look at that couch and hesitated to lie down. Still, he reasoned, the nightmare had also occurred when he tried to sleep in his car. It wasn't the couch. He lay down and closed his eyes . . . and the nightmare returned.

TWENTY-NINE

"C'mon, Jason, get your shoes. Derrick, find your backpack. You're going to be late," yelled Hannah up the stairs to their two youngest children.

Anson donned his coat while Elizabeth placed her books into her backpack. Jonathan, their sixth grader, walked out of the kitchen through the front room. Anson noticed he had stopped at one of the windows overlooking the front.

"Get a move on, Jonathan. We need to leave." He walked over to his wife and kissed her on the cheek. "I'll be back as soon as I've dropped these guys off. The lawyer might get here before I get home. Her name is . . ." He retrieved the note from his pocket. ". . . Alicia Somers. She's with some Milwaukee firm that works with the MJFDA."

Jonathan looked over at him. "Dad, there's a lot more TV trucks out there."

Anson heard him but was unsure what to say. He'd grown more concerned the previous night when a third satellite truck had joined the first two. *Why?* he had wondered. He's not sure what led him to do it, but he dug out two old nanny cams used when the kids were younger and powered them up to make sure they still worked. One he placed in an upstairs window overlooking the front and angled diagonally to capture all of their front yard. The second he placed in a window in his garage, pointing across the yard along a diagonal perpendicular to the other camera. He captured both cameras' Wi-Fi signals with an old desktop computer he allowed the kids to play games on. As of dawn, all activity across the front of their home was being recorded by these cams, as well as their Ring doorbell.

As the two youngest came down the front steps, Jonathan's cry was one of distress. "Daaaddd!"

At that moment, the front door came crashing in and six fully armed men stormed into their home. Their body armor said FBI in big letters. The girls shrieked and began to cry as they rushed for the protection of their mother. The youngest boys screamed and ran back up the steps. Hannah began yelling, "Stop! Stop! What the @#% are you doing?" Jonathan stood still, his mouth gaping at the scene playing out 12 feet away from him. Anson stood there with Derrick's coat in hand, bewildered . . . as much by the word coming from his wife's mouth, a word he had never, ever heard her say, as by the armed home invasion taking place.

"FBI!" . . . "FBI!"

"On your knees!"

"Hands behind your head. Fingers interlaced!"

"On your knees!"

Anson dropped the coat and complied. Did he have any choice? He gaped through the opening that once was their front door and saw neighbors milling around the news vans, watching the event unfold. Many had their cell phones up to their faces. The news crews had video rolling as well. And several additional agents, plus local police officers, stood at the ready in their front yard. Was this truly happening? To him?

An agent placed handcuffs on both wrists, shackles on his ankles, and pulled him roughly to his feet. Now, Anson was getting mad.

"Was this really necessary? All you needed to do was ring the bell, introduce yourselves, and ask me questions. Did you need this circus, scaring my kids and wife to death? Tearing apart my home?"

He looked over to his wife. "Hon, I think the kids need to stay home today. Let the attorney know what happened."

"Quiet!" Two of the agents began to drag him out of the house.

"Hey! I can walk. Just tell me where you want me to go."

They continued to drag him along, and he realized this was for the cameras. It all made sense now. The media had been alerted ahead of time so they could prepare their crews. Their agenda became clear. He was to become the face of angry parents. He was to be the example of what could happen if you protest the actions of your school board as they implemented their indoctrination of your children. These officers were following a script, one that took orders from someone higher up on the food chain.

Anson saw that they were headed toward a car with the back door open. He kept trying to stand and shuffle with the shackles on his own, but the agents didn't offer him that dignity.

"What's the meaning of this? What are you doing? Where's

your warrant?"

The woman's voice rang out to his right somewhere. There was an authoritative tone to the voice, and yet as he glanced toward the voice, he saw a petite blonde in a hunter green, skirted suit, and heels storming toward them. She had fire in her eyes.

"Let my client stand up! Who's in charge here? Where's your warrant?"

The agents dragging Anson stopped and allowed him to stand up. He tried to straighten himself and his clothing. The woman marched up to him. She didn't extend her hand, as it was obvious that he couldn't return the greeting and her doing so might have looked comical for the cameras. An agent in a black suit with an FBI vest over it approached. He did not look happy, but she met his gaze with fierce determination.

"I'm Agent-in-charge Torres. Who are you?"

"I'm Alicia Somers with the Midwest Justice and Freedom Defense Alliance, and we're representing Mr. Hardy here. What's the meaning of this? Where's your warrant?"

At the mention of the MJFDA, several of the agents showed concern. The firm's reputation preceded it. Torres fished out the paperwork from his suit coat and handed it to her. She perused it within seconds, and Anson figured she knew just where to look for salient details.

"Are. You. Kidding. Me? You sent eight cars and over a dozen officers to arrest him on a misdemeanor charge? You broke into his home, in front of his family and neighbors on a misdemeanor charge? Who authorized this raid?"

No one spoke up.

"I want all of your credentials and numbers before you

leave here, or else. You're all on video. We *will* be able to identify you by day's end. And if we don't have the name of who authorized this before you leave, *all* of you will be named on the lawsuit, qualified immunity or not. This is outrageous."

One of the agents tried to lead Anson toward the car. Alicia put up her hand.

"Oh no, you're not. You're not going to lead him away in handcuffs and shackles for an alleged misdemeanor trespassing charge. Take off the cuffs and release his legs."

The agent looked at his AIC, who nodded. The man pulled out a key and removed the handcuffs, followed by the shackles. Anson rubbed his wrists.

"Thank you," he said.

"Now, AIC Torres, I also suggest you get a contractor out here this afternoon to replace this family's door. You know, I don't know who you pissed off, but giving you this assignment was a sure way to get you in trouble."

She walked up to Anson, and this time extended her hand, which he took with gratitude. "Thank you, Ms. Somers. I can't believe this is happening."

"Nor can I. Please call me Alicia. I know we'll be working together a lot, particularly after this debacle."

Anson heard feet running toward him from the house and turned to see Hannah and their kids running up to him. The group hug nearly knocked him to the ground. He heard some applause from neighbors as well.

"Anson, please come with me. Mrs. Hardy, if you and the kids want to come stand behind us, that would be great."

She led the family to a spot in front of the news vans. In an instant, they were almost surrounded by cameras and reporters.

"Ladies and gentlemen, I am Alicia Somers of the Midwest Justice and Freedom Defense Alliance. What you watched here . . ."

THIRTY

Caleb felt uneasy as he and Ted drove to Madison. With Caleb's ability to practice his profession being threatened, Ted had requested, and they had been granted, an expedited hearing with the Medical Examining Board, which had the legislative authority to investigate all complaints against physicians, as well as to terminate their licenses. They were to meet with an investigator at the board's offices across from the southwest end of Lake Mendota.

As they sat in the waiting room, Caleb couldn't help but cross one leg over the other and then reverse them, repeatedly. His nerves were getting the best of him.

"Relax," said Ted. "This is just a preliminary interview, to let you tell your side of the story." Then he gave Caleb a Cheshire grin and added, "Besides, I hear Home Depot's still hiring."

Caleb's first reaction was "that was cruel." "Not funny," he replied. But in a way, it was, and it got Caleb's attention. The jitters seemed to dissolve and be replaced by resolve.

After several minutes, they were called back to a meeting room where they sat at a long, boardroom table. No water or coffee was offered them, but then, Caleb reasoned, the inquisitors had no need to butter up their subjects before beheading them. A slim man of about 50 years, with slicked-back hair and a bushy, black mustache, entered the room.

"Good morning. I'm Mario Renzoni, chief investigator for the board." Introductions followed, and all sat down.

Caleb refrained from smiling. The man's mustache seemed fitting with his name, but he doubted the guy had a plumbing background.

Ted had instructed Caleb to let him lead the way and do most of the talking, except where the medical issues were involved. So, Ted started.

"Thank you for expediting this interview. Dr. Wahlburg seeks to clear up this matter as soon as possible so that he can proceed with the next phase of his OB/GYN career."

Caleb liked the positive spin.

Investigator Renzoni nodded. "I agreed to do so because this is something of new territory for us, too."

Ted sat forward. "May I ask what statute the board is using to authorize this investigation? There are no issues regarding informed consent or death certificates, and as a Christian, Dr. Wahlburg doesn't do abortions."

The man opened his folder. "That's true, so statutes 253.10 (3), 448.30, 450.13 (2), and 69.18 are not being applied."

Caleb tried not to let his eyes glaze over. He needed to be attentive. Ted had gone over the various statutes under which the board could initiate a hearing, but the numbers went in one ear and out the other, like an otoscope light in a politician.

"Let's see. We received word that ACOG was investigating your credentials."

Ted jumped in. "My understanding is that ACOG is investigating because you're investigating, and now you're saying that this board is investigating because ACOG is doing so. That sounds like circular reasoning to me. Plus, are you saying that ACOG is an affiliated credentialing board attached to this one? They are not a state board, so how are they attached to this board? Under 49.45 (2) (a) 12r, this board can only investigate issues of decertification by attached credentialing boards."

The to-and-fro continued for several minutes, leaving Caleb impressed with one thing: Ted truly had read all of those volumes of Wisconsin statutes in his meeting room. In the end, it came down to the board's receiving notice of Caleb's termination from the hospital, which automatically triggered an inquiry based on statute 50-point-something or other.

The investigator turned to face Caleb, "Dr. Wahlburg, as I said, this is new territory for us. By that, I mean the reason for your termination. As I understand it, social media is involved. Would you explain this to me?"

Ted nodded for Caleb to proceed. He told the man of the increases in stillbirths, miscarriages, and the like that he was seeing. He mentioned finally getting to the point where he posted his observations, as well as a link to a study by a prominent maternal care specialist, on social media. That had prompted a threat of termination from the administrator, which was something of the final straw for him. He made another post and was terminated. He acknowledged that in anger he'd made that final post right in front of Massey and was open about the fact that the two of them often rubbed each other the wrong way.

"My concern was and always has been the health of the women in my care, and their babies. Mr. Massey's lack of caring really upset me."

Mr. Renzoni looked contemplative. "Can you provide us with specifics, statistics from your practice?"

Caleb shook his head. "No. Mr. Massey forbade me access to the data and told me that would be another cause for termination."

"I see." The man paused. "As I said, this is uncharted waters for us. Do you have any materials to support your claims about these issues being caused by the vaccine?"

Caleb pulled a stack of papers about four inches thick from the chair next to him. "Dr. Thorpe's paper is on top. It's a well-done analysis and very comprehensive."

Renzoni pulled the papers toward him. "Well, looks like I have enough bedtime reading to last me a few weeks."

While Caleb assumed that the comment was meant to be lighthearted, it caught him two ways. On the positive side, it appeared that the man would indeed read the material. Of course, he could just be saying that. On the negative side, however, was his mention of bedtime. If he was going to try to read this stuff when tired, he'd be reading it for more than a few weeks as he'd likely fall asleep well before finishing any given study. And until he finished and came to a conclusion about the need for a full hearing, Caleb would be sitting there in limbo.

THIRTY-ONE

For Aric, Mondays had become his toughest morning. The weekends had their mix of study and fun, with Sundays being filled with church and young adult activities. Of course, those always included time with Jess. The previous day had been no different. But on Monday he had to be up earlier for class than for his other morning classes. He felt convinced the professor added that extra half-hour lab session to the beginning of class on Monday just to hassle the students who'd spent too much time partying over the weekend.

As he left the dorm for that early session, he stopped just yards into his walk toward class. Despite the dense fog coming off the lake, he saw it a hundred yards away—the white van. He looked around and saw no one else except a handful of students wending their ways to class, the gym, or the library. He picked up his pace, put up the hood on his sweatshirt, and headed toward the classroom. He had no other choice. To try to detour around it would make him late.

As he neared the vehicle, he saw that it was idling, but he saw no one milling around it. He checked the rear tag and recognized it as the same van. As he passed by, he saw two men sitting in the front, but they made no effort to exit the vehicle as he walked by. Had they not seen him? Perhaps they hadn't expected him so early. Or maybe they didn't recognize him thanks to the hoodie.

He made it into class without being stopped and breathed a sigh of relief. Was he simply being paranoid? Boy, he would feel stupid if he discovered they were on campus for an entirely different reason that had nothing to do with him and Adam. But no, deep in his gut, he believed they were there to find information on Adam. Why else would they have entered his room?

After the early morning lab, they gave the students a 15-minute break before the main class started. He grabbed both phones, jammed them into pockets, donned his hoodie, left his backpack and books behind, and made a beeline toward where he had seen the van. He expected them to have disappeared, but what he saw made his heart skip a beat.

The two men had stopped Jess and Chris on the sidewalk. They wore FBI windbreakers this time, not jogging suits, and they looked quite serious. Other students gave them wide berth as they passed by and gave the pair questioning looks. Jess saw him and used her eyes to warn him off. He stopped, turned, and retreated to a bench around the corner behind a stand of burning bushes, their leaves resplendent in crimson.

A few minutes later, Chris came around the corner.

"Where's Jess?"

He took a deep breath. "She insisted on talking with them alone. Don't ask me why."

Aric suspected he knew why, but he had never expected her to, well, to fulfill his plan. Her parents were against it. She had been willing to go along with it, to save Adam from discovery.

"Hey, I gotta get to class. She should be along in a minute." Chris hurried along.

Aric checked his time. He, too, would have to get back to class, and he knew he'd never be able to focus on the lecture without knowing what had happened. As he debated leaving, she rounded the corner.

"Aric! Oh, I'm so glad you didn't come over. I don't think I could have done it with you standing there."

"Done what? What happened?"

"It was like you said. They approached us and stated that they knew we were friends of yours and asked if we knew your brother. They said they were conducting interviews for Adam's security clearance. They asked questions about his whereabouts, which I thought strange if they were working on his security clearance, but I didn't let on. Chris just followed my lead."

Aric sighed in relief at that revelation. He hadn't had time to brief Chris himself and had asked Jess to fill him in . . . with as much as he needed to know.

"Fortunately, they asked if we knew where he was, not where he lived. We could answer 'no' without lying. We were asked if we knew a Robert Holmes and had ever been to his house in East Troy. Again, Chris could say no on both counts. I played the game we'd talked about. Hemmed and hawed. Suggested that Chris head to class, and I could finish."

Aric had a feeling he was about to award Jess with an Oscar.

"I told them I didn't know a Robert Holmes but had been

to the house with you. Again, all true, just like you said. I told them you had been asked to check on the place off and on, and that I went with you. And just as you predicted, they started getting pushy. They asked if Robert Holmes was really Adam. I said I didn't know Robert Holmes and had never met him. They started to suggest that I was lying about going to the house, that I had actually gone with you to see your brother, and that they needed to find Adam."

Aric was right. Their only reason for being on campus was to glean information on Adam.

"In hindsight, I should have confronted them right then about lying about security clearance interviews, but I started getting nervous and didn't think about it."

"And . . ."

"And I finally burst into tears and told them yes, I'd been to the house but not for the reason they suggested. I stammered about being college students, in love, and needing a place to, well, be alone. They took the hint and asked why we couldn't find a place nearby. As you had suggested, I told them my dad was a prominent pastor with church members from as far away as 40 minutes and that I didn't want to embarrass him or myself. I even managed to blush about the same color as these leaves here." She fingered several of the leaves on the burning bush. "They added two and two and got five. I never had to lie about anything, just as you said." She gave him a coy smile. "It was actually kind of, well, fun, leading them on like that. They took it hook, line, and sinker."

He gave her a big grin and leaned over to kiss her. "You are an all-star. Hey, we're late. See you at lunch."

THIRTY-TWO

The weekend had been among the worst Adam could remember. Was it the location? Had being there triggered some sort of psychosis? His sleep had been interrupted by the dream on several occasions, and during those periods of wakefulness that followed the nightmare, his mind could not focus on anything else. His attempts to fall back to sleep became a struggle. He knew he needed sleep, but his thoughts kept circling back to the image of him being in a cage while Grace stood in the arms of the figure of light.

He fought the idea that the figure was Christ and the idea that He was somehow sending a message to Adam. Yet, in this fight, the nightmare was winning.

The previous morning, he found himself driving out of Camp Douglas toward the town of New Lisbon. On his drive to the Dells, he had noticed signs for a couple of churches there. He couldn't explain the feeling of being drawn there, but he knew he needed to get hold of a Bible. He needed to read it for himself. He didn't want to talk with Aric, his folks, or even Lynch Cully, although he knew any of them could talk with him about the Bible. If this was just some kind of psychotic break, he didn't want them to know about it.

He pulled off the interstate and headed toward town. Just after passing a Dollar General, he saw a church. The building looked little bigger than the dollar store and very utilitarian. The Cobra helicopter and tank were interesting touches for a church, but then he saw that the building was also the home of the local American Legion. Even so, the lot was at least three-quarters full.

He had pulled into a parking slot and steeled himself for going inside. He didn't want to get roped into staying or talking with someone; he just wanted a Bible, if they had one to spare.

As he walked in, a balding man in his fifties greeted him. Adam must have looked and smelled ripe. He hadn't had a shower or shaved in three days. He hadn't slept well. He could only imagine how he looked to others and what the man thought of him, but that hadn't stopped the man from welcoming him.

He asked if they had a Bible he could borrow. The man asked where he was from, whether he had eaten recently, and where was he sleeping. Adam figured he must look homeless but just reiterated his request. At one point, he had admitted to not having slept well for the past few nights and having a recurring nightmare. He hadn't meant to open up like that and didn't understand why he'd divulged that, but it was out there. The man seemed genuinely concerned, and while Adam might have pushed for more information if he'd been in that man's shoes, the guy didn't. He seemed to know that Adam needed some space. In the end, he gave Adam a Bible, said he could have it, and gave him a business card with the invitation to call him at any time.

Adam couldn't remember the last time he'd ignored his computers or the results that UltraNet brought him. But yesterday, he hadn't even powered them on. Upon returning to the lair, he parked himself on the couch and began to read . . . and read . . . and read. He found himself quivering by the time he finished the Book of Matthew and tears came to his eyes as he read John.

Now, Monday morning, he finished the New Testament. He had no nightmare that night because he'd spent the entire night reading and trying to absorb what he read. He flipped off the light, sat back on the couch, and sank into a deep sleep.

At some point, he began again to dream, but this time, it was different. Grace was not there, but the figure was, and he seemed to be beckoning Adam to join him. All Adam had to do was push open the door to the cage and walk to Him. But Adam hesitated. He couldn't seem to find the strength to push open the door. Instead of terror, sadness engulfed him.

When he awoke, he checked his phone to discover it was mid-afternoon. He flipped on one of the battery-powered lanterns and found his way to the generator. With full power again, the wells would provide water, and with a little luck, the water heater would provide hot water to the shower he'd found during his first inspection of the building a few days earlier. He wondered if the children had used it. He hoped they had.

While he waited on hot water, he shaved and pulled together a clean outfit. He tested the water . . . lukewarm. As he sat on the couch, replaying things he'd read the night before, he realized he had never had a clear picture of who

Jesus was and of what He did for mankind. Yet, he still had lots of questions.

He pulled out the business card he'd been given and which had been his bookmark during the night. Ralph Bursiek. Top Gun Mechanicals—Plumbing and HVAC. *At least the guy should be down to earth*, he thought. *I hope he knows enough to answer some of my questions.*

He took a deep breath and dialed the number. The task wasn't as difficult as he'd expected.

"Ralph here."

"Um, Mr. Bursiek, I, uh, hope I pronounced that right."

"That you did. How can I help you?"

"I, um . . . I'm the guy you gave a Bible to yesterday. I spent the day and night reading the whole New Testament, but I, well, I have questions. D-do you think you might have the answers?"

"Son, I might, and then, I might not, but I know how to get 'em. Do you have a name?"

Adam started to say Robert but stopped. That was a lie. It was a convenient one when it came to evading certain people, but this was not the place or time to keep up the lie. "Adam," he replied.

"Well, Adam, you have plans for dinner? I'm on a job right now, but it's almost quitin' time. Why don't you join me and my missus for dinner? I'll let her know we're havin' a guest."

"Really, sir, I don't want to impose. Maybe we—"

"It's no imposition. I mean that. And my wife won't see it that way either. Six o'clock. We'll eat and then see about gettin' you some answers."

The man wouldn't say no, so Adam finally agreed to dinner

and jotted down his address. Adam—having lived in DC, where no one would invite a stranger, especially one who had looked so ragged as Adam had the day before, right off the street into their home for a meal—sat there wondering about this man. But was it so difficult to image someone that generous? He realized Aric would do the same. Even his parents had invited an immigrant family they'd never met into their home to experience an American Thanksgiving. Sure, that event had been sponsored by a ministry that had already vetted the family, but a willingness to serve and reach out was still required.

A few minutes after six, Adam rang the bell at the front door of the man's home. The home was just down the road from the church, a 1970s-vintage two-story at the end of a farm lane behind a field of corn. The corn appeared to have seen its final days of the season, having been nipped by a heavy frost. Two pole barns sat to one side of the home. One appeared to hold his business and the other, farm equipment. The whole place looked well-tended and tidy.

The door opened, and the man Adam recognized from the previous day stood there, welcoming him inside. Ralph had a surprised look on his face.

"Adam, you certainly clean up nice. Almost didn't recognize you."

Adam offered a weak smile. "Thanks. I'm pretty sure I looked a wreck yesterday."

If the man wanted to agree, he didn't. "Well, welcome to our home." A middle-aged woman joined them from the back of the home. "Hon, this is Adam. Adam, my wife, Paula. Best cook in this part of the state."

She smiled and swatted her husband on the shoulder with her dish towel. "He's biased." She held out her hand. "Adam, nice to meet you."

Adam felt her gaze as it scanned him from head to toe. No doubt Ralph had told her about the crazed man at the church. He wondered what she might be thinking now.

He glanced around. The home was tidy and not overly burdened with knick-knacks. Family photos lined tabletops and the mantle. A welcoming fire had been started in the wood-burning fireplace.

Dinner ended up being a joint effort on the part of Ralph and Paula. He had smoked brisket over the weekend, and she added delicious cheesy mashed potatoes, homemade yeast rolls, green beans from their garden, and a dessert that demanded seconds—English trifle, with hunks of angel food cake, surrounded by a vanilla pudding-ice cream mix and fresh strawberries. Paula seemed pleased when he asked for that second portion.

"That was delicious. Thank you so much for a wonderful meal."

"Our pleasure. Glad you enjoyed it. Coffee?"

Adam shook his head. "Um, no thanks. I, uh, I don't want the caffeine keeping me awake tonight." He didn't want to bring up his nightmare with her, although he suspected Ralph had already shared that with her. He still could not understand what led him to share that with the man the previous day.

"Then, why don't you fellas head back to the living room to talk. I know that's what you really came here for."

"Thanks, hon."

Ralph gave her a peck on the cheek as he passed by on his

way to the other room. Adam followed. Ralph pointed to a chair for Adam and then poked the fire and added a log.

"So, you have questions. We all do, but first, why don't you tell me a bit about yourself."

Adam hadn't anticipated that but realized that he should have. The man would need to know some things about Adam if he was to help.

Adam decided to avoid any talk about his current situation, or what led to it. He had little doubt that the man had probably heard about the FBI raid two years earlier on the facility outside Camp Douglas. The place was, after all, only 10 miles away via the back roads.

Adam told him about his upbringing, his family, his skepticism, and how college had confirmed his belief that the Bible was a collection of myths and ancient letters about how to live a good life. He talked about his belief that Jesus was a good man, but the Son of God? Was there a God?

Adam knew he would have to explain the nightmare since he'd already mentioned it. He told of the abduction of his daughter and that she'd been found, but that something recently had triggered the fear he'd experienced in his search for her.

Then he described his nightmares.

Through it all, Ralph looked contemplative. He listened patiently as if guided by experience in counseling others. Adam suspected that he had done just that, many times.

Finally, Adam stopped talking. After a moment of silence, Ralph spoke. "So, let's address the biggest question here. Is there a God?"

Adam nodded. He had to admit that was the primary

question. If God didn't exist, then Jesus couldn't have been His son.

Ralph waved his hands around him. "Tell me, where did all of this come from? I mean everything, the world, our bodies, the air we breathe. Where did it come from?"

Adam had a ready answer. "Well, science tells us it started with the Big Bang, and then various chemicals formed, one thing led to another, and through evolution over millions of years man evolved."

"Yep, that's what science teaches today. Of course, 175 years ago no one had ever heard of such. Darwin's theories didn't exist, and most folks believed in Biblical creation or cultural myths. But, think about it, the Big Bang. What takes more faith, to believe that first there was nothing and then it exploded to create the cosmos or to believe in an intelligent designer? What about the laws of physics? If there is conservation of energy in a system, the first law of thermodynamics, where did the energy come from for the Big Bang? What about the second law that says everything in a closed system shares energy until that system reaches a common, shared level of energy? Heat only transfers to colder objects, not the other way around. Over billions of years, why hasn't the earth lost its heat to the moon or the cosmos in general? Why hasn't the sun burned out by now? Where did its energy come from?"

Adam tried not to let his mouth gape open. This guy was a plumber? Laws of thermodynamics? Clearly, Adam had underestimated the man.

"Let's take this from another angle. Why do we still have mountains? In fact, why does dry land exist at all if the earth is billions of years old? Modern-day science tells us that mountains erode from rain and wind at an average rate of 39 inches every 1,000 years, while tectonic uplift only adds 6-7 inches over that same time. Erosion by rivers reduces their basins over time, ranging from four-one-hundredths of an inch to 750 inches per 1,000 years, depending on the river. With an average height of 2,000 feet, the continents would have disappeared after several million years just from water erosion by rivers. A plateau as high as Mount Everest could be leveled by China's Yellow River in 10 million years. What's easier to believe, that the earth is billions of years old, yet defies basic physics and geological forces, or that it's only seven thousand years old?"

The man gave Adam a wry grin.

"Okay, that gives me a lot to chew on, but what about evolution?"

"What about it? Is it truly plausible to think that proteins and enzymes and such came to be in some kind of random fashion, in some kind of primordial soup? They postulate that high oxygen levels and maybe electricity from lightning started the first reactions, but they ignore that such high levels of oxygen cause oxidation, one of the most *destructive* chemical reactions we know, not a creative one. Besides, what are the odds of a protein forming at random? Most proteins have 400 carbon atoms, over 600 hydrogen atoms, 100 nitrogen atoms, and over 100 oxygen atoms as their base. The odds of this coming together by chance are astronomically against it. But, getting back to proteins and enzymes, it's kind of a chicken and the egg proposition. Look at enzymes. Enzymes are built from proteins, yet enzymes are needed to build the proteins. Which came first? Plus, the process is based on instructions from our DNA. DNA alone makes our supercomputers look like abacuses. The entire system has to be in place for life as we know it to happen, but the odds against such are so great that billions of years aren't long enough for this to have happened randomly."

Adam's mind was spinning. "What about chimpanzees being close relatives to man?"

"Ah. Well, that's flawed science. When the first genetic sequencing was performed, the technology was still in its infancy. Where they had gaps in the ape's DNA sequence, they simply filled it in with known human sequences because, after all, everyone knew that man evolved from apes, right? Well, two separate studies in two different labs in 2018 and 2019, using better tech, confirmed each other's findings that chimps and man only share about 85% of DNA, not 98.5% That knocked the whole man evolved from apes thing right off the table."

Adam took a deep breath and sighed. "Wow, and that was only one question."

Ralph nodded. "Sorry, but that question underlies all the others you might have. Seeing everything around us, as well as us, as the results of intelligent design is much easier than believing all that evolutionary, old earth stuff."

Adam nodded in response. He had a lot to process, but if he took the man's statements at face value, how could he not believe in God as the Creator of all things? The concept of an intelligent designer struck home with Adam. The fact that some portions of DNA were found in common among different species was no different than automotive engineers using the best ideas and designs among different cars.

He came up with another question. "So, if good people go to heaven, why exactly did Christ come to earth?"

"Another great question. First, who says good people go to heaven? The Bible teaches that being good isn't enough. Just as apple trees produce apples and kangaroos beget more kangaroos, sinful man begets more sinful men. The Bible teaches that there is no one, not one person, good enough to earn a way into heaven. Too many people believe that man is born good and can become wicked because of how he's raised or by circumstances beyond his control. The Bible teaches that all of us are sinners. None of us can earn our way into heaven. If good deeds could earn us eternal life, Christ wouldn't have had to come. And if you don't believe man is born a sinner, just spend some time watching little kids. They're selfish and have to be taught to share. They'll lie to get what they want and have to be taught not to lie. They're often disobedient. What does that say about their underlying nature? You see, God doesn't differentiate or grade sin. A lie is just as sinful as murder. Adultery is just as sinful as homosexuality. Christ came to give us a way back to God's presence, to heaven as it were. Plus, he's the *only* way. The Bible is clear that only one road leads to eternal life and that path is Christ. Not Islam, or Buddhism, or being good, just God's gift of grace through accepting Christ."

"Okay, I got that from my reading, I think, but does that mean just believing in Jesus as the Son of God is enough?"

Ralph shook his head. "Sadly, no. Even demons accept Christ as God's Son. One must accept Christ as both Savior *and* Lord, not just as a savior. Repentance is key to that. We are to strive to live our lives as God wants us to, to be more like Christ. We won't be perfect, but we're to try. In this case, our good deeds become a demonstration of our faith."

"So, the people who say that God is love and a loving God won't condemn anyone to hell are wrong?"

Ralph nodded. "In several places, the Bible teaches that while God's grace is sufficient and that He is love, we must still accept Christ as our Lord. We can't go on living in the same sin, whether that's homosexuality, fornication, lying and cheating others, stealing, or whatever, and expect God's love to save us from an eternity of torment, outside of God's presence. Without repentance, your beliefs can be meaningless."

That prompted another question. "So, that brings up hell. What is heaven and is there a hell?"

"Well, that produces a lot of debate. As I read it in the Bible, heaven isn't floating about in the sky playing a harp or some other realm of sunshine and lollipops with everybody being happy. A new heaven and new earth are coming where we'll exist with Christ, in God's presence for eternity, living in the Eden that He first created the earth to be, pursuing the life He intended for all of us. Hell, on the other hand, is described as a lake of fire, a place of eternal torment outside of God's presence. Curiously, the only person to describe hell in the Bible is Jesus."

Adam felt emotionally spent. If he had ever been taught these concepts, he didn't remember them. He had a lot to think about.

"Adam, don't overthink these things. The Bible isn't supposed to be confusing. Its teachings are pretty straightforward. The Bible also says today is the day of salvation. Putting off a decision could mean you're too late. If you die without accepting Christ, it's too late. There's no do-over, no second chance."

"I . . . I have to—"

"Adam, it's your decision to push open that gate on the cage or not. It's not locked by anything other than your indecision."

THIRTY-THREE

The day had come. Everything was set for George's plan. The only variable that could throw a kink in the plan was the weather, but the forecast remained in his favor. He went to the roof that morning and was greeted by a glorious sunrise and crisp, autumn air that seemed to force the exhaust from hundreds of vehicles down to the ground.

"Hello, Mike from floor twelve."

He almost ignored the voice but recalled having used that name when he met Cassandra . . . if that was her real name. He turned to find her in almost the same spot as two days earlier.

"Good morning. Cassandra, right?"

She nodded and smiled. Her crooked smile seemed straighter today. He hoped the Bell's Palsy would not be a lifelong issue for her. Her found her attractive despite that minor flaw, but he wouldn't be around after that day. He considered asking for her contact info but realized that his giving a fake name would not sit well.

"Well, today's the big day, eh?"

Her comment caught him off-guard. Indeed it was, but how could she have known that?

"Big day?"

"Yeah, the big sculpture dedication at PfenRich. Dusk tonight. I hope it's a total flop."

He grinned. If all went well, it would be more than that. Of course, he couldn't say anything to her about that.

"I'll second that," he replied. "So, do you plan on going?"

She nodded. "I guess so. I mean, it is supposed to be quite impressive when lit up. Besides, I want to witness it fail. Give me something to tell my grandchildren, if I ever have any."

He so wanted to reassure her that she would have quite the story to tell, but he couldn't. They talked for a while.

"Would you like to join me for coffee?" she asked.

"I'd like to, but I can't. My work here ends today, and I'll be leaving this evening at some point."

"Oh."

She looked disappointed. He felt disconcerted, confused about the feelings he felt growing inside. He hadn't been attracted to anyone since Isabella died. His attraction toward Cassandra seemed like cheating somehow. He was intent on his revenge but now questioned his leaving. Yet he had no choice. He wasn't about to drag her into his plan. If he got caught and went to prison, that was one thing. He'd never forgive himself if she got involved and went to prison, too. Besides, while his work in the city would be done, that didn't mean his work was done.

"I'd like to keep in touch, but, honestly, I don't know where I'll end up after this. My contract work takes me all over the country."

She nodded. "I understand. I just thought . . ." She turned away from him and toward the city.

"Yeah. If I was going to be around for a while, I think I'd enjoy getting to know you."

After a moment of awkward silence, she looked at her phone and said, "Well, I need to get to work, too. It was nice meeting you. Good luck with your next position." With that, she left him alone on the roof.

He stood at the rail watching the growing activity along the streets below. He pensively reflected on his chance meeting with her, but in short order, his thoughts refocused on the task at hand. He walked over to the HVAC units and found his tanks where he'd left them two days earlier. *So far, so good.*

He pulled a small balloon from his pocket, put it to his lips, and blew it up. After tying a knot on the stem, he walked to the spot he had previously chosen for the balloon launch and released the test balloon. Initially, an updraft of air from the building caught it and sent it skyward. A moment later, the breeze took it toward the PfenRich headquarters. *Perfect*, he thought.

He spent the day killing time. He packed the device inside a backpack that he could more easily attach to the balloon by a customized harness. He also added a battery-powered fan, like those people could buy at summer sporting events to keep cooler. If the air was calm, it would help propel the package in the correct direction. However, he still debated about its use. Should the bag get oriented differently, the fan could just as easily propel the balloon the wrong way. Its use would be a last-minute decision.

He packed his clothing, toiletries, laptop, and other belongings into his carry-on case. Not that he was flying out, but it was just the right size for his stuff. He had a car parked in a long-term garage about a mile away. After lunch, he decided to take his gear to the car so that he wouldn't have to deal with it in a hurry later.

The eight-block trip, to and back, was uneventful, but he arrived at the apartment later than he had desired. He hurried to a small nearby diner and ordered food to go. As he waited, he noticed Cassandra alone in a booth near the back. He hesitated, but then offered her a subtle wave. If she saw him, she ignored him. That was probably for the best, but the snub still tugged at him.

With food in hand, he took the elevator to his floor, retrieved the package from the apartment, and proceeded to the roof. Sunset was less than 30 minutes away. He hurriedly ate while preparing the balloon and its harness for the package. He wolfed down the last of the double cheeseburger, followed by the last of his mineral water.

With his mind no longer focused on the food, he noted something amiss. What had happened? He stuck his index finger in his mouth to wet it and raised it over his head. Noooooo! The winds had shifted.

What was he going to do? Today had to be the day. The lighting ceremony offered him the maximum effect with the news coverage already assembled there. Plus, he had "promised" Cassandra a story to tell her children and grandchildren. He couldn't explain why, but he didn't want to fail her, or his, expectations.

The winds were coming from the west, from the river. He had previously scouted out an area near the water where he had relative seclusion. He could fill and launch the balloon from there with the current winds. He would need to add a bit more helium to get lift. From the rooftop where he now stood, he already had the height he needed. He did a quick recalculation on his phone. He had enough gas.

He made the snap decision to move ahead and repacked everything into the backpack, thankful he had chosen that style of bag. He slid one arm into a strap and hoisted it onto his back. Secured on his back, the grabbed the tanks.

He didn't look forward to lugging those things back down the stairwell but going down proved to be easier than moving them up. He waited on the elevator, tapping a foot with impatience. He hoped to have a clean ride to the lobby but instead the car stopped several times as people got on and off. Some gave him a strange look with his tanks in tow, but no one asked any questions. As the lift neared the lobby level, he checked the time. Sunset was almost on them. With speeches and other ceremonial activities, he had maybe 20 minutes to get there and get ready.

Ten minutes later, he stood by the water, separated from the crowds assembled for the lighting by being six feet below grade with shrubs above for further cover. The location was also a blind spot for security cams. He rushed to assemble the harness, tether, and package. With the balloon secured within its harness, he began to inflate it. This process he could not rush. The gas would leave the tank of its own accord based on pressures within the tank as well as inside the balloon. A nearby bike rack provided him with an anchor for the whole rig as the balloon tried to ascend with its increasing size.

The tall building now added its shadow to his cover. The sun had set. The balloon was almost ready.

With the small tank empty and the large one nearly so, he disconnected the regulator from the balloon, untied the cord from the bike rack, and tested the lift of the balloon. It had enough lift to rise above the trees surrounding the plaza before potentially getting entangled in them. And by the time it passed the sculpture and neared the building, it would have enough altitude to do its job.

Now was the time. He untied the tether from the balloon itself, lest someone be able to snag the rope from below and stop the package. As he did so, he saw someone approaching from the corner of his eye.

He positioned himself away from the shrubs and other potential obstacles nearby. After one more glance around, he pushed a button to set its timer and released the package.

As he watched it rise above the closest trees on its way toward the building, he heard a female voice from behind. "Mike? Mike? Is that you?"

THIRTY-FOUR

Edvin met Werner at the airport. His boss had flown back to the city to attend the sculpture lighting ceremony. Werner looked tired, but Edvin knew better than to call attention to that. Unknown to his superior, Edvin had become privy to some of Werner's private health information. The man had had an arrhythmic attack some time back that had required a pacemaker to be implanted. Edvin wondered if all was well.

"So, Edvin, what is the latest on our search for Adam Afton?"

They drove along I-495 from Farmingdale toward midtown Manhattan. The sun was setting quickly, as it seemed to do this time of year.

"Sir, we have confirmed that the death certificate was no more than a cleaver ploy to fool anyone looking for him. We have at least three people who have confirmed that he is alive and well."

"Why then haven't we found him? We have the full power of the government intelligence and police authorities behind us. We have the growing abilities of AlterNet2. And yet, we can't track down one man?"

Werner's surly attitude caught Edvin unaware. He had heard of the man's temper from others, but he had never experienced it firsthand.

"Sir, he knows how those authorities work. He clearly doesn't want to be found, and he knows how to evade any search. Granger told me they've discovered a few tripwires on the web as they've searched for him. He believes the man placed those out there and knows where we're searching."

Werner did not look placated.

"I had suggested using the old-fashioned way. Have agents been out there asking questions, looking for him?"

Edvin nodded. "Yes, sir. That's how we know he's still alive. Two neighbors of the parents in St. Louis, and the brother's girlfriend. The agents told them they were updating his security clearance."

"And . . ."

"And we thought we found him. Granger hacked into and downloaded the brother's GPS from his car. It showed several trips to a cabin an hour northwest of the college. Records show the place registered to a man in his seventies, an old friend of the Afton family it turns out."

"I don't believe that for a moment. Do you? If Afton has a quarter of the talent we believe him to have, he could have faked those property records and backstopped the alleged owner's history."

Edvin took a deep breath. The man was truly cranky this evening. He debated asking his boss about his health. Something was going on.

"I would agree, sir, but the FBI agents who interviewed the brother's girlfriend said that after some pressure, she admitted going there with the brother to have sex where no one might recognize her and embarrass her pastor father. The agents are both convinced she was telling the truth."

"I see." The man drifted off into thought once again.

"We have also placed taps on the brother's and parents' phones. So far, only routine calls to family, friends, and business colleagues. All numbers verified."

"He could have a throw-away phone."

"Yes, sir. They placed cell sniffers at the boy's dorm and parents' home. No other phones have been detected."

Werner looked at Edvin. "Good job, but we're missing something."

"Well, sir, we have not found him. That is for sure."

The remainder of the trip to PfenRich headquarters was taken in silence. Edvin kept a close eye on the older man. He seemed to be labored in his breathing.

"Sir, if I may ask, are you feeling well? You seem to be short of breath."

Werner waved his concern aside with a gesture. "I will be fine. The cool evening air should help."

As special guests to the ceremony, Werner's car was allowed into a barricade set up to separate VIPs from those milling about. Edvin offered the man assistance in exiting the car, but Werner brushed him off again. He would have nothing to do with anything that might make him look unwell or frail.

Edvin had to admit that he looked his usual dynamic self on the walk to and up onto the platform set up for the VIPs. Werner sat in the front row, while Edvin was honored with a seat behind him. As the sun set and the building behind them cast its deep shadows across the plaza, the ceremony began.

Edvin noticed Tucker, the security chief, on his phone nearby. He had marshaled his troops to monitor the proceedings and be alert to any threat. Edvin easily identified several of the security teams' men and women which he thought would make them easy to avoid by an attacker.

Mr. Bouras, the CEO, welcomed the crowd and then introduced the governor. The man's five-minute speech became ten and then the mayor took his turn. Then the podium returned to the CEO who spoke of the history and symbolism of the sculpture. The time finally came for the debut of the sculpture. The CEO pushed a button on a ceremonial controller and the light flared up through the middle of the hands into the torch where its crystals divided the light into four beams of red reaching for the four corners of the globe. It was stunning.

At the moment of the lighting, Edvin heard voices being raised and people pointing up. He thought they were pointing to the light at first, but then he noticed the movement of something above them. He looked up and saw it—a large balloon carrying some sort of pack.

At that second the pack exploded, and yet no debris fell. Instead, the entire block went dark. Cars, buses, and trucks died in their tracks. The yellow flashing lights on the barricades went black. Silence engulfed them and everything came to a standstill. He grabbed his phone. It, too, was dead. Chief Tucker began yelling instructions as it appeared his phone was out as well. The people in attendance began to panic and many began to run toward the lights still evident a block away. Sirens could be heard, but only in the distance. Inoperable vehicles blocked all access to the area around

PfenRich headquarters.

Tucker came running up onto the platform to talk with Bouras. Edvin overheard him say, "Everything electronic is toast. If it had circuitry or required electricity, it's useless now. We've been hit with an EMP."

EMP? Edvin knew the term—electromagnetic pulse—but he thought that was only a byproduct of a nuclear detonation. How? Who?

That's when he noticed his boss not moving. He placed his hand on Werner's shoulder and the man fell forward to the ground. His pacemaker. The EMP had taken it out, too.

"Mike, what are you doing? What's that?"

"Cassandra, um, you'll see in a moment, I gotta do something real fast."

He had maybe a minute before the device went off and his burner phone would become a useless block of plastic and metals. He hit the speed dial key that had been lined up. Once the connection was made, he said, "Seth, this is Noah. Package sent. Time to drain 'em."

He no sooner disconnected when everything went black. Cassandra started at the sudden calm. The only lights were from a block away. Cars stood still, their power gone. He threw the phone in the Hudson River.

"Wha . . . what just happened?"

"Long story, but the short version is you got your story to tell your children and grandchildren. Look, I have to go. I told you my work here was done today. PfenRich will now pay for all the lives they've taken or ruined."

He turned and began to walk upriver along the bike path toward his car, which was safely out of range. In 20 or so minutes he would be inching his way through traffic toward phase three. At that point, he would also learn whether or not phase two had succeeded.

As he neared the edge of lights at the perimeter of the damage zone, he felt a tug on his shirt. He turned to see Cassandra. A look of wonder filled her face. "I-I don't know what you just did, but for everyone hurt by that company, me included, thank you."

He nodded. "You're welcome. The best is yet to come, though." He didn't want to come across as impatient, but he needed to go. "Look, this area is going to be locked down real fast, so I'd like to get out of here."

"I understand. I, uh, I want to come with you."

His eyes widened in disbelief. "I don't know. If things go south and I'm caught, I don't want to drag you down with me."

"I understand that, too. I'm willing. I don't know how to explain this, but I feel we made a connection. Yeah, I know we've only talked, what, twice? But you looked beyond this palsy and at me, as a person. That hasn't happened since I woke up like this. And I feel like I'm sharing your pain over losing your fiancée. Maybe it's just me. Maybe we'll discover we don't like each other, but I don't have anything here to keep me in New York. It's a dead-end job, and I'm barely scraping by. I want to come with you."

"We don't have time to go back to the apartment. The elevators might not even be working."

She shook her head. "Don't care. They can give it to Salvation Army. It's only a few sets of clothing and some cosmetics and toiletries. All replaceable."

He shrugged as if to say, "I guess so," but inside he felt excited at the prospect. "Let's go then."

As they reached the boundaries of the first cameras, he donned a mask and ball cap. She followed suit with a mask and beret. They didn't rush along. That might look suspicious. To blend in, she reached over and grabbed his hand. He smiled . . . not that anyone could tell.

THIRTY-FIVE

Adam awoke that next morning feeling refreshed for the first time in days. No nightmare. He wasn't aware of any REM sleep at all. A calm had fallen over him, but things still didn't feel settled. He knew what he needed to do. He simply hadn't committed yet.

He contemplated the information Ralph had provided the day before, but he didn't want to base any decision on what one man said, as convincing as he had been. He powered up the generator and realized he was going to need more diesel soon. That could come later. With the electricity flowing, he powered up his computers and sat back. Alerts chimed from multiple searches, but they would have to wait. Ralph's admonition about not getting a second chance rang true.

He began a basic search on the man's first argument. How much sense did a Big Bang make? After reviewing the three laws of thermodynamics, the law of entropy, and other basic principles of physics, he recognized that such a thing made little sense. He wondered why he'd never questioned it until now.

Next, he reviewed the geologic claims made by Ralph.

Numerous sites from both the creation science and traditional science points of view confirmed erosion rates. The traditional sites, however, took that no further. They didn't follow the logic that made their old earth teachings seem flawed. Only the creation science folks followed up with the implications of what such erosion meant over history.

Likewise, Darwinian evolutionists ignored the power of oxidation when postulating the origins of the first biochemicals. He tried to run a statistical analysis of the probability of just one amino acid forming but couldn't due to a lack of information. Far too many assumptions had to be made to make that plausible. Taking it another step, he tried to determine the odds of multiple amino acids forming *de novo,* and those odds reached the level of mathematical impossibility. And if that was mathematically impossible, how could anyone fathom them forming into proteins?

He looked up the studies about chimpanzee DNA. As Ralph had stated, these two groups had come to their conclusions independently and, yet, corroborated each other's findings.

He found a couple of other pieces of information he'd never heard before. Not only was the earth perfectly positioned around the sun for life as we know it, but so was the moon. Without the moon in its current orbit, there would be no life on the planet because of its gravitational effect on the tides and winds.

So, did all of this just happen by chance? Not a chance.

Adam bowed his head. "God, I believe you exist now. And Jesus, I understand now why you came to earth. All the stuff my brother's been saying for years now makes sense to me. Please forgive my sins and help me to become more like you."

If someone expected something mystical or supernatural to happen upon accepting Christ, he'd be disappointed. Adam felt little different, but yet, there was a sense of freedom, of a weight being taken from his shoulders. He recalled the words of Jesus saying that His yoke was easy and His burden was light. However, he knew from Aric that accepting Christ wouldn't make life all rosy and easier. He had commented before that many aspects of life would get harder because the world was at odds with followers of Christ.

He wanted to dig into the Bible more, to reread the New Testament over and over, but another alert chimed from his second laptop. He'd ignored the alerts that had accumulated over the past day, and at least six alerts that had tried to get his attention while he was searching for confirmation of Ralph's words. In thinking of Ralph, he wanted to call the man and let him know he'd finally made that life-altering decision. It was the least Adam could do.

However, as he glanced at the screen on that laptop, the headline being displayed caught his breath.

Terrorists Strike PfenRich Headquarters, Three Dead

He started to read the article linked to *The Epoch Times* homepage. Sculpture dedication . . . at 6:17 pm terror struck . . . all electronics inoperable . . . included phones, computers, vehicles, lighting, elevators, and more . . . entire PfenRich building affected . . . hundreds of millions of dollars in damage . . . buildings in the surrounding area also affected . . . three dead from apparent pacemaker malfunctions . . . authorities suspect some sort of EMP—electromagnetic pulse—device.

Then it got worse for PfenRich. He found a follow-up article that detailed a massive data dump from PfenRich's backup servers before those servers were erased overnight. The data was sent to multiple conservative news organizations, as well as the Children's Health Defense and National Vaccine Information Center non-profits.

A preliminary review of those documents revealed that the company knew all along that their vaccines could result in major side effects and even death, and that their efficacy was limited. Emails about legally mandated safety testing showed how they rigged their tests, if they did them at all, so that no safety signals would arise in the tests. Other documents showed the lengths they went to in securing people favorable to their drugs to perform studies and to take positions at the FDA and CDC. Emails mentioned secret meetings over safety issues in which no cell phones were allowed, and no recordings were made. Finally, numerous damning communications with the World Order Council showed them to be working in concert to depopulate the world. Werner Koch was mentioned as a casualty at the ceremony but had survived his pacemaker malfunction.

Adam sat back and let it all sink in. PfenRich had just taken it in the chin with a knockout blow. Every byte of data at their headquarters was toast. The backup of that data had been released for the world to see. Their building would require total rewiring, new controls for everything mechanical, new HVAC systems, new computer systems, new backup generators, new lighting, and more. Attempting to restore their operations using data from their many research and production facilities would take months, or even years, after rebuilding.

Out of curiosity, he checked one other item. As he suspected, their stock had taken a swan dive off the top of their 40-story building, having lost 98% of its value overnight. Would they survive? *Could* they?

Wow! he thought as he sat there shaking his head. Three thoughts entered his head after the sense of disbelief waned. One, who had done this? He knew a lot of hackers by reputation and their skills. Only one person stuck out as being capable of the data dump and erasure at such a cyber-secure company: Seth. Could he use this event to track down the man?

Secondly, if Seth was involved, where did he gain the skill to build an EMP device? He'd been the guy who almost cut off his fingers trying to cut a 2x4 to length. Was someone else involved?

The third thought, however, was of a more immediate danger. The people behind the rebirth of AlterNet would be fit to be tied. The size of the target on Adam's back had just enlarged and with it, the danger to Aric. They would want Adam's abilities at all costs now, if for no other reason than to hunt down the perpetrators of this attack on one of the Deep State's darling pharmaceutical companies.

THIRTY-SIX

Following the photo-op raid on his home the day before, Anson and his lawyer went to police headquarters where she led him in responding to the alleged trespassing charge. Alicia already knew the charge to be bogus. She had reviewed multiple videos of the school board meeting and in none of them was any announcement made about clearing the room, the board going into executive session, or of Anson being arrested. Anson and the others had a legal right to be in the room, a public forum.

She predicted that the charge would be dropped within 24 hours. After all, how can they allege trespassing in a public building on public property at a meeting open to anyone? More than that, Anson had been at the mic at the board's open invitation, and anyone with a stopwatch could see that he wasn't given the promised two minutes.

Now, they sat in Anson's living room using the boarded-up front doorway as a backdrop for the camera set up in front of them. Anson sat next to Alicia.

"Denton wanted to be here, but this has all happened so fast that he couldn't get out of other engagements. I hope you don't mind my taking his place."

Anson shook his head. "Are you kidding? You've been a Godsend to us."

"I've worked with Sam Sussman several times. He's great to work with, so this shouldn't be difficult."

"Good to know. I am a bit nervous." Who was he trying to kid? He hadn't been this nervous since getting down on one knee to propose to Hannah.

The Newsmax team adjusted their sound levels and made a few adjustments to the lighting. This interview would last roughly 15 minutes, which would be edited to a segment lasting only a few minutes. Then the camera team would clear out leaving enough time for the Fox News team to repeat the process before lunch.

The local crew leader looked at the duo and with both fingers and voice, counted down, "Three - two - one" at which time he simply pointed to them.

Anson watched in the monitor as Sam Sussman joined them remotely. Although the interview would appear to be live, they were recording it roughly an hour ahead of his noon program. This allowed time for editing and fixing any technical glitches.

"Many of you have already seen the video. Today we have more. Our next guest is Anson Hardy, along with Alicia Somers of the Midwest Justice and Freedom Defense Alliance. Welcome, Anson and Alicia."

"Thank you, Sam. Good to speak with you again," said Alicia.

Anson nodded before realizing no one hear his head moving. "Good morning."

"Our viewers no doubt recall the video of Anson at their local school board meeting. Alicia, would you like to cover that again for us?"

"Certainly. Anson was . . ."

Anson listened as she went through the salient details of what happened at the school board meeting. As she did so, the video replayed on the monitor in front of them.

"Thank you. Now, as I understand it, the situation there took a sudden turn for the worse yesterday morning."

"That's right, Sam. As Anson was preparing his children for school . . ."

Again, Anson watched the video of their home being invaded by the FBI and of him being cuffed, shackled, and dragged from their home.

"Anson, how are you and your family doing today?"

Alicia turned to him and nodded in encouragement. The nerves seemed to have evaporated while watching the video of his home invasion.

"Well, Sam. You can see the damage done to our home behind us. Earlier we had to move our kids to a private school, and now, with yesterday's invasion, we've had to keep them home completely. After yesterday, they're all having nightmares, so none of us got much sleep last night. As for me, well, I never expected this in our country. I lost my job and have been vilified in the press, all because I spoke out against things happening in our local schools that I wouldn't have seen coming in a million years. Our children are becoming victims of a political agenda that goes against God and all that we believe in."

"Thank you, Anson. Alicia, anything else?"

"The home invasion you saw on the video was approved at the highest levels of the FBI. And why? That show of force was over an alleged misdemeanor *trespassing* charge. The FBI has labeled Anson as a domestic terrorist because he chose to speak up at a public forum. The FBI now considers concerned parents to be terrorists. The current administration has weaponized our government against the citizens of this country. All of us need to be concerned and ready to defend our freedoms."

Anson nodded again. "We *will* be fighting back. We can't let them win if we want freedom. If we sit back and do nothing, we lose. We lose our freedom, our rights to raise our families as we see fit, and our constitutional rights to life, liberty, and the pursuit of happiness. We become no different than communist China or North Korea."

They wrapped up the interview without giving away any of the strategies they were discussing with regard to fighting back.

"Well stated there, Anson," said Alicia. "I guess you got over the nervous butterflies."

"I did. Watching that video of our home being attacked made me angry all over again."

An hour later, they repeated the process with Fox News. Anson began to feel like this was old hat. His confidence in speaking about the issue grew. A phone interview with *The Gateway Pundit* followed. Curiously, but not unexpectedly, not a single mainstream media network or cable outlet called to request an interview.

As the afternoon wore on, he noticed an uptick in encouraging emails from friends. Then came the negative emails and death threats. Someone had doxed his email address. His concern rose that his home address would also become publicly and widely known. They'd already seen some local protesters but being doxed could open the floodgate holding back the real crazies. He had no idea what they would do or where they would go if that were to happen.

Hannah had missed the excitement of the day due to in-person meetings at work. However, just before Alicia had to leave, she showed up earlier than Anson had expected. She did not look happy. She walked straight to the kitchen, grabbed a glass, and filled it with wine. That was not a good sign.

Alicia followed him to the kitchen. Hannah looked up at them as they walked into the room.

She sighed. "Well, your interviews looked great, but they got around at work and several people complained."

"Complained about the interviews?" Anson didn't understand.

"No, complained that I was married to you and by default agreed with your statements. Which I do, but that has no bearing on the work I do there. I guess that didn't matter. They fired me." She took a big drink.

THIRTY-SEVEN

The night before, as they reached his car in the long-term lot, George received a text on his regular phone, which he had shielded from the EMP. Still concerned about dragging Cassandra into his plans and making her an accomplice, he excused himself to the restroom at the garage and suggested she do the same. He had no idea how far they might be driving that night.

The text read:

Nice work. Phase two complete. On to phase three.—Seth

He replied:

North or south?

The answer:

North.

With that, he and Cassandra climbed into his car and headed out into late evening traffic in the city. He headed for the 495, from which his goal was to pick up I-80 and head west. Central Michigan held PfenRich's largest manufacturing facility. With his second EMP device and its rig in the trunk, he planned to deal their death blow to the company.

Seth had postulated that word would go out after the previous night's attack to alert all helium retailers within a hundred miles of a PfenRich location. That seemed reasonable. The helium balloon had been a rational choice because of the proximity of the apartments to the headquarters building. Although a drone would have delivered its package before anyone could deal with it, drones were illegal within the city and people were encouraged to report them as soon as spotted. That might have led the police to George before he could escape. Besides, the balloon was a nice stealth move and held the element of surprise. Did it ever.

However, this time the delivery would be more high-tech. The manufacturing campus was over 1,200 acres in size and a balloon would take too long to reach the center of the facility. Its path would also be less predictable over such distance. This time a drone would be utilized both for its speed of delivery and its accuracy. They were targeting the power plant for the production center.

Having pulled off I-80 at New Columbia, PA, they found a mid-range motel for the night. Cassandra had surprised him by insisting on sharing a room . . . and a bed. He hadn't expected that. It had been a long time since he'd felt the warmth of intimacy with a woman. Still, this was so sudden. It wasn't a matter of *hardly* knowing each other. It was a matter of not knowing each other at all. Yet, his fleshly desire won out.

As he awoke, he found the bed empty next to him. He sat up.

"Cassandra?" No answer.

He hopped out of bed, donned his boxers, and checked the bathroom. Empty. He looked out the window and felt relief that his car was still there. He grabbed his jeans, and his anxiety was further eased to find his wallet, keys, and phone still in the pockets. But had she checked them? He was still "Mike" to her. One look at his driver's license would unveil that lie. As he finished dressing, the door's lock beeped, and the door eased open. Cassandra pushed it open with an elbow as she held a cup of coffee in each hand.

She smiled. "Hi there. I wondered if you'd be awake when I got back." She set the cups down on the dresser. "Didn't know if you took it black or not." She fished two packs of creamer from a pocket in her coat and set them next to the cups. Then she eased up next to him and stroked his cheek with a fingertip. "Um, that was nice last night. Up for another round?"

He was . . . but he wasn't. He had a schedule to keep.

"Not this morning, Cass. Got word on a new job and have a long day of driving ahead. Let's grab breakfast and get going. If we push through, we can get to the new town with plenty of time for lots of fun this evening." He kissed her fully on the lips. "Something to look forward to."

She smiled, but something still seemed off with her. Needy? Too willing? He couldn't put his finger on just what bothered him.

Edvin walked off the elevator onto the floor holding the cardiac step-down unit where his boss had been admitted. He knew better than bring flowers but wondered if he should have been bringing something else with him. What that might be, he didn't know. It just seemed appropriate to bring something to a person in the hospital, and he was empty-handed.

He stopped at the nurses' station and identified himself. He was there only because Werner had insisted upon it. Non-family members weren't allowed as visitors. A clerk pointed him to the correct room.

He knocked at the door and waited for a response.

"*Komm herein*," came a familiar voice. Werner sounded like he was back to his usual form.

Edvin entered the room and approached the man's bed.

Werner continued in German. "Edvin, I need to know what happened last night. These nurses will not tell me anything. They will not get me a newspaper or let me watch the news. If I have another cardiac event, as they keep calling it, it will be their fault."

Yes, the man was back to his gruff German self. Those nurses had to be some toughies themselves if they were able to hold him off. He could only imagine what Werner was calling them in German behind their backs.

"Well, sir, you had a cardiac event at the sculpture dedication." He gave his boss a devilish grin.

Werner saw through him. "Yes, yes. I will back off. You are right. I am being too harsh."

"Do you recall anything, sir?"

"Only the speeches and then some kind of commotion."

Edvin nodded. He explained what had happened, that an EMP device was suspected, and that Werner's "cardiac event" was due to a malfunction of his pacemaker. He added that three others with pacers had not been so lucky.

"I have been told that there was no heart damage, but that my pacemaker needs to be replaced."

"Yes, sir. That's the information that I have been given as well. The next question is where would you like that performed. A flight home might be risky."

Edvin knew that the original pacemaker placement had been done by Germany's top cardiac surgeon at the University Hospital Frankfurt am Main. He had been flown to New York Presbyterian Hospital-Columbia, ranked #4 in the U.S. Even though an ambulance could make the trip between PfenRich and the hospital in under 20 minutes, getting an ambulance into the area near PfenRich had been nearly impossible with all of the dead vehicles blocking the way. Edvin would personally be quite content to see the procedure performed here, but the decision was Werner's.

"I agree. I am not opposed to having it done here. I am told they could do it as early as tomorrow."

Edvin nodded. "*Sehr gut, Herr.* I can assist with making the arrangements if you wish."

"Yes, thank you, Edvin. I assume you have already notified my wife."

"Yes, sir. She is concerned, obviously, but pleased that you are in a top cardiac hospital. Anything else, sir?"

"Perhaps. I did not trust the security team at PfenRich to be thorough. It appears I was correct. However, I admit that no one could have expected an EMP device carried by a balloon. Anyway, I had our people place observers in a number of buildings around PfenRich. They were to observe the rooftops, lobbies, and streets around the company. My effort paid off. We have a lead."

THIRTY-EIGHT

Adam had slept well again until that early morning period of light sleep right before waking during which his mind engaged in contemplating the most pressing problem at hand. How could he eliminate the threat posed by those attempting to rebuild AlterNet? He couldn't simply barge into their servers and try to knock them out. They would shut him down quickly and then have the means to partially trace his trail. They might not be able to find him at Hotel CD, but they might narrow down the state or even the region within the state. That would be cutting things too close.

As he awoke, he thought about what Aric would do in a quandary like this. What came to mind was something he had seen his little brother do many times—he prayed for wisdom. When that thought came to him, he grabbed the Bible and began to search out where he'd seen that before in God's Word. After some searching, sure enough, there it was. James 1:5 said, *"If any of you lacks wisdom, let him ask God, who gives generously to all without reproach, and it will be given them."*

Adam bowed his head. "God, I'm new at this, and I don't know how to pray to you, but I need wisdom for the situation

I'm facing now. Would you please give me that wisdom? Thank you."

Adam grabbed the two five-gallon gas containers he'd filled the day before, added that ten gallons of diesel to the fuel tank, and powered up the generator. With full power, he cooked some breakfast on the hot plate for the first time since he'd arrived. Cold cereal had gotten old. While he ate, he reviewed the latest news on PfenRich. In doing so, he noticed some memes that were already surfacing on Facebook. That's when it hit him. Rebecca was addicted to Facebook.

Perhaps he could use her Facebook account to penetrate their network. She had always been overconfident in her ability to separate work devices from personal ones. Yet, he recalled seeing her using both to access that social media platform.

He finished eating and cleaned up. Then he got to work.

Despite Facebook's programming to forbid access through virtual private networks, he was able to create a bogus profile using a VPN to gain access to one of their servers. From there, finding the correct Rebecca Olsen, now Stiles as he learned, was easy. With the necessary parameters, he then programmed UltraNet to find every IP address and every MAC, or media access control, address within the networks that she used to create a list of those that had accessed her account. He also added date parameters to find those addresses recently used. He left the program to do its thing. It would alert him when the task was complete.

With UltraNet off and running, he returned to his other two problems. He still had no luck tracking down Seth. But what if there were two people involved in the PfenRich incident? Could finding the person who launched the EMP device lead him to that man's accomplice? His working hypothesis was that Seth was that accomplice. He might be wrong. Yet, whoever it was who was able to dump all of PfenRich's files into the public domain was someone Adam wanted to meet. So, Seth or someone else as proficient. It was a win-win if he could find that person.

He directed his software to scour the New York City security cam grid within two blocks of PfenRich for anyone with gas tanks within an hour preceding the incident. He doubted anyone would have ventured near the building in broad daylight with one or more tanks. They would have been easily spotted and possibly questioned, given the security concerns for any event like that of the sculpture dedication. He set UltraNet to work on its second task, expecting it to also take a while.

He began to code the worm he would launch through Rebecca's system that would take out their new AlterNet and its entire system. He hadn't progressed far when he had an NCIS-Kasie Hines moment—his computer alerted him to having results far too fast to be real-life.

He checked and indeed, someone with both large and small gas tanks on a dolly was spotted on the street heading toward PfenRich on its south side. The figure appeared male, carried a backpack, and walked with determination. The man's mask prevented any attempt at facial recognition. Adam followed the man's course through a series of cameras until he lost him near the Hudson River. Additional views did not reveal the guy moving on. The man had discovered a blind spot for the cameras.

Recognizing that the cameras would be useless after the EMP, Adam programmed UltraNet to locate anyone of that approximate size with similar clothing and mask who left the area within a short period after the blast. He started with a 15-minute span figuring the guy wouldn't dawdle in leaving. But which direction should he focus on first?

He stood up and began to pace. If he were that guy, how would he want to leave the island? The subway would have cameras galore and bright lighting to easily track him. The streets would expose him to cameras, as they had on his way to do the deed, but now it was dark, and recognition would become more difficult. However, walking would only get him so far. All public transit had cameras. A ride-share vehicle would be an option, but that, too, left a loose end—a driver who could give a description. Adam decided the man would likely have a car available. Short-term parking options were expensive and few.

Back at his computer, he focused on long-term parking options. The closest one would require escaping to the north, so he directed his search to begin on the streets just north of the damage zone. Fifteen minutes later, he had him, but he had a woman with him. Adam hadn't expected that. Was she part of the team? Was she the hacker? Maybe he'd been wrong about Seth.

Adam checked the progress of his first search and decided he had time to continue tracking the couple. Using sequential cameras, he followed them for about ten blocks. They entered a long-term parking garage complete with its own cameras. A minute later, he had the make and model of the car and most importantly, its tag. With this information, he would be able to find this car pretty much anywhere in the country, and in short order, UltraNet was doing the search for him.

While Adam held no endearment for PfenRich, he didn't feel that the thousands of people who relied upon the company for employment and who were simply doing their jobs deserved to lose their livelihoods. Plus, while unintentional, the three men who died from pacemaker malfunctions didn't deserve that fate. The decision-makers who put their greed above safety and people's health deserved what they would get, and he hoped they would soon get the justice due them.

Adam faced one more dilemma. Did he turn over what he'd learned to the police? To do so would open a huge can of worms, like how did he get that information? Could he do so anonymously? He would have to wrestle with that idea for a while. One thought did ease his mind though. If he could come up with that information within just a couple of hours, why shouldn't he expect the authorities to do so as well? That would save him from having to decide.

He saw dilemmas piling on top of quandaries on top of more dilemmas. And then it hit him. He now faced a moral crisis unlike anything he'd encountered before. How could he reconcile what he himself was doing with what he'd read in God's Word?

THIRTY-NINE

Four hours closer to his next destination, George took time to fill up the car while Cass went inside the convenience mart to use the restroom and gather some snacks. He'd given her ten dollars to get whatever she wanted. Soon, though, his cash reserves would tap out.

Alone, he pulled his phone from his pocket and made a call. The man he knew as Seth answered.

"Glad you called. Your car has been made."

That shocked George. "What? I was really careful. How?"

"Police found you on video surveillance moving the tanks toward PfenRich and caught you again leaving the area."

George shook his head. He couldn't have been followed. "No way they could have followed me. I changed jackets, masks, and hats twice en route to the garage."

"But the woman didn't. Who's she?"

He explained how he first met Cassandra and what had happened that night.

"Give me a minute."

Seth came back on the line as George was hanging up the gas nozzle.

"No one by the name of Cassandra renting a room at that building. You sure you know who she is?"

George took a deep breath, pursed his lips, and shook his head. Yet, he recognized that he had no room to make accusations. He was still known to her as Mike.

"Nope, but I'll find out. What about the car?"

"They tracked you to the garage and ID'd the car. Good news is they don't have the ability to track your car across the country like they once did. But I'd be careful once you get to the plant. Every PfenRich facility has been alerted."

"Got it. I'm gonna need more cash."

"Okay. Use the debit card. I'll make sure the money's in the account by tonight. Enough for another used car."

"Thanks." George had no idea where the money came from. He was too frugal to throw it away on unnecessary things, but the cash seemed never-ending. He'd learned not to ask about it.

"I'll call or text to keep you updated." The line went dead.

George grabbed his receipt from the gas pump and looked up to see Cass, or whatever her name was, leaving the store. He passed her on his way into the store.

"Be out in a couple of minutes."

As he entered the restroom, his phone rang. CallerID was blank so he expected Seth on the other end as he answered.

"Your car has been ID'd, but they have no idea where you are."

The voice was not a familiar one, and George began to freak out. Clearly, this guy knew where he was and also managed to get his phone number.

"How? W-who is this? What do you want?" His heart began

to race.

"How is unimportant. What I want is one thing? Are you working with a guy code-named Seth?"

George's eyes widened. "H-how do you know Seth?"

"I'll take that as a yes."

"Yeah, I'm working with Seth. How—"

"Tell Seth Adam is looking for him." The guy hung up.

George hurried into a stall and sat down. He needed to regain his composure as he'd been seconds away from peeing himself. His car had been ID'd, and PfenRich folks were on high alert for it. Cassandra wasn't Cassandra. Some stranger named Adam not only knew where they were but had traced his phone number. And the guy wanted to find Seth. Seth was not someone to be toyed with.

With his breathing under control, he used his phone to text Seth.

Someone named Adam knows where I am and has my phone number. He's looking for you. Delaying phase 3 by a week. Going to ground.

A reply came back in an instant.

Thanks. He's cool. Relax. I've got this.

George took a deep breath. That news calmed his nerves. He meant what he said about going to ground. Things were too hot around PfenRich. Plus, he needed to deal with the car . . . and Cass.

FORTY

Aric worried about Adam. He texted him several times and kept checking the burner phone for messages. Nada. He had asked Ryan almost daily about word from his brother, but the security officer, too, had not heard from him.

And then there was the whole PfenRich Pharmaceuticals thing. It was all anyone on campus talked about. There was speculation about other companies being next, dismay that the authorities hadn't caught and tried the perpetrators yet—as if this was an episode of some Hollywood crime show, and even quips about Antifa and BLM being jealous. Aric shuddered to think what might happen if that technology ever fell into the hands of those two groups. He hoped this attack hadn't spurred them on to copy it.

What Aric found most astonishing was the alleged total surprise of the event. Even in hindsight, the authorities claimed they had no hint of what was about to happen.

Of course, they could be hiding that fact. The bombing of Pearl Harbor was known in advance, but the government withheld that information to sway public opinion and draw the country into WWII. There was advance intel chatter about the World Trade Center attack but, like Pearl Harbor, no action was taken, and the country was sold on entering the War on Terror. Time and time again authorities knew *something* was about to happen but either failed to act on that intel or chose to ignore it.

And each time, word leaked out shortly afterward about their knowing about and failing to act on the information. But not this time. It was as if they truly didn't expect this and were caught totally unaware. The fact that the target was PfenRich—one of their darling companies, favored by most, if not all, of their billionaire benefactors—seemed to support this. It was one of "their own." Surely, they would have spared no expense in protecting it against a known threat. The Deep State wasn't known for abandoning those that served their purposes.

While Aric had mixed feelings about the PfenRich event, his more immediate concern was Adam. Surely, the pressure on those hunting him would be increasing under the belief that a new AlterNet might have discovered the potential attack and allowed the authorities to stop it.

Despite his concern for Adam, he had to admit that since Jess's performance earlier in the week, he'd seen nothing of the van or any other suspicious men on campus. Maybe she truly had convinced them.

He called Jess. "Hey, up for a road trip?"

"What did you have in mind?"

"Well, not the cabin," he whispered.

"Quit. You know what my dad said when I told him what happened."

"Okay, okay."

Both had been thoroughly chastised for going through with that plan. While acknowledging that they had cleverly avoided lying, they had been deceitful, and the Bible made it clear that God disliked deceit as much as dishonesty. Plus, not only were they to avoid any impropriety but also the appearance of such.

After all of the ego-building of getting that hero's award, Pastor Larson's "sermon" to them had humbled him. He shouldn't be joking about it.

"I'm worried about Adam. I've not heard from him at all."

"I thought you didn't know where he was."

"I don't for sure, but I have an idea. Problem is, it's a three-hour drive from here, so that means an all-day trip. And if I'm wrong, then it ends up just being a day of driving."

"Well, it promises to be a beautiful day and the fall color is peaking. I've got my classwork under control, so, sure, if nothing else, it'll be a beautiful country drive seeing the foliage. I'm ready whenever you are."

"Great. Pick you up in ten."

Aric headed off to his car, double-checked to make sure the GPS was disabled and no new AirTags had been taped to it and headed toward the Larsons' home. Jess met him at the door.

"Almost ready." She led him to the kitchen where Mrs. Larson was busy making sandwiches.

"Hi, Aric. Jess told me you two were going to take a drive in the countryside, so I thought I'd prepare you a picnic."

Jess looked at him and rolled her eyes. He winked in response.

"That's sweet of you, Mrs. Larson." She stopped her

preparations and gave him a look. "Um sorry, thank you, Sue." He continued to find it hard to break the habit of calling his friends' parents Mr. or Mrs. so-and-so. Her dad hadn't been a problem. Everyone called him Pastor Tom.

With food and drink in hand, they loaded into Aric's car. He took his regular phone and removed the battery. Without needing to explain, Jess handed him her phone, and he repeated the process. With that done, off they went.

Three hours later, and satisfied that they hadn't been followed, he pulled off the interstate and into the small town of Camp Douglas. He remembered the way, and before they could blink, they left the town behind and drove through beautiful rolling farmland.

"Wow, this is beautiful. As a family, we've taken the interstate to Minnesota before, but I've never been into the countryside in this part of the state. How did you find this place?"

Aric shrugged. "I don't think you want to know."

"Oh. Is this where—"

Aric nodded. He'd told Jess and her family a little bit about what he and Adam had done two years earlier. However, he had seen no reason to go into any detail.

Minutes later, he pulled into what seemed like a private drive leading onto a wooded hillside. A hundred yards later, they came to a tall fence and chained gate. Aric exited the car and walked to the gate where he inspected the lock and chain. Jess joined him.

"Yeah, I think he's holed up here. Look, the lock is new. No signs of weathering."

He tested the gate. No give. There was no way of squeezing

through. He looked about. His only way in would be to go over the top of the fence, but it was lined with razor wire. Maybe he could find a spot where the wire was broken or missing.

"I don't think anyone will bother us here, but why don't you get back in the car and lock it, just in case. Here's my key fob. I'm going to walk along the fence and see if I can find a place to climb over or crawl under."

She scrunched up her face in dislike. "Ewww, I don't like that idea. Maybe I should come with you."

Aric shook his head. "No, please stay with the car. If anyone shows up, you can honk the horn to alert me. If someone asks, I'm in the woods taking a pee or looking for something or whatever."

With a bit more persuasion, he convinced her to stay and headed off into the woods to their right.

Two days had passed since he contacted the man behind the EMP attack and asked about Seth. He had been correct in his deductions that his old colleague had been involved. Yet, he still hadn't heard from the guy, and now he wondered if the message had been passed along or not. If it had, though, he would not be surprised to discover that Seth was trying to locate him first and validate the request to contact him. It's what he would be doing if he were in Seth's shoes.

The past two days had been spent developing the worm to take down the new AlterNet. The programming would have to sniff out all backup copies, isolate them, and overwrite that code before dealing with the main servers and network devices. This is where Seth's expertise could helpfully come into play. It had to be perfect. He would only have the one chance.

He also ran and reran and reran his search for Rebecca's devices. That, too, had to be perfect, and to date, his searches had corroborated each other. Now, he would have to discern which device would gain him the easiest access to the AlterNet network. This was proving more challenging.

He took a break and perused the latest news about the PfenRich event, the war in Ukraine, the elections coming up in just over a week, and more. The Nord Stream pipeline sabotage had waned in the news cycle, but he had anonymously provided detailed information and links gathered by UltraNet to a Pulitzer-prize-winning journalist he trusted. That data proved that divers from an elite U.S. team, with assistance from Norwegian divers, had planted the explosives during a joint naval exercise earlier in the summer and that a sonar buoy had sent signals to those devices on September 26th to detonate the explosives. The data was definitive in showing that President Sidon had authorized the incident. Of course, he knew that the writer would make every effort to validate the information before publishing anything. Adam guessed it might be early February before being released.

As he continued reading, he was startled by an alert from the motion detector. He ran for the stairs and bounded up to the first floor. Cautiously, he found a vantage point where he could look out a window toward the main gate without being detected. He smiled and started laughing at seeing Aric's car outside the gate. *Of course. Why should I be surprised?* he thought.

Using a side door that he could prop open, he left the security of the building and walked out to the gate. Unlocking it, he waved to Jess and motioned for her to pull the car inside the compound. He closed and relocked the gate before walking up to her.

"Where's Aric?" he asked.

She laughed. "Trying to find a place to climb over the fence. Boy, won't he be surprised?"

He walked around to the passenger side and climbed in. "Pull around back over there so the car can't be seen from the gate." He pointed to the drive along the side of the building. "Keep going a bit more. There's parking a bit farther along the drive. Yeah. There." He pointed again.

Outside the vehicle, he laughed. "I've walked the perimeter to check for my own security here. There's only one spot where I think he'd be able to get past the razor wire, but he won't have fun getting there."

"Why in the world did I do this? I should have just turned around and gone home," Aric mumbled to himself. At first, close to the gate, the underbrush had been cleared and the going was easy. The farther he went, the heavier the brush became.

He figured he had moved maybe a hundred yards from the gate when he came to his main nemesis—thick briers. Maybe he needed to turn back. *No*, he thought. *I need to know if Adam's here and if he's okay.*

He first tried stomping on the briers to forge a path through them. However, as he stomped on one clump, another would lurch up to snag his clothing or block his way. About ten feet into the patch, he thought he heard a car, and he worried about Jess. He looked back at the way he'd come and couldn't make out any path at all. It was as if he hadn't been there. He looked about for the shortest way out and decided to push ahead.

That's when he saw it. A tree branch had fallen across the top of the fence and pulled the razor wire down with it. The area on the other side of the fence was cleared for about five feet and then the woods resumed. He would decide which way to go once he got over the fence.

He began to climb. At one point he had to push away a strand of the razor wire, but he was able to secure it within a link of the fence and get it out of harm's way ... his harm. From that point on, the climbing was easy.

He hopped to the ground from about halfway up on the other side. He looked back to where he'd been. "Man, I sure hope he's here," he mumbled. "I don't want to have to go back that way."

As he debated whether to follow the cleared area and hope that it led to the parking lot or to work his way through the woods toward the building and the drive that encircled it, he stopped. What did he hear? Was that laughter? Jess?

FORTY-ONE

Caleb and Ted had talked at length during the trip back home from the Medical Examining Board inquiry. They both shared similar insights after meeting and talking with Mr. Renzoni. One, that the concept of "spreading misinformation" was one the board had never wrestled with. To sanction physicians over such accusations was new territory for them. Two, Mr. Renzoni himself seemed sympathetic to Caleb's plight and seemed impressed with the materials they had given him in support of Caleb's arguments.

Still, the week had been another one of unrest. Caleb considered opening a new private practice, like in "the old days" before hospitals owned all of the practices. But that would never work without hospital privileges. After all, he was an obstetrician and gynecologic surgeon. He needed a place to deliver babies and do surgery. In addition to being unable to practice, he had the Medical Examining Board's decision hanging over his head like a Sword of Damocles. And under him, like a trapdoor, was the decision from ACOG.

Privately, he considered other options, choices his wife knew nothing about. He preferred to keep it that way, despite his understanding that keeping secrets in marriage invariably led to "problems."

He sat in the kitchen drinking coffee and mulling over their future. He felt his wife's hands touch and begin to massage his shoulders from behind.

"You're awfully quiet," she said.

"Lots to think about."

"I know. We'll be fine. I can go back to work if need be."

"It's more than that. Financially, we can make it as long as we skimp a bit here and there, maybe sell this big place and downsize. Honestly, I'm wondering whether or not I even want to practice medicine anymore. It's become so political."

"Like everything else these days."

He nodded. "True, but for doctors, these political issues have real-life consequences. It's not the administrators and politicians facing malpractice lawsuits. They dictate the policies, and we take it in the chin when things go wrong."

She sat down in the chair next to him and reached for his hand.

"I feel like Ignaz Semmelweis."

"Who?"

"Ignaz Semmelweis was a Viennese obstetrician in the 1850s. He worked in Vienna's Lying-in hospital where one in two young women died in childbirth. They didn't know about bacteria in those days, and the doctors had all sorts of contorted ideas about why. He ultimately figured it out. He noted that the women who died were those who were examined after doctors did their autopsies in the morgue. The need for washing hands wasn't known then. He began washing his hands after doing his autopsies and between examining patients and his patients stopped dying. He began to promote hand washing and was laughed at, driven out of practice, and ultimately died penniless in an asylum."

"That's awful, and we see hand washing as basic hygiene today."

"Yep, because of Ignaz Semmelweis. Back then, it was their equivalent of today's Medical Examining Board and ACOG that drove him out of practice and ridiculed him."

Ally nodded. "Now I see why you feel like him. More coffee?"

"Sure. Thanks."

She stood, grabbed his cup, and refilled it for him.

"I was thinking about something else when I said you've been quiet."

"Oh?"

"Yes. The whole world seems to be talking about the PfenRich event, and yet, I don't think I've heard you say one word about it. That's not like you. You're typically pretty outspoken about things like that."

He shrugged. "Do I think they deserved it? Yes. It's their vaccine that's been causing all the problems despite what the so-called fact-checkers, CDC, FDA, and mainstream press all keep telling everyone. And Google, Microsoft, Facebook, and other Big Tech companies are in collusion. If you Google something like 'miscarriages COVID vaccine,' all you'll get is page after page of links supporting the vaccine and promoting it to pregnant women. Not a single alternative link is offered. It's total censorship on their part."

She sighed. "I know. It's sad really. The government can't legally censor anyone, so they get their corporate buddies to do it for them. Folks might complain and criticize them for it, but they can't stop them."

"But somebody did." Inwardly he smiled. "Stopped PfenRich, anyway. It's now all out there for the world to see." The doorbell rang. "I'll get it," he said.

As soon as he saw the postman standing there, his heart rate accelerated. He could think of only one reason for the carrier to deliver to the door.

"Hey, doc. Have a registered letter for you. Sign here if you would, please." He offered Caleb a stylus to use on the electronic pad. Caleb complied. "Thanks." The man handed him the letter. "Have a good day."

Too late for that, Caleb thought. "Thanks."

As expected, the letter was from the examining board. He closed the door and stepped back a step before opening the envelope. He sighed as he read it. It wasn't the worst scenario that he and Ted had conjured up, but it might as well have been. The board was recommending a ten-hour remedial class on social media posting and the spreading of misinformation. Caleb had 30 days to comply. Without it, they would be taking away his license to practice.

FORTY-TWO

Anson should have known that what concerned him most—the doxing of his address—would be inevitable. Seeing news vans line up along the street had become a harbinger of bad news. How did the vultures know when to circle?

The kids had no school that day, so Hannah had taken them to her parents' place out on Eagle Lake. It was a beautiful autumn day, so they would be able to escape the madness that had engulfed them and enjoy some boating and board games at the cabin. Hannah had even mentioned lunch at one of their favorite places, Michael's on the Lake. She expressed her hope that he'd be able to join them.

However, the appearance of the first news van did not bode well for that. With the arrival of the third van, he called Alicia.

"Anson? What's up?"

"The news vans are encircling the camp again." He heard some muttering on the other end that he took for legalese swearing.

"Okay, stay safe. Don't go outside to engage anyone. If things look rough, call the police. If the police don't respond, at least we'll have the 9-1-1 recording to use as leverage. It's going to take me close to an hour to get there."

"Got it. I'll call ASAP if they go away for some reason." He couldn't think of what that reason might be other than whatever staged event was planned got called off for some reason.

He made sure the nanny cams he had installed previously were working. The MJFDA had taken the video footage he had recorded from the FBI assault and was putting it to good use. They had filed a complaint against the FBI the previous day calling for a retraction, the clearing of the names of those parents who had been labeled terrorists, and a public apology to those parents. And as Alicia had expected, the trespassing charge was dropped within 24 hours.

The home invasion and arrest had been arranged for the optics only, to scare others into obedience. That plan had backfired. Conservative media was having a heyday with it and more people were beginning to stand up. Anson could only wonder what sort of optics they wanted today.

Their front door had been replaced two days earlier. Anson half expected a bill, but to date, nothing had come to the house. While their original door had sported a full plate of nicely decorated glass, he had a premonition that something stronger would be required. However, they had not been given a choice. The building crew had arrived with an almost exact duplicate of the original. He hoped his foreboding would prove to be false.

Anson didn't have to wait long for the "optics" to begin. Half an hour after calling Alicia, a horde descended upon their normally quiet street. Protesters of all shapes, sizes, and ethnicities began marching back and forth in front of his home. A number of his neighbors came out to their front porches and walkways. He phoned those he knew well, apologized, and asked that they, too, call the police. He did the same, as requested by Alicia, but saw only one patrol car arrive . . . ten minutes later. The officers did not even leave their car.

The crowd became more vocal and active. Several protesters ran up to their front door in sequence, pounding on it and screaming profanities. He was glad his family had left for the day. Via the nanny cam, he saw several protesters, carrying something in their hands, running up toward his garage door. Unfortunately, he had no view of the front of their home. What he did have on video was a lackadaisical police "presence" that allowed it to happen. Should he later discover vandalism had occurred by those "people" he would have further recourse to sue the police to cover those damages.

He wondered why no additional police had been dispatched to the scene. He was tempted at one point to call 9-1-1 and report that he was prepared to shoot anyone who came through his front door. He would have been legally justified, not that he ever wanted to injure or kill someone, but he recalled Alicia's comment about having the 9-1-1 call recordings. That would not have been a call that would help his cause, so he refrained from making that call.

All in all, he decided that it was time to move.

An hour after they arrived, the crowd dissipated. He figured the news crews had recorded enough. Or maybe they'd gotten bored by his not responding. As much as he'd wanted to and as goaded as he'd been to react, he had taken Alicia's advice to heart. But where was she?

As the last news van pulled away, Anson took a chance and walked outside. His fear was confirmed. His garage door was "repainted" in a Jackson Pollack abstract; the broken balloons carrying the paint littered at the base of the door. He pursed his lips and waggled his head. It wasn't half bad, as abstract art went. He doubted the HOA would appreciate it, but unless they complained, it gave the house a certain distinction.

As he surveyed the "damage," a car pulled into the driveway. Alicia climbed out of the driver's side. She was obviously perturbed.

She kept shaking her head as she exited the vehicle. "I never . . ." She looked up and glanced at him standing near his garage. "Oh my . . ."

He nodded. "But I didn't confront any of them. I didn't leave the house."

She sighed. He gave her an account of what had happened and then discovered that she had been detained three blocks away for at least fifteen minutes. While only one patrol car had shown up on their street, the police had been busy alright . . . assisting the protesters. All streets leading to his had been blocked to traffic, except for those who could prove they lived within the cordoned-off area and those planning to protest. She saw any number of them pass through the cordon. The police had been in on it the whole time.

FORTY-THREE

The laughter seemed to be coming from some point beyond the trees now in front of Aric. He decided to head toward the sound. At least there were no briers.

As he worked his way through the underbrush, the voices became clearer—his brother and Jess, having a laugh as he slogged his way through the woods and briers. As he emerged from the trees, Adam pointed at him.

"Tadaa. Didn't I tell you that's where he'd come out?"

Jess grinned as she nodded. Then she shook her head. "You're a mess, Aric. I think the woods won." She walked up to him and carefully began to pull twigs, thorns, and burs from his clothing.

"Go ahead. Have your laughs. That's what I get for being so concerned about you that we drove all this way, and then I fought my way to get into this place to make sure you were okay."

He was not happy, but at the same time, he felt relief that Adam was well. As he continued to observe him, he seemed more than well. Aric couldn't remember the last time he'd seen his brother so relaxed and jovial.

"You could have just texted me."

"I did. You never answered." He pulled the burner phone from a back pocket, tapped the messaging icon, and held the screen up to show Adam the texts.

"Oh. Sorry. Reception is lousy here. I've got a cell booster and satellite transmitter, but they only work when I have the generator running, which has been sporadic lately."

Aric brushed off some debris that Jess had missed. "Well, are we just going to stand out here, or what?"

Adam nodded his head toward the building. "This way. I've got the side door propped open."

As they entered the building, Aric noticed Jess looking all around and then wrapping her arms around herself. Knowing what he had shared with her about the place, he wondered what she might be thinking. Yet, he didn't want to broach that topic as it might spur on a need for even more details.

"This place is eerie."

Adam nodded. "Wait till we get downstairs. It's even creepier."

"Gee, thanks. Can't wait. It's like a horror movie where the teens head down to where the creep with the chainsaw is waiting. Everyone knows they shouldn't go that way, but they do anyway."

Aric noted a change in temperature as they descended the stairs. While he had expected it to be cooler, he was surprised to find it warmer.

"Hey, it's getting warmer."

"Yeah. I learned the place has zoned heating and cooling, so I set it up to just heat the area where I've set up camp."

Moments later, they arrived at Adam's "camp." Jess's eyes

widened as she looked around.

"You're actually living here?"

Adam nodded. "Yeah. Cozy, right?"

"Yep, love what you've done to the place, bro," quipped Aric. "But then, anything's a step up from what we first found here."

Adam grimaced. "That's an understatement." He turned toward Jessica. "This is where—"

"I don't think I want to know."

Adam shrugged. Aric agreed with her. She didn't need the details.

As he glanced around and saw the couch, something sitting on it caught his eye and surprised him. He walked over to the spot and picked up a familiar book . . . familiar to him, not to his big brother.

"What's this?"

Adam smirked. "Gee, I thought you'd recognize it."

"Adam, you've never been interested in the Bible, so what gives?"

Adam took a deep breath, and said, "Have a seat. This might take a few minutes." He proceeded to tell them of the recurring nightmare that started that first night in the building. He mentioned how the dream had changed with time and what his perceptions about the dream were. He then told them of his trip to the church, getting the Bible, and of his having dinner with Ralph and his wife, Paula. He had even gone to the midweek evening service at the church three nights earlier.

"I've accepted Christ as Lord and Savior."

Adam's smile seemed the brightest Aric had ever seen. He

jumped up and embraced his brother with a huge bear hug. Tears welled up in his eyes at the good news. As the two brothers separated, Jess came up with her own hug.

"Yayyyy! Adam, that's incredible. I'm soooo happy for you."

Adam nodded. "Thanks. I-I feel, well, I don't know how to describe it."

"We need to celebrate," said Aric.

"Yeah, well, that'll have to wait. I have to work here to finish up, and then I have to face up to a major life decision, and I-I'm really torn about it."

Aric had a sudden insight into the dilemma facing his brother. Working for Chamberlain with AlterNet, Adam had done some, well, no, many illegal things, bad things. Personal privacy meant nothing if Chamberlain could use what they found for blackmail. And Adam had been partly responsible for that invasion into personal matters. Some of the things Adam had discovered led to suicides. Some led to Chamberlain's "troubleshooter" Buckner dealing out death or injury. Adam's conscience finally got the better of him, and that led to Chamberlain's and Buckner's deaths. It also led Adam to destroy AlterNet.

Aric could understand it if Adam again felt compelled to destroy the efforts to reproduce that program. But what might that lead to? Other deaths?

And what about his own UltraNet? True, Adam now used it to put away the bad guys, to right wrongs, and generally do good. But, in most cases, it still required illegal means to do so. Aric could understand his brother's moral quandary, but he couldn't know the depth of feeling he must be facing.

But now was not the time for discussion. This was not something Jess should be a party to.

"I think I understand," said Aric. "Maybe that's a discussion for you, me, and Lynch."

FORTY-FOUR

George didn't like what was happening. He wasn't supposed to be identified. His car wasn't to be linked to the incident in New York. His jitters had also put Cassandra on edge, which seemed to have had the effect of making her clingy.

Their second night together had been okay. She had allayed his worries by appealing to his fleshly desire once again. But on the third day, she began vocalizing desires for something long-term. Nothing outright, like did he want kids or not, but the hints were obvious. The attraction he had initially felt in New York dissipated quickly. She was coming across as needy and possessive, traits he wanted nothing to do with.

They had spent the last four days in Ann Arbor. He wanted to avoid big used car operations like CarMax and dealerships. The odds were greater that they might receive alerts about his car. So, he posted his car for sale on the university campus. A cash sale to a student would delay potential identification until the sale worked its way through the state's DMV for titling and licensing. There, things would get dicey for the buyer since the title wasn't as clear as it might seem. By then, he'd have a new ride and be out of town.

"Do we have to move again?" Cass whined.

They had moved daily to reduce the risk of his car being spotted and identified.

"We've been through this before. You know what happened in New York. You were there, and at this point, since you've made no attempt to turn me in, they'll see you as a willing accomplice."

She winced. He had hung that over her head since that first night. While there was some truth to what he said, he doubted she would face any serious legal consequences. The authorities could verify that she'd been working in New York for months in an unskilled position. They would track down her education history and realize she hadn't the brains to pull off anything like he'd done. She could even claim that he'd forced her to go with him. After all, she depended on him for food, lodging, and even the clothing on her back. She could point to the few new outfits he'd recently purchased for her. She could lay on him all of the traits of a trafficker, short of selling her for sex. Using her for sex, though, was just as bad.

But then, his conclusions were based upon what she had told him. Seth's caution about really knowing her added to his anxiety. What if what she'd told him was fabricated? Or worse, what if she was the hunter and *he* was the prey? Maybe the sex was simply her way of keeping him on a short leash until the police swooped in to nab him.

They packed up the car and left the motel. He drove to the outskirts of the city on the opposite side of town. A new motel every night *was* getting old. About that, he had to agree with her. He kept his fingers crossed that someone would call about the car and make a reasonable offer. So far, every caller had wanted a super bargain. If every caller expected him to give it away, he had a different plan for it.

He found a low-end motel, pulled into the lot, and went into the office. The guy was a bit surprised that he wanted the room for the entire night and not just an hour or two. That told George what kind of clientele frequented the place. The room he requested was on the back side of the building where his car couldn't be seen from the road. Evidently, that was more in line with the usual guests.

Upon entering the room, Cassandra frowned. "Each night, they're getting worse. This place is a dump."

George thought so, too, and wished he'd asked to see a room before giving the man cash payment.

"Sorry. I didn't expect it to be so bad. I'm running low on cash 'cause I need to get a different vehicle. I'm . . ." He started to say something about the car having been made but decided against it. "In fact, I need to do that today. Make yourself as comfortable as you can here, and I'll be back as soon as I can. We passed a used car lot about half a mile back. I'm gonna check it out."

Cass did not seem happy. In some ways, he couldn't blame her, but at the same time, she was the one who latched onto him, not the other way around. And he was feeding her and had bought her clothing, which had further depleted his immediate cash reserves. What would she do if he abandoned her there?

As he walked toward the car lot, he used his phone to check in. Seth did not return his text right away, so he checked his debit card account. Another $15,000 had been added to it, just as Seth had promised.

He had told Cass the truth about needing a new vehicle that day. His deadline was closing in. He had to detonate the device within the next 48 hours . . . something to do with a timeline involving PfenRich's ability to begin downloading critical data from its widespread facilities and restoring some semblance of normal operations. Seth had argued that crippling their largest facility would be the death stroke for the company. For George that didn't seem adequate. It was the COVID "vaccine" that had killed Isabella and that had earned PfenRich billions in profits.

He'd managed to walk about a third of the car lot uninterrupted before hearing a voice behind him.

"Hi there. How can I help you today?"

George turned to face the salesman. The guy didn't exactly fit the stereotype of a used car salesman, except for the big welcoming, fake smile.

"G'morning. I was on my way back home to Montana, and my old Buick Rendezvous bit the dust on the interstate not far from here. Engine exploded, so it's been towed to the great scrapyard in the sky, so to speak. I need something reliable enough to get me and the cargo I was moving to Helena. Nothing fancy. I'll worry about something more permanent once I get there."

The salesman nodded. "What kind of cargo requirement? You know, size?"

He gestured to display the dimensions. "Two boxes. One's, oh, about three by three and a foot-plus deep. The other is about the size of a medium, moving box. Sorry, guess I should have measured them. They fit in the old car, so I never thought about needing to." His eye caught on an old S-10 Blazer. "Oh, and my suitcase."

"Well, I have a couple of nice SUVs this way." The man pointed toward a later model, white Yukon sitting next to a silver Ford Explorer. They were off to their right while the old Blazer was to their left.

George didn't want to come across as picky, which might make him memorable, so he complied and followed the man to the two SUVs. They were nice, clean vehicles, about a decade old, fewer than 100,000 miles on each, and their prices were within range, even with the post-pandemic price inflation for automobiles. He pretended to examine them, but his thoughts kept going back to the old Blazer.

"I saw an old Blazer over there. What about it?"

The guy looked disappointed but led George to the older SUV. George looked it over.

"A little rust, but the upholstery is in good shape. It's a 2004 with only 82,000 miles."

"How's it run? Like I said, I'm in a pinch and forced to get something here, and I just need it to get me to Montana."

The guy waggled his head. "Runs great. It's my uncle's. He owns this place. He's always had a fondness for this S-10, and I think he doesn't really want to sell it. That's why it's priced like it is, twice what the blue book value is."

Twice or not, George's frugality kicked in. It was still a third of the cost of the other two. And it didn't truly need to get him to Montana. He didn't live there any more than he owned an old Rendezvous.

"Can I test drive it?"

The man nodded. "Sure. C'mon into the office. Just need a copy of your driver's license."

George's first instinct was to hesitate. He didn't want to divulge his license data. But then, he remembered it was the old car that had been identified, not him. It wasn't registered to him, so no one would be looking for him by name. There would be no alerts out on his name or license.

Half an hour later, after a test run and some paperwork, and cajoling the salesman to accept payment by debit card—which went through without a hitch—the car was his. He pulled up next to his old car and moved the crates holding the drone and his second device into the Blazer. He knocked on the room's door and was greeted by a litany of complaints about the room.

And then she glanced at the Blazer. "What? First, this two-bit room, and now this piece of junk for a car?" She turned and plunged back into the room.

The thought he'd had earlier crossed his mind again. What would she do if he abandoned her there? At that moment, her well-being no longer concerned him.

He followed her inside and looked about the room. A nearly empty bottle of Jack Daniels sat on the bedstand. Where in the . . .? Then he recalled seeing a Price Cut Wine and Spirits store across from the motel. She must have been keeping the change from him whenever he gave her money for snacks and the like.

"I gotta pee," she announced as she marched into the room's tiny bathroom.

He saw his chance. He checked his suitcase and confirmed that she hadn't tampered with it. He tossed the keys to the old car onto the bed with a couple of twenties, grabbed his suitcase, and marched out the door. As he pulled away from the motel, he saw her staggering around the side of the building chasing after him. *Too bad. You're a nutcase, lady*, he thought.

As he neared the interstate, he had a choice to make. Two hours west lay PfenRich's largest plant. Ten hours south sat the Research Triangle unit outside Raleigh. However, he'd had time to read some of the data Seth had managed to release. He had learned that the website was a ruse when it came to their vaccine research.

Eleven hours east—back to where he'd first started—was its real vaccine center and the facility where the mRNA derivatives were created. Seth argued for the Michigan facility. With this new revelation in mind, George saw the southern New York center as its biggest cash cow, particularly for the future. His old vehicle was in Michigan and could be used to draw attention there. He texted Seth and then pulled onto the interstate heading east.

FORTY-FIVE

Edvin knocked on the door of Werner's suite at The Plaza. Following his pacemaker replacement, his boss had decided to begin his recuperation in New York. While he fully trusted his cardiologist at home, the brand of pacer was not yet available in Germany, and he wanted to be able to follow up with the team that had inserted it and understood its technology. Edvin also guessed that he wasn't yet up to the long flight home, although the man would never admit such.

Elisha, the personal chef, opened the door for him. They greeted each other.

"Herr Koch will be out shortly. If you like, I have made apple strudel this morning. It is at the bar."

Edvin grinned. "*Danke.*" He loved Elisha's strudels.

At the bar, it became clear that someone else had been loving the dessert first. A third of it was already gone. Edvin restricted himself to a portion smaller than he would have liked. As he took his first bite, he heard footsteps from the other side of the room.

"Ah, Edvin, I see you have already found the strudel."

He finished his bite. "Elisha offered it to me."

Werner smiled and laughed. "And I see he's forcing you to eat it, too. Come, sit."

The man sat on one of the lavish couches in the main room where the windows opened onto a vista of The Pond at Central Park with the Upper West Side of Manhattan in the distance. Edvin never tired of the view. He sat opposite his boss.

"How are you feeling, sir?"

"Great. Back to my old self. The sutures come out in two days, and if the pacemaker is functioning properly, which it has so far, then I might consider flying home this weekend."

Edvin nodded as he chewed. He resisted the temptation to talk with his mouth full. After swallowing, he said, "I am glad you are feeling better. I have some news."

Werner pointed to the strudel. "Go ahead. Finish that, and then we can talk."

Edvin savored every bite. He noticed the older man gazing out the windows in contemplation. He wondered what might be going through his mind. His boss' insights and intuition had never failed to amaze him.

To his surprise, as he swallowed his last bite, Elisha was at his right side to take the dish. "Again, *danke*, Elisha. That was delicious."

The chef responded with a curt bow before turning and leaving the room.

"So, you have news."

Edvin turned back toward the older man. "Yes, sir. Perhaps follow-up is a better term. The state police have tracked the ownership of the dark blue Impala that we believe the bomber used. It was registered to a Harold Bishop of Lancaster, Pennsylvania."

"And have they tracked him down?"

"Yes and no. It appears Mr. Bishop died three years ago. They have not yet tracked down any next-of-kin or anyone known to be using the car."

Werner frowned and furrowed his brow. "That is disappointing, but not surprising. Someone ingenious enough to create and deploy an EMP device would not be so stupid as to use his own car."

"Well, sir, the good news is they have located the car and caught the woman seen in the security videos. She was driving under the influence, and the police pulled her over. When the officer ran the plates, he discovered the alert for the vehicle. She is currently in jail in Ann Arbor, Michigan. The FBI will interview her when she is sober enough to be questioned."

"And the man?"

"Nowhere to be seen, and the car was empty except for a bag with the woman's few items of clothing."

"Fingerprints? DNA? Do they have anything that might identify the man?"

Edvin shook his head. "Nothing yet. It is in progress."

"Have them expedite it."

"The FBI director has already assured us that they will. However, even that could take 72 hours."

Werner stood and walked over to the windows. He had that contemplative look again. He retrieved his phone from a pocket and took a moment to review something on it.

"Seventy-two hours might be too late." He paused and turned to face Edvin. "So, why Ann Arbor?"

Edvin nodded. "I have been thinking about that. Perhaps he is not finished with PfenRich yet. Their largest production facility is in central Michigan. Maybe that is another target."

Werner nodded. "Possibly, but that does not answer the question of why Ann Arbor? I just checked the map of Michigan. He could use two interstates to get to the PfenRich plant. The slower route would go through Ann Arbor, not the faster one."

"Maybe he suspected that security around all PfenRich facilities would be increased and that to move on one too soon was risky. Maybe he hoped that security measures would ease up after a short time when nothing else happened."

"Yes, perhaps. What other reasons might there be?"

"Maybe he anticipated that he might be identified through the security cam network in New York and that the car would likewise be identified. Then, he would have to switch to another vehicle."

"Yes. And how could he make that switch?"

Edvin pondered that for a moment. "He could have another car stashed someplace and simply swap them. He could steal one. He could sell it to someone, maybe a car dealer., and buy another one."

Werner nodded. "The first is a possibility. With the second, I don't see him stealing a car. That would send out alerts quickly. The third is also a possibility, but who would he target? Not a car dealership. They, too, were sent alerts. But an unsuspecting college student would know nothing about the car until he tried to register it."

"A small used car lot is another possibility. They did not receive the alert." Edvin paused. "But the fact that the woman was caught with the car goes against his selling it. He might still be in Ann Arbor, or he might live in Ann Arbor. Also, he could be using another car to head toward the plant."

Edvin knew that PfenRich was important to his boss. He suspected that the man had taken a beating when the stock price took its nosedive. Werner had invested heavily in the pharmaceutical giant because it played such a vital role in the World Order Council's plans. And companies endorsed and used by the Council had such a high level of support that they never failed. Until now. However, the Council's support of the company was likely a more important reason for Werner to want to see PfenRich rebound. The loss of PfenRich and its mRNA vaccines would set back the Council's plans of complete global dominance by months, if not years.

The older man again nodded. "We must assume the latter while not ignoring the idea that he is still in that city. We need to ask the FBI to increase security at the PfenRich plant." He paused for a moment. "On second thought, we should ask them to increase it at all PfenRich facilities. We must assume and be prepared for the worst scenarios."

FORTY-SIX

"I still don't understand why I have to go to Washington for this. Couldn't they just do the interview from our living room again, or some local studio?" asked Anson.

Alicia smiled as she took her carry-on luggage from Anson who pulled it from the back of the Uber at Milwaukee's General Mitchell Airport. Denton Pierce had arranged for them to meet him in the nation's capital for a personal on-air appearance with Perry Carson. Anson grabbed his carry-on next, as Alicia paid the driver.

Both had their RealID and TSA Pre-Check cards readily available. As such, and having only carry-ons, they had arrived at the airport an hour ahead of the flight anticipating no delays.

"You've done so well in previous interviews that Denton wants you to become more visible. Perry agreed."

Anson frowned. Denton had told him the same thing, and he felt torn. On one hand, he only wanted to slide back into the shadows and try to find a new job, put bread on the table, rebuild their lives, and live the "quiet" life they'd once had. Well, as quiet a life as possible with five kids. On the other hand, he didn't want anyone else to go through the unjust persecution he'd been encountering for simply speaking up against immorality. To accomplish that he needed to speak out and expose that injustice.

In the end, the latter won out. And the promise of a speaker's fee for appearing on the show helped cement that decision. After all, both he and his wife had lost their jobs over the situation and the money was needed.

At the ticket kiosk, Alicia scanned her ID and e-ticket and printed out her boarding pass without a problem. Anson, however, seemed to be having trouble. The pass wouldn't print, and he was directed to an agent at the ticket counter.

"May I help you?"

Anson nodded. "Yes. I can't seem to print my boarding pass at the kiosk." He handed the agent his ID and ticket.

She scanned the items, and a serious look crossed her face. "One moment. I'm sure this is probably just a mistake."

She walked to the far end of the counter and talked with another agent. That agent picked up a phone and began to talk as the first agent returned to Anson.

"Someone will be here to help in a minute. Could you step to the side so I can help the next person? Thank you."

Anson and Alicia stepped aside. A couple of minutes later, a TSA officer with three stripes—a supervisor—walked over to him. He motioned with his hand. "Please come with me."

Alicia stepped up. "May I ask why?"

The man looked at her. "And who are you?"

"Alicia Somers, an attorney with the Midwest Justice and Freedom Defense Alliance. Mr. Hardy is one of our clients."

"I see. Well, Ms. Somers, you'll need to stay here while we

clear your client for flying."

"Clear me for flying? I have TSA Pre-Check. You folks have cleared me for flying. My family and I went through here to fly to Colorado just three months ago."

"Excuse me, officer, but there's been no indication that he was selected for secondary security screening."

"No, ma'am. The DOJ asked that he be put on the no-fly list."

Anson's eyes widened. "The no-fly list? What the—"

Anson was well aware of the "dreaded" Quad S designation—the four esses. He had gone through the Secondary Security Screening Selection before. Even with the TSA Pre-Check, he could be randomly selected for the enhanced screening which might include a thorough exam of his carry-on contents, a complete pat down, and lots of questions. But to be placed on the "no-fly" list like some terrorist or felon was way beyond his comprehension.

The officer led him away to a room off to the side of the TSA screening area. Two other officers were there as well. They had him open his carry-on and empty its contents, which they examined in detail. All the while they asked questions about where he was headed and why, what did he do for work, whether he was affiliated with any groups such as the Proud Boys, and more. Throughout it all, Anson kept his cool.

And then the supervisor said, "Please strip down to your underwear."

That hit Anson as uncalled-for. "Strip down? Why? I criticized my local school board for allowing boys in my daughter's locker room and you're treating *me* like some criminal? You do realize my attorney's just outside that door waiting to add the TSA to our lawsuit against the DOJ and FBI. She no doubt already has your names and numbers."

The three officers looked at him with blank expressions. He shook his head and complied. He resisted voicing the snide comments going through his head and redressed. After another round of questions, he was released.

He repacked his carry-on and rushed out the door where Alicia awaited him. She started to ask him questions.

"We can talk on the plane. We need to get to the gate or we're going to miss the flight."

At the gate, he was stopped once again, and another round of questions began. Anson heard the gate attendant announce the final boarding.

"Ms., that's the final call. We need to board the plane."

"I'm sorry, sir, but we have a protocol to follow. You're going to miss this flight."

FORTY-SEVEN

Adam had enjoyed Aric's and Jessica's company for the afternoon and found the visit to be far too short. That in itself surprised him. He'd never had trouble being alone, and visitors often became distractions if they overstayed their welcome. But something within him had changed. He had valued their fellowship and was saddened to see it end. Still, he understood their need to leave. They had another three-hour drive to return to Kenosha.

Yesterday, he joined Ralph Bursiek and his wife at their church. He met more people that morning than he could possibly keep up with by name. The Bursieks invited him to join them for lunch, which he readily accepted, and during that time together, he had peppered the man with more questions, all of which were answered. Sometimes his response was qualified with "as I understand it, but some disagree," but he provided Adam with a level of comprehension that hadn't been there previously. Adam realized he had a lot of learning to do.

He also now recognized why Aric commented so frequently about the deterioration of society. As pointed out in the book of Romans, chapter 1, verses 18-32, God allowed those who denied Him to follow their debased passions and allowed them to be *"filled with all manner of unrighteousness, evil, covetousness, malice."* It was God's ultimate permission of free will.

Now, two days after Aric's surprise visit, Adam paced within the basement of the old lab and found it depressing and lonely. He had a difficult time focusing on his work while wrestling with the moral dilemma of continuing his white hat hacking. He made no money from his efforts. There was no conflict of interest in that sense. Truth be told, he had made such good money previously, lived a spartan lifestyle, saved, and invested well that he was financially set for life. Not that he advertised that fact, even to his little brother.

He liked Aric's suggestion to consult Lynch Cully. The man's experience and level of understanding of both the law and the Bible made him the ideal adviser. Now the question was, when? Did he risk coming out of hiding to see the former detective, turned professor?

There was one thing he was determined to do, though— stop the efforts to rebuild AlterNet2. To allow that program, with its power to spy on and track people, to return to the hands of the unscrupulous, global elites would be a disservice to all freedom-loving peoples.

He sat at his makeshift computer station and tried to review the code he had written to infiltrate Rebecca's computers and ultimately the AlterNet servers . . . all of them. Something seemed to be missing but he couldn't put his finger on the issue.

Per custom, he stood and began to pace as he mulled over

the problem. On his second lap around that part of the basement, an alert sounded on his computer. With hopeful expectation, he hurried back to his chair.

Yes! He pumped his fist in the air. It was Seth . . . purportedly.

He forced himself to be cautious. As with any online situation, he needed to confirm the individual's identity.

Hello, Seth! It was a dismal day in Eden.

The response:

But a sunny day in Eden West. Hi, Adam. Been a while.

Adam smiled. The coded response was correct, but that alone didn't confirm Seth's identity. Rebecca, aka Eve, would also know that code, and she now worked for the "enemy." Adam needed to use something that Eve wouldn't know.

Eve is as hot as . . .

The reply came quickly.

. . . the only woman on earth could be.

Adam grinned. Only he, Sam Renner, aka Abel, and Seth knew that phrase, and Sam was gone. None of them considered himself a misogynist or to the other extreme, a womanizer, but Rebecca Stiles was far from comely. She was an excellent database designer who could hold her own against anyone in that arena. However, Seth had originally made the comment—when it came to looks and womanly curves, to be considered "hot" she would have to be the only woman on earth.

With the code names given to them, it seemed highly appropriate at the time. Today, Adam recognized it as disparaging, whether true or not.

It has been a while. I see that you, too, have left the planet. Lol

Not as well as you, however. You found me.

Pure luck and a gut feeling. The PfenRich event was genius but I felt sure you didn't have the skills to create the EMP device. It was the dumping of their data that convinced me you were involved. All I had to do was track your accomplice and contact him.

Which really freaked him . . . and me . . . out. Then I started thinking. Who could have tracked him like that? Do you have AlterNet?

Adam pondered that question for a moment. Did he want to admit that he did? Then again, Seth would see right through him if he denied it. Some surveillance programs, like that in New York City, might be able to track someone across a city or region, but only a program like AlterNet could have tracked his partner across several states.

Sort of. I destroyed CSS's copies and servers after they killed Abel but kept a copy of it for myself. I call it UltraNet now.

Sweet. I figured you had it. It's the only way someone could have found me.

The reason I've been looking for you is that someone like Wallace Chamberlain is trying to resurrect AlterNet. Eve is working for them. If they succeed, our freedoms are over.

They already are. Look at the COVID mandates and lockdowns. Look at WHO wanting global jurisdiction over all medical responses to pandemics only they will define. Their vaccine passports are just a slippery slide away from becoming mandatory for all buying and selling.

Adam hadn't thought about that. He'd read in the Book of Revelation about the mark of the beast being required to buy and sell. Aric had mentioned something about Lynch saying the beasts of Revelation had already risen. Now it appeared that the mark of the beast was about to come on the scene, too.

Perhaps, but why make it easier for them?

There was a pause.

Good point. How can I help?

Adam outlined his idea, which Seth agreed to assist.

Werner had personally contacted the security chief at PfenRich, as well as the director of the FBI, to request continued surveillance and a beefed-up police presence at all PfenRich facilities. The Michigan plant was given the highest priority, but Werner had expressed his doubts to Edvin that this was the target.

Edvin had returned to the AlterNet2 facility to continue their hunt for Adam Afton. As he sat at his desk, he noticed the programmers huddling around Rebecca's workstation. The discussion appeared somewhat heated. He arose to go see what was going on.

As he approached the desk, all of their heads turned toward him, and the conversation dropped off. Granger nodded in greeting as he joined them.

"Sir, we might have a problem."

"Oh? What kind of problem?"

"Maybe I should let Rebecca explain."

The woman looked as if she'd just been thrown under a bus. And maybe she had.

"Sir, come around here and look at this."

Edvin did she asked. He looked at her screen to see a chat thread open. The text read:

Eve, it was a dismal day in Eden.

But a sunny day in West Eden. Who is this?

A member of the team you never met. I spotted your request on the DW for information about Adam Afton. He's a figment of your imagination. His name was Adam just as yours was Eve. He was first on the team. Afton was a name pulled from a hat for its alliteration with Adam. Cain died by suicide and Abel was killed by Chamberlain because he knew too much. Might you be next?

Who is this?

They called me Seth. I was the fourth man on the team. Then came Enoch and Irad, but you didn't know them either. Be careful whom you search for.

Rebecca spoke up. "The first line was a code phrase we were to use to identify and confirm others on the team in online conversations. Only someone else on the team could have known this. The DW refers to the dark web."

"So, who are these other people? You led us to believe only this Adam fellow was the missing part of the team, and now his identity is in question."

The woman looked troubled. "Sir, I-I . . . he was the only other one I ever worked with. Sam Renner was Abel, and he is dead, but I didn't know why or how. I often wondered if there was a Cain, but this suicide thing is news to me, too. As for the other names, I never met them or even heard of them. I told you before that Wallace Chamberlain liked to compartmentalize the work."

Edvin felt distressed as well. How could he present this to his boss?

"How do we know this isn't Adam Afton himself trying to throw us off the trail?"

Granger shook his head. "We don't, sir."

Edvin took a deep breath and ran his hand through his hair. Were all of their efforts a waste? The FBI had come up empty regarding the brother at the college campus. Was that because they'd been trying to track down someone who never existed? Then he remembered that the FBI had not come up empty in St. Louis and that the girlfriend had acknowledged knowing Adam Afton. But was this truly the Adam they were looking for? It had to be. Only someone with his programming skills could erase his existence as this man had done or fake a death certificate as he'd done.

"Where did this come from? Have you been able to trace it? This should be easy for the program to track, even at this stage."

"No, sir, we haven't. That's what we were discussing when you noticed us. We thought the program could handle it, too, and it's still working. But it hasn't helped so far."

Edvin rubbed his face. Did he dare to take this to Werner? The man had given the project to him. He needed to prove himself. What should be his next move?

FORTY-EIGHT

George glanced at the time: 10:50 pm. He had made excellent time even when considering the time zone change. He made several passes along the roads surrounding and leading to the PfenRich vaccine research facility.

He pulled off into the shadows of a local eatery across from the main entrance on the north side of the property and simply watched for half an hour. Of concern, but not unexpected, was the exceptional police presence not just at the entrances to the plant but also patrolling nearby parking lots and residential neighborhoods. He was almost spotted at one point. He moved to a neighborhood to the east and noted less of a security presence.

After observations along the south and west sides that took him into the early morning hours, he realized the police were focused most heavily on the west and north. That made him smile. Clearly, they weren't out-of-the-box thinkers. After his balloon attack in the city, they appeared to expect the same here and were covering the areas where the prevailing winds favored a balloon launch.

Yet, his new toy was the best he'd produced yet. Not only

could the four-prop drone carry the payload of the EMP device, but it was programmable. He needed no controller or to guide it visually whether by line-of-sight or by an onboard camera. He didn't care about FAA requirements for maintaining a line of sight on his drone. He needed only to set the GPS coordinates, flying altitude, and altitude for detonation; launch it, and sit back and watch. Well, he didn't even have to watch. He could launch it from as far away as five miles, although he planned to do so no further than two miles away to have a margin of safety.

Still, despite being the best, the drone and its results would not bring Bella back. His world had collapsed with her death, and if he was honest with himself, he didn't much care whether he lived or died after getting his revenge. Perhaps death would be preferable, the ultimate escape from his pain.

He expanded his radius from the plant and found a suitable parking lot for the launch about a mile and a half away as the crow flies. Now it was time to catch some ZZZZs. He needed to strike when the company was likely to have the most electronics in operation. That meant late morning before lunch or mid-afternoon. He was tired after the full day of driving, so he decided upon an afternoon time frame unless he should wake in time for the late morning option.

He decided, too, that he'd had enough of two-bit rooms. He'd saved enough by buying the old Blazer that he no longer had to string out his finances. He had little remaining cash, but his endeavor was almost to its end. He decided to use the debit card and find a nicer motel. A short drive down the road brought an answer to his quest, and he pulled into the Doubletree to see if they had a room.

FORTY-NINE

Caleb and Ted had a long talk that Saturday afternoon after his receipt of the letter from the examining board . . . over several beers at the Wahlburg residence and without charge by Ted. Their basic conclusion was that Caleb had two options.

First, he could refuse the remedial course and lose his license for sure. That would, in turn, lead to being unable to secure a license elsewhere since the revocation would be public record, and he would be obligated to report it to other states should he apply for a license. Other states would be highly unlikely to issue him a license to practice with that on his record. Second, he could comply with the dictate. That led to two other choices—to comply fully and not post anything controversial to social media or to take the program and continue his current course of social media posting. The latter would no doubt be seen as a challenge to the state board if those posts were deemed misinformation.

Ted hadn't pushed him one way or the other. The decision was Caleb's, and Ted had said as much. Now, three days later, Caleb still wrestled with a decision. He had leaned toward a fourth option: taking the course, but then leaving medicine altogether. He would then allow his license to lapse and not renew it. This way he wouldn't have the stain of having his license pulled on his record. But as he thought about it, why not just quit his license to start with? Why take that stupid ten-week course and waste his time? The decision seemed to have taken him to the mat with the referee counting down.

Ally found him in his study.

"Where'd you disappear to last night? I woke up in the middle of the night, and you weren't there."

Caleb knew that it wasn't just the previous night. He'd been up most of the night, each night, for the past week, and it wasn't the nightmare keeping him awake. He had previously decided that Ally shouldn't know about certain aspects of his life prior to their meeting. But keeping secrets in marriage was problematic and usually did not turn out for the better, as he kept reminding himself. Still, some things required secrecy, as anyone with or who once had a Top Secret clearance would understand. He understood. His security clearance had once been two levels above Top Secret.

However, he was bound to secrecy for only seven years after leaving that job. Well, bound to secrecy for certain aspects of his position. Some of what he knew required a lifetime of zipped lips.

He stood from his desk and walked up to his wife. He embraced her and kissed her gently on the lips. It was time that she gained a better understanding of what his life had been like before they met. He led her to a couch in the next room and motioned for her to sit.

"I appreciate that for all of our years together you haven't prodded me about life before we met. I think it's time I open up a bit more."

He noted tears welling up.

"You don't have to if you're not comfortable with it. I have no real complaints about our life together."

He shook his head. "No. I think you need to know where I came from. You already know about my Korean heritage, my parents and their deaths, my adoption, my first wife, and how she died. I've never held back on that."

He gauged his next words carefully.

"Right out of college, I worked for the military. I can't provide details about that but suffice it to say I had a high-security clearance and worked on some pretty serious stuff. I was a computer programmer and was recruited for a very special project. After the conflict in Afghanistan, that program was taken over by a civilian company with, shall I say, less than moral scruples. Heck, no scruples if I'm to be honest. The program I worked on began to be used to hurt people, for blackmail, and for all kinds of things I couldn't agree with. To get out alive, I was forced to disappear. My name was Simon, and I used my programming skills to remove all traces of my previous identity and create a new one, the Caleb Wahlburg you know. I went to med school to help people, and I couldn't think of anything better than to help bring new life into the world."

Ally grabbed both of his hands and squeezed. "I don't want to know who you were. I know and love who you are."

He squeezed back and offered her a wan smile.

"I love you, too. But a few days ago, my old life found me. Our work was highly compartmentalized, but I got to know two of the other programmers fairly well. One of them was murdered while trying to blow the whistle on that company. The other disappeared as I did. He succeeded in taking down the company and eliminating the program that caused all the trouble. Or so I thought."

Her eyes widened. "Oh?" She took a deep breath. "Are we in—"

"Danger? No, I don't think so. The bad people at that company are also dead now. My old colleague found me. I don't know exactly how, but he did. And he told me that another programmer from the old team was recruited by Werner Koch to help rebuild the program. She's on a team that's trying to resurrect what we called AlterNet."

"Werner Koch? Why do I know that name?"

"He's head of the World Order Council. He's an elitist trying to bring a global government about."

She shivered at that thought.

"And this AlterNet program?"

"It would become a master surveillance program that could eliminate freedom for all of us."

"And this old friend wants your help?"

He smiled at how perceptive she was.

"Yes. That's exactly why he contacted me . . . and why I was up most of the night. He doesn't want to see a new AlterNet develop. He has a plan to destroy it but asked me for, well, to review and refine the code he's already written."

She sat back looking stunned. He hoped he hadn't overloaded her with information, or worse, disappointed her somehow.

"Is something wrong?"

She shook her head. "No. I'm just trying to wrap my head

around the fact that my husband, besides being a great OB doc, is some computer mastermind." She smiled. "Whatever he needs, help him. Big Tech isn't a friend of freedom, so if you can fight fire with fire, go for it." She leaned over and kissed him on the cheek. "And of course, my lips are sealed. None of this will leave the room by me."

He laughed. "Glad I didn't have to use the 'if I tell you, I'd have to kill you' line."

She smiled again. "I do have one question though."

"Oh?"

"The timing of this with respect to the attack on PfenRich is suspect to me. Was he involved in that?"

Ally's perceptiveness once again shone, and Caleb's heart rate began to speed at the mention of PfenRich. He hoped his sudden anxiety wasn't obvious as he forced himself to remain calm. Some things were meant to remain secret. But then when she asked her question, he felt calm engulf him as he realized that wouldn't have to lie to his wife.

"No, dear, he wasn't."

FIFTY

Edvin arrived early at the AlterNet2 lab. He hoped for good news. Randall Granger had not yet arrived, but as soon as he did, Edvin cornered him.

"Well, have we tracked down whoever sent those messages?"

Granger replied, "Give me a minute to check, sir." The man signed in on his computer and began to type. A frown crossed his face, and he furrowed his brow as he typed some more and scrutinized the information on his screen. After a couple of minutes, he shook his head. "No, sir. We ran into an unforeseen roadblock. The program triggered some kind of trip wire that launched a virus set to infiltrate our servers. Our firewall stopped it, but the program stopped the search as a result." He looked up and directly at Edvin. "That was a protocol we set up to prevent any back-tracing effort to damage our servers from an outside source. It worked as designed. We have the virus quarantined and will examine it. It might give us a lead on who created it and its origins."

Edvin felt disappointed, but he appreciated the work the team had done to protect itself and AlterNet2. Far too much effort and financial resources had gone into their work to risk losing any of it now.

He watched as others from the team filtered into the lab, most carrying extra-large cups of coffee. He knew that some of them had worked past midnight. He decided that their dedication would be rewarded handsomely should they manage to find this Seth, or Adam, whoever he really was, and if he still existed.

He pursued his own work and prepared a report for Werner on the fallout of the PfenRich attack. They still had their vaccine development labs and production plant, and an attack on the mid-Michigan production plant would not have as big an impact as Werner had expected. That facility produced mainly older drugs. Their main profit maker now was the COVID vaccine and future mRNA products, and they would be able to rebuild from that work alone.

As midmorning rolled around, he noticed one of the programmers, Matt, jump up, agitated and panicky. He let out a string of four-letter words that were unmistakable.

"Shut it down! Shut it down!"

Granger rushed into the area of the workstations, took a look at Matt's screen, and screamed in disbelief, "We're being hacked. Pull the plug."

Rebecca, too, ran back in from the break room where she'd grabbed a Monster™ Energy drink, and rushed to her workstation. "No, no, no, no, no!" She looked desperate as her fingers flew across the keyboard. After a minute, she sat back in her chair, tears flowing down her cheeks. "It's gone. It's all gone."

He noticed the same defeat on Granger's face, as the man

took off his glasses and rubbed his face. The man slowly stood and walked over to Edvin.

"Sir, may I borrow your laptop?"

"Mine?"

Granger nodded. "Yes, sir. It's the only one here that wasn't connected to the network using AlterNet2's interface."

With reluctance, Edvin complied. If what he thought just happened, happened, he didn't want his laptop compromised. He couldn't afford to lose the material on his computer. The idea of such made him resolve to back up his system ASAP.

Granger made use of the laptop for a few minutes, shook his head, and sighed. Tears welled up in his eyes. "It's all gone, sir. All of it." He handed the laptop back to Edvin.

Edvin furrowed his brow. "What do you mean, all of it is gone?"

"Everything we've worked on. All of AlterNet2. Our workstations, our servers, our remote backup servers, our backup of the backups. Everything. I can't access any of it."

Edvin's heart sank. What was Werner going to say? Surely Werner wouldn't blame this on him. Would he? No one could have foreseen this. Then a thought hit Edvin. As a precaution, the backups were located off-site, and Granger was trying to tie into the servers remotely. Maybe there was another way, like in the movies where the hero had to make a daring intrusion into the enemy's building, find the server room, and connect directly to their computer to destroy it. Maybe there was a lifeline here.

"What about connecting directly to those servers? We should drive to their location and try to connect by cable or Ethernet or whatever. Maybe we will find something left."

Granger shook his head. "It's not like that, sir. It's not that we can't connect to those servers. I can see them remotely. It's that everything there was deleted and overwritten. There's nothing to salvage, whether I connect remotely from here or by Ethernet there."

Edvin kept shaking his head. "No. There has to be some—"

"No, sir, there isn't. Everything we've done over the past year is gone."

Adam and Seth had worked through the night to complete the worm code that Adam would use to infiltrate and destroy the new AlterNet effort. Of course, he had no guarantee that they wouldn't start all over. He could only remain vigilant for such an effort and hope to keep them from any level of success. They had progressed too far this time, further than Adam felt comfortable about, but he knew now what to watch for and to set trip wires to detect such efforts earlier. Such detection would be easy if a new effort utilized Rebecca's database structure and search algorithms. Should they start afresh with something completely new, the task would be more difficult.

He sat at his computer workstation and made one last review of the code. Seth was satisfied with it and confident that it would work. He had created a virus to back-trace any attempt to find him, but its purpose was mainly one of diverting attention from their main assault. Now, Adam, too, felt the last of his reservations evaporate.

He checked the time. While he knew all too well that programmers kept strange hours, he also knew how such corporate teams operated. There would be a supervisor who would live by corporate hours and expect the others to accommodate their bosses to a great degree. The odds were greatest that all of the team's workstations would be up and running in midmorning. And being an hour ahead in the eastern time zone, now was the time.

Adam took his time and with great caution wove his way through Facebook's servers and into Rebecca's computer. Once there, he used his familiarity with her database structures and their backup procedures to confirm that the full network and its backup servers were operational. Then he waited.

He used her laptop's webcam to spy on her and anything else within range of the camera. He needed to wait for her to take a break and step away before moving ahead. His patience was soon rewarded as he watched her sit back in her chair, stretch her arms, and scoot back from the desk. She stood and left the camera's field of view. If she was anything like she had been, she was heading to get caffeine, either in the form of coffee or an energy drink.

Satisfied that his timing was right, he set up the worm and launched it. Without her working on her computer, it would distribute itself throughout their network and backup servers before she could ever notice the unusual activity on her computer.

Less than five minutes later, he heard pandemonium break out in their facility. Several voices began screaming in chorus, "Shut it down!" and "We've been hacked" and strings of words he hadn't heard in the years since he'd escaped Wallace Chamberlain's hit squad. A moment later, Rebecca was back at her computer frantically hitting keys in the hope that some key combination would stop the rampage occurring on her system.

And then all went black on her end. That was the final act of the worm. Her computer was now a useless electronic brick.

Adam pumped a fist in the air. *Yes!* He knew the action was a bit anachronistic, but it seemed fitting.

He glanced about the old lab's basement and nodded at the thought that it had been a fitting place to bring down the attempted resurrection of AlterNet. Now, it was time to leave, and he began to dismantle his workstation and pack the car.

FIFTY-ONE

George had slept well. His confidence in his plan and his electronics had enabled him to fall asleep and stay asleep. The fact that he'd driven nearly eleven hours to return to southern New York and then spent three hours surveilling his target had certainly helped. His body had crashed upon lying down.

He awoke about 8 am, surprised that his body's biorhythms hadn't kicked in earlier. He still had a couple of hours to take advantage of the WakeUp Doubletree Breakfast™ he had purchased. He looked forward to a hot breakfast, juice, and coffee. It had been a while since he'd eaten something other than fast food. As he thought about it, after yesterday's drive, it had been over 24 hours since he'd eaten anything other than a bag of chips washed down with a soda.

After showering and shaving, he descended to the area off the lobby where the breakfast café was located. He indulged himself with scrambled eggs, both bacon and sausage, as well as a biscuit with sausage gravy. He added an apple-cinnamon muffin to the meal and sat down to enjoy it. A tall glass of orange juice and a mug of black coffee accompanied the food.

The thought of it being a condemned man's last meal flit through his head. He shook off the idea. The sound sleep and promise of good food had diminished his depressive thoughts. His plan was going to work, and he'd be home within two days of driving.

He was nearly finished when a young man entered the café and walked right toward him. The man appeared upset, and his pants were stained with coffee.

"Sir, the front desk pointed you out to me. Are you the owner of the old dark green Blazer in the parking lot?"

George wasn't sure how to respond. Had his purchase of the vehicle in Michigan somehow been traced? How had they found him here, at the Doubletree? His initial anxiety eased as he realized the man was not a police officer. His nametag announced him as "Scott" with some company that sounded like a tech firm.

"I am. What's up?"

"Sir, I am so sorry. My hot coffee tipped over in my truck and spilled all over my legs as I was backing out of my parking slot. My foot jerked on the accelerator, and I hit your Blazer. My tow hitch went right through the back hatch of your car. It did a job on the hatch, but I took a peek into your car and everything in the back seems okay." The man handed him a copy of his driver's license, phone number, and insurance.

George's initial response was one of "so what." He had no insurance on the vehicle, and it would soon be disposed of. As long as the crates in the back were okay, he was okay with what had happened.

"You said the crates in the back were intact?"

The man nodded. "Yes, sir. Looked like it."

"Okay. Not a big deal. That thing's so old, I was planning on getting a new vehicle once I got back home from this trip. As long as my cargo's intact and it's drivable, I don't think I'll even worry about making a claim."

The man looked relieved. "Oh, it definitely looks drivable. Even the bumper's intact. Just my tow hitch got it."

George nodded. "Well, give me a minute to finish my food, and I'll walk out with you to check everything."

The man looked antsy again. "Sir, if you don't mind. I'm heading to a trade show to deliver some of our products, and I'm already late. Would you mind if I got going? You have my contact info and stuff if you need to contact me."

George hesitated at first but realized that under the circumstances he wasn't about to call and file a police report. Still, he didn't want to come across as unconcerned.

"I'd prefer inspecting it with you . . . but, I guess so. Give me one sec." He pulled out his burner cell phone, dialed the number on the paper, and waited. Sure enough, the phone in the young man's pocket rang. "Okay, just wanted to make sure you weren't giving me a fake number. If something's amiss, I'll let you know before calling the police to file a report."

Again, relief flooded the man's face. "Thanks. Thank you, sir. Again, I'm so sorry."

The man rushed from the room and out the front doors. George's gaze followed him outside until he could no longer see him. He heard the loud grumble of a big truck start up and looked outside to see a large, jacked-up pickup rumble past the windows of the café. As it turned onto the street, he noticed that it had a large tow hitch sticking out the back, like those for oversized trailers.

The thought of that penetrating the back of the Blazer caused anxiety in an instant. *But the guy said my crates were intact*, he thought. Yet, were they?

He rushed through finishing his meal, ascended to his room, gathered his things, and headed toward the old sport-ute. The four-inch hole gaping through the metal of the tailgate didn't appear that bad, and from the windows, all looked good inside.

It required a bit of effort, however, to open the back. When he succeeded in getting the door open, he gasped. The hole in the tailgate continued into the crate of the drone.

He quickly dumped his gear onto the back seat and worked to open the crate. His heart dropped as he saw the drone. Its electronic guidance package, which he had so lovingly designed and built, was shattered. Would the machine even fly now?

He closed the tailgate, climbed into the driver's seat, and headed for the abandoned strip mall with the crumbling asphalt parking lot where he had intended to launch the system. Behind the stores out of view from the street, he again forced open the gate and lifted the two crates from the back. He took the drone and powered it up. All the props worked. He more closely inspected the guidance package and recognized that he would not be able to repair it. At best, it would need to be rebuilt, but he hadn't the time or resources for that.

He had no time. He needed to launch this third and final phase of his attack today before PfenRich had time to retrench and begin to rebuild upon its vaccine products. He would have to pilot the drone with its original controller…and that would require doing so with a direct line of sight if he wished to detonate the EMP device in the optimal location.

He removed the EMP from its crate. Satisfied that there was no damage to the cargo structure he had fashioned on the bottom of the drone, he assembled the two into a single unit. He grabbed the controller. Under direct vision, he was able to launch, fly, and land the drone with its special package. He smiled. Not ideal. Not what he had expected upon awakening that morning, but so far, so good.

Leaving the crates behind the building, he returned the drone unit to the back of the Blazer. Having it already assembled would save him valuable time at the launch site. Now, he just needed to decide where that site would be.

He mentally reviewed his surveillance of the previous night. As he recalled, he had but few options. He couldn't very well stop on the shoulder of the main highway. He would stick out like the proverbial sore thumb. The highway was also elevated, so he had few locations to choose from on the side opposite from PfenRich. The two main entrances to employee parking were also too conspicuous. Plus, they would be well-guarded.

His target buildings were along the southeast corner of the company's campus. He needed a direct view of those buildings because the EMP needed to be deployed right between the two.

As he drove one more time along the main highway, he pulled off onto the main interchange outside the facility. The two employee entrances lay to his right and left, but to his left, the elevated highway would obstruct his view. He turned right.

As he drove along the road, he saw several locations that might be suitable, but the car repair shop's lot was in plain view of the road and patrolling security. There was a church lot, but his view of the target was blocked by large pine trees on the PfenRich property.

He had only one choice, a Mediterranean restaurant. He could park and launch in its back lot. He had a clear line of sight of his target and there were some small pines to hide behind so he could follow the drone to its final destination. He pulled into the back.

At the moment, the eatery's lot was devoid of cars except for those he suspected to belong to employees preparing for the lunch crowd. He checked the place's website and saw that it didn't open until noon. He had plenty of time.

He tugged the tailgate open one more time and lifted the drone from its cradle in the back. He placed it on the asphalt about ten feet away from the Blazer and out from under any trees. It was showtime. He had no reason to delay, and the sooner he did this, the sooner he got on the road out of there.

"Once again, this is for you, Bella," he said to the open air, his face gazing toward the heavens.

The drone lifted off without effort and darted toward the PfenRich vaccine facility. His original program would have had it flying five times that high, with a final descent to 100 feet upon reaching the GPS coordinates. Now, he took it to an altitude of 100 feet as it sailed toward the desired spot between the two main buildings. The flight time would be so brief that he didn't care if it was spotted en route.

Almost there. Two police cars came screeching to a halt in the front lot. Four officers jumped out of the cars, and one looked off toward the drone. He was too late to shoot it down, even if he was that good a marksman with his service weapon. He'd be shooting toward a populated area if he fired now.

The others started running up the lot, guns in hand. That's when one of them spotted George in his semi-secluded spot.

"Drop the controller!"

"Hands off the controller and behind your head!"

"Stop the drone or we'll shoot!"

At that point, George didn't care. Fifty, maybe sixty feet to go. He heard a gunshot in the distance. Someone was trying to shoot it down as it neared the buildings. George laughed. A sudden drop of just six feet in altitude would set it off. He'd had the same safeguard on the original device should someone have attempted to shoot down the balloon.

But the gunshot had a different result. The anxious officers just 40 feet away from him reacted to the sound as if they had been fired upon, even though they could clearly see his hands. George felt the sudden burning of bullets entering his chest and left thigh. His femur shattered, and he collapsed to the ground.

He almost lost his grip on the control, but he focused on maintaining his hold on the controller and on watching the drone. It began to dip and swerve but he managed to lift it to the optimum height from the ground. His breathing became ragged, and his vision began to dim.

The last thing he saw was the flash of the explosion as he managed to press the detonation button. The last thing he thought was, *I'm coming Bella*.

FIFTY-TWO

Anson and Alicia were unable to board the last direct flight from Milwaukee to Washington because of a lack of seats. Indirect flights were available, but Anson would have to go through the same harassment at each airport, and then again for the return trip. Were they to schedule flights for the next day, he would have to start the process all over again.

Yes, to personally meet Perry Carson would be the highlight of his year. To make his case on the man's show would be the epitome of his new fight against the push to socially re-engineer the public schools to favor what Anson saw as not just being inappropriate for young children but as immoral, too. However, the DOJ and TSA had succeeded in restricting his travels. Until those restrictions were lifted and his Pre-Check status restored, the minuses of air travel outweighed the pluses.

It was now midmorning and Anson, Hannah, and Alicia sat together watching the Fox News crew once again set up its remote "studio" in the Hardy's living room. The doorbell rang, and Anson met Denton Pierce at the door. The head of the MJFDA had been expected.

Anson extended his hand. "Welcome. Nice to meet you face to face."

Denton smiled and nodded as they shook hands. "Likewise." He looked right and left. "Nice door. Alicia told me they did a good job replacing it."

Anson nodded. "They did. One of the few positives to come out of this whole mess. Come in."

While Carson did his show live from the Fox News studios in Washington, they were going to have to record this segment for use later that night.

Half an hour later, they were told that Mr. Carson would be with them remotely in five minutes. They all sat on dining room chairs that had been moved into the living room. Last-minute lighting adjustments were made. And then they were "on."

On-air introductions were made, followed by a brief statement of thanks made to Carson by Denton for having them on the show.

"So, Anson, we've been following your story over the past week. I understand some new complications, if that's the right word to use, came up yesterday. You were supposed to fly here and be on our show live today, but our government had different plans. Actually, for our viewers, why don't you give us a synopsis of what's happened to you and your family up until today."

"Thanks, Perry." Anson proceeded to give a short description of the ordeal they were facing, including the loss of their jobs and reactions from the neighborhood. He finished by detailing his experience at the airport.

"Wow. I'd say you must be doing a good job if the DOJ is so

scared of your message that they put you on the "No-fly" list to curtail your travels. What's next?"

Denton spoke up. "If I might, Perry. Twice now in the past two weeks, Anson has been placed in handcuffs and literally dragged away to a police car. One of those times he was also shackled. And why? Not because of the bogus trespassing charges brought by the local school district, charges that were later dropped because it was clear that he was on public property, at a public meeting, and publicly invited to speak. No, it was because the school district didn't like what he had to say. It's because he spoke up against social engineering in their public school system. He spoke up to protect his children. Someone decided that he needed to be taught a lesson, and not in the form of reading, writing, and arithmetic, which our schools don't seem to teach very well these days. No, he was to be made a scapegoat, an example of what might happen to you if you go against the communist-inspired agenda of the elites who think they should control you and your children."

"So, again, what's next?"

Anson listened as Denton went on to talk of the lawsuits being prepared against the school district, the police and each individual officer involved, the FBI and each agent involved, the DOJ, and the TSA. He still found it hard to believe they were going through this.

Denton concluded by saying, "It's time that people wake up. Our government is no longer one of the people, by the people, and for the people. The government believes you work for them, not the other way around. If people don't stand up to this, the elites, who think they know better than us, will win. Next week, at the voter's box, people need to elect those who will fight for *them*."

"Thank you, Denton. I fully agree. It's not a time to be complacent or apathetic. Hannah, let me ask you something. As a mother of five, how has this affected your family?"

Hannah nodded to acknowledge the question. "Perry, we've had to sit down and have long talks with our kids. On the plus side, our friends, family, and church all stepped up to help put our kids into a great, positive school setting, and that has helped. But our kids have trouble getting to sleep. They get anxious whenever they see a police car. They worry that their dad might get arrested again and taken away. And they worry about other basics in life. We both lost our jobs because of this, so they've voiced concern about getting food, getting kicked out of our home, and more. It's going to take some time to work through this as a family."

"Well, I understand your sister is trying to help. She launched a GiveSendGo campaign to help raise money for your family. Is that correct?"

"Yes."

"Well, we want to help, too. Folks, here's the website for that account. Please consider helping out this family."

Tears came to Hannah's eyes upon seeing the website listed at the bottom of the screen on the monitor in front of them. Anson's eyes got misty as well. He didn't recall ever seeing Carson promote a giving website like that before.

"Thank you, Perry," he said.

"So, we need to close out this interview, but first, Anson, I've been told that you have some big plans in mind."

Anson nodded. "I do, Perry. Whenever I've been interviewed about this, I've promoted our need to get involved. If we want to take back America and make it the constitutional republic it once was, we can't sit back and let the status quo continue. We need to get involved politically. As such, Hannah and I have talked this over. I'm too late for next week's mid-term elections, but I will be filing to run as an independent for our local congressional seat two years from now. Our current congressman, a Republican by the way, has been lackluster at best and has shown no interest in our situation. He seems interested only in the status quo. Next week, he goes unchallenged. Two years from now, he won't."

FIFTY-THREE

Werner received the news as he was being driven back to the hotel from his pacemaker follow-up appointment. As much as he trusted Edvin, he had learned long ago to have multiple sources of information. It was particularly helpful when several lines of inquiry all matched and corroborated one another.

He tipped his head and closed his eyes. This was devastating news . . . in more ways than one. Why hadn't AlterNet2 been able to track down the perpetrator and stop the second attack? He texted Edvin to contact him by phone as soon as able.

A text response came quickly: *Awaiting your arrival at The Plaza.* Even better.

As Werner entered the main lobby, he saw Edvin emerge from the Champagne Bar. He noted that it was too late for breakfast and doubted that he was there for an early lunch. It seemed obvious that the news had hit him almost as much as it had Werner. For Werner, the financial loss was significant.

Edvin approached him and offered a curt bow. "Sir, they told me you had arrived."

Werner nodded. He scrutinized his assistant. He could understand the young man's wanting a drink to "fortify" himself before sharing bad news, but he looked like he'd had more than one. That was out of character for Edvin.

"Let's talk upstairs."

Werner noted that the young man kept looking down at his feet as the elevator rose. Was something else going on?

Upon entering the privacy of the suite, Werner decided to spare the young man any further anticipation.

"I have already heard about the second PfenRich attack. Mr. Bouras called me directly."

Edvin's eyes widened in shock. Had he misjudged the reason his aide looked so shaken?

"A second attack? Where? The Michigan facility?"

He hadn't heard. Now Werner felt concern creep throughout his mind. If it wasn't the PfenRich attack that led him to drink, what had? Was Werner prepared for what was to come?

"No, the vaccine facility outside of the city here. The attack was carried out by a drone carrying another EMP device. It took out everything within the two main buildings. The attacker is dead. Preliminary investigation points to the attacks being revenge for the death of a loved one that the attacker blamed on the COVID vaccine. That was based upon the contents of his wallet."

Edvin sat down and took several deep breaths as he shook his head. "I'm sorry, sir. I should have been the one keeping you up to date. I will do better."

"Edvin, you're an excellent aide. You couldn't have stopped this, but I'm upset that AlterNet2 wasn't able to find this man so we could stop him. I thought the program was further along than that."

Edvin turned white. Why?

"Sir, AlterNet2 is gone. Completely destroyed by a malicious worm. All of its systems were rendered useless as well as if EMP devices had gone off in the lab and the off-site server building."

Now Werner sat down. His heart sank. All that work. All the potential that the program held for their coming world order. Two major setbacks on the same morning. He was glad his pacemaker was given a thorough check and a final approval because he felt as if his heart could stop at any moment.

Edvin told Werner about the surprise discovery of other programmers having been involved originally, of the name Adam Afton being a code name, and about the sequence of events leading up to the program's destruction. Like Edvin, he wondered if the name Adam Afton was real or fictional. There certainly appeared to be a man by that name, who had a brother and several sisters. But was he the programmer they sought? Perhaps he had other reasons to disappear as he had. Or maybe the AlterNet2 prototype had failed in this as well.

"Sir, I have let you down."

"No, Edvin, no one could have anticipated, much less prevented, both of these setbacks for us. I cannot hold you responsible."

Indeed, Werner recognized that he, too, would not have fared better. What to do now would depend upon decisions to be made by the WOC. The executive committee would have to decide whether or not to pursue a new surveillance program.

Perhaps a different route would work. The WHO was meeting to make changes to the International Health Regulations. As Werner thought about that, changes to the IHR could work. He had been in talks with various health ministers about those changes. Indonesian Minister of Health Budi Gunadi Sadikin was specifically interested in an international "digital health certificate acknowledged by the WHO" to enable the public to "move around." Such a "vaccine passport," as many have called it, would be much easier to track. Yes, perhaps it was time to prioritize the IHR changes.

"My pacemaker checkup is complete. We have no further obligations here. Please have my plane prepared for this evening. We leave for Munich after dinner."

FIFTY-FOUR

Aric was excited to hear that Adam was moving back to the lake house an hour away. While the town itself didn't offer much, he always enjoyed the serenity of the small lake. It was a peaceful getaway from college.

Yet, more than that, Adam would now be in a place where he could join Aric at church on occasion. Still, as eager as he was to help his brother mature in his newfound faith, it was more important that Adam reunite with his family. That time had come.

Also, his return showed that Adam no longer lived in fear of being discovered. This was something Adam wanted to talk with him about. So, he was anxious for the day's classes to end early, like now. That would suit him just fine, although Adam had announced that he wouldn't be picking Aric up until dinnertime.

True, it had only been a couple of days since Aric and Jess found Adam at the old lab. Aric had been reluctant to leave, and he would have stayed if Jess hadn't been with him. But her father's talk about not having even the appearance of inappropriate behavior weighed on him. The last thing he wanted was to keep her out overnight. Besides, the lodgings offered by Adam—the back seat of his car—made "roughing it" seem like glamping.

Aric forced himself to focus on class, but as soon as it ended, he bolted for the dorm. There he changed into some cleaner jeans and a nice, button-down shirt, which reminded him that he was overdue in doing his laundry. He'd already had to pull some underwear from the dirty clothes basket. If his mother knew, she'd shoot him. Actually, she'd probably grab it all, wash and fold it, and return it to him a day later.

He still had half an hour before Adam's arrival, so he killed time with some class reading. When his phone chirped with a message, he felt surprised that he'd gotten so engrossed in the material that he'd lost track of the time. Adam was outside, waiting. He rushed down the stairs rather than wait on the elevator.

"Hey, welcome back," he said as he climbed into the passenger seat of Adam's car.

"Thanks. Glad to be back. That basement had become depressing." He looked Aric over. "Glad you changed into something a bit nicer than your usual. My treat tonight. The HobNob. We're celebrating."

"Wow. That's some celebration."

The HobNob was one of Wisconsin's iconic supper clubs. Overlooking Lake Michigan, its food was fabulous . . . and pricey, and its atmosphere was nostalgic of the days when celebrities ate there as part of the entertainment circuit between Chicago and Milwaukee.

"After dinner, I've arranged to meet Lynch at their house. You can join us if you want. I'd like you to . . . if you don't have too much studying."

Aric was pleased that Adam had taken up his suggestion to talk with Lynch. "Sure. I'm caught up. Well, close enough anyway."

During dinner, Aric brought up the subject of Adam's being discovered. "Aren't you worried about being back at the lake house or finally going home to your family?"

Adam shook his head. "Not really. Adam Afton is no longer a ghost. I used UltraNet to restore my identity. For every database where I made a change, I kept a record. Every major transaction I made under an assumed name, I tracked. And my software reverted everything back to me in just a couple of hours."

Aric was concerned. "But that means they can find you now."

His brother nodded. "Yep. And now they'll really question whether their new AlterNet truly worked or not. If they come looking and find me, they'll be scratching their heads over why they couldn't find me before. That will send them down some rabbit trails that never end. But I don't think that will happen."

"Why?"

"Because their resurrected AlterNet is no more. I found and reconnected with an old colleague. Ends up we're just as like-minded now as we were then. We teamed up to destroy their effort. The last thing we need is for a program like mine to fall into the wrong hands. Plus, he planted some large seeds of doubt by telling those folks that Adam was a code name, just as we had Eve, Cain, Abel, Seth, and others on the team. Between that, and the seeming flaw in their program, I doubt they'll restart the development of a new program."

"But what if they do?"

"I've planted a few safeguards out on the web. If they try, we'll learn about it sooner rather than later."

Upon finishing his prime rib, Aric sat back, satisfied. "That was delicious."

Adam nodded in agreement. The HobNob was also known for its alcoholic ice cream desserts, but Adam refrained. He'd been sober for over two years. He had no reason to tempt himself now.

The Cully home was just minutes away from the restaurant. Adam texted Lynch before starting his car and got the okay to come over. Less than five minutes later, they pulled up in front of the home.

Amy answered the door and welcomed them inside. "Lynch is in the den. Go on back."

The ex-detective-turned-professor stood as they entered the room. They exchanged handshakes and brotherly hugs and sat down.

"Coffee? A soda? Water? It's filtered."

Adam waved off the offer. So did Aric. "Adam just treated me to dinner at the HobNob. We're celebrating."

"Oh?"

Adam nodded. "Yeah, celebrating the return of Adam Afton. I'm no longer a ghost." He proceeded to tell Lynch about everything that had happened over the past few weeks. Aric added some details about how he had been tracked and followed, too.

Lynch took a deep breath before responding. "Well, you two seem to have a knack for finding trouble. Reminds me of someone else I know." He nodded his head toward a nearby room where Amy had gone to watch the kids. "Before we got married anyway." He laughed. "I agree. It certainly sounds like that was a program we wouldn't want in the wrong hands. So, Adam, you mentioned having some questions for me. What's up?"

Aric was aware that Lynch knew a bit about Adam's programming skills and his previous involvement with the original AlterNet. Was that why his brother wanted to talk with Lynch?

"Lynch, you already know how I found those kids and that lab in Camp Douglas. What you don't know is that I still have that program. I took what was called AlterNet, built upon that framework, and developed a superior version I call UltraNet. I've been using it to find data and build cases against corrupt politicians and businessmen. In the two years since Camp Douglas, I've given prosecutors information on over two dozen corrupt individuals, and three-quarters of those people went to court and got convicted."

"And all of the information came via your program?"

Adam nodded.

"Were you hired by these prosecutors to find this information?"

"No. More often than not, I stumbled across something fishy and developed the case from there. Often what I discovered led to someone else just as involved. Anyway, I turned over the data anonymously along with the sources so they could corroborate what I sent and build their legal cases."

"Was the data easily discoverable by, say, the investigators working for the prosecutors?

"Some, but not all."

"Was the data legally obtained?"

Adam waggled his head back and forth. "I think you know the answer to that question already. Not usually. No search warrants or anything like that. Just an everyday citizen coming across incriminating evidence, turning it over to authorities, and letting them handle it via warrants or whatever. At least, that's how I looked at it . . . until I read the Bible."

Lynch smiled. "Sounds like a convincing argument, except that everyday citizens don't hack corporate and government databases to just 'come across' such information." Adam shrugged, trying to look innocent. "So, you've come up against a moral dilemma, as you put it when you called me. Can you still be this white knight hacker looking to bring justice to corrupt people and be biblically justified in doing so?"

Aric had been right in his assumptions about why Adam wanted to talk with Lynch. The man knew both the law and the Bible and could give Adam the answer he sought. Yet, Aric saw where this was headed. Adam had spent the past two years bringing down bad guys, and it looked as if he would have to stop. Could he stop? What would he do instead?

Lynch looked at Adam. "Your turn. I think *you* already know the answer to this."

Adam took a deep breath and sighed. "Yeah, I think so. The Bible tells us to follow the law. So, if I'm breaking the law to do what I do, I need to stop. But what if the law is flawed? What if it favors the corrupt because it was created by the corrupt?"

Lynch nodded. "Therein lies a true dilemma. We saw examples of this during the pandemic. Churches in Canada held services against the law of their provinces. People refused to wear masks in disdain for what some saw as laws, even though they were just mandates. Arguments flew on both sides of the church aisle. Some said to obey all laws. Others said we need to obey laws that were moral or biblical, but that we were morally obligated to ignore those that weren't. We see that in the abortion fight. Pro-death politicians put laws into effect to protect the murder of the unborn, while pro-life protesters break those laws because they're seen as immoral."

"Exactly."

"Except that those protesters often end up in jail or charged with the crime."

"Yes, they're willing to break an immoral law and risk the consequences. They bring both the immoral law and, in your example, the immorality of abortion into the light for all to examine. I've always accepted the fact that at some point I might be caught."

"True, but there's a difference. Are the laws you're breaking immoral? Do they protect just the corrupt, or do they protect the innocent as well? Privacy laws protect all. Anti-hacking laws protect corporations but in doing so, they protect not just bad actors but also proprietary information that might be critical to staying in business. They have a fiduciary responsibility to their investors to stay in business. The life savings of innocent people could be lost. So, are these laws immoral or unbiblical?"

Aric wasn't going to say anything. He saw that Lynch's arguments were likely to win out. Would Adam see that, too?

"Let me say this in a different way," said Lynch. "The fact that you're torn between the two sides, that you see this as a moral dilemma, means one thing. Well, to me anyway."

"What's that?"

"That God is already speaking to your heart that you need to quit what you're doing. If it was okay to continue, then you wouldn't be having this argument in your head. I've always found that if I have a sense of peace in what I'm doing, then I'm still in God's will. If I don't have that peace, then I need to find a way to do things where I am at peace. His Spirit typically leads us this way."

"Amen" whispered Aric. Both men looked at him. "Sorry, I didn't mean to say that out loud, but I agree with Lynch on that. One of the hardest things I've had to learn as a believer is how to follow God's lead, and having a sense of peace over a decision or action is what I've discovered to be the best way."

Adam wanted to resist what Lynch was saying. He'd had such success in exposing the corrupt and in helping to make them pay for their crimes. But as Lynch spoke, another thought came to mind. God had promised His judgment of these people. Of *all* people, in fact. Only by the grace extended through accepting Christ as one's Lord and Savior would one be spared that righteous judgment. One way or another, the people he sought to expose would ultimately pay for their actions . . . for all eternity.

He didn't want to compromise his growing faith by continuing to inject his personal judgments into his actions. In his brief experience, he already had come to realize that many who called themselves Christian accepted bits and pieces of what the Bible taught while mixing in unbiblical concepts taken from various worldviews. They might condemn homosexuality as wrong while living together outside of marriage. Both were equally sinful from a biblical perspective. As imperfect as he was, he wanted his life to emulate Christ's. That meant learning to accept God's lead and His prescription for a godly life as found in His Word.

Aric's corroboration of Lynch's advice about letting the peace of the Holy Spirit help guide you struck home. He had seen that in action in his younger brother's life, time and time again.

By the end of their conversation, he agreed. UltraNet would be mothballed. He couldn't bring himself to totally destroy all of that work and reasoned that there might come a time—an emergency—in which he might be led to use it. Until then, all traces of it on the dark web and elsewhere would be eradicated, and the program itself moved onto CDs for storage in a safety deposit box or similarly secure place. He chose CDs over a flash drive because the latter was too easily lost, misplaced, or taken.

As he and Aric said their goodbyes, he wondered what life ahead would be like. Still, he had reinvented himself once before. He could do it again.

Author's Note

While the U.S. is dominated by Dispensational teachings that include a rapture, an Antichrist (capital 'A'), a seven-year tribulation period, and such, many of the rest of the world's Christians don't accept those ideas, despite the spread of these ideas in popular culture (movies, books, etc.). For more detail on these concepts, I suggest you look at the two study guides I wrote about the End Times: *Still Here! Surviving the End Times*, and *Still Here! The Apocalypse is Now.*

I once accepted the Dispensational teachings. I didn't know any better and trusted that those teaching me did. Still, something didn't seem right about those teachings, and I began to study eschatology (the End Times) and the Book of Revelation for myself. Now, I recognize that, unlike those who accept Dispensational theology, the Book of Revelation can't be taken literally. The numbers used in it are symbolic. The images presented are symbolic. And to understand it, you need an understanding of Old Testament scripture. That is, after all, what John had available to him when he wrote the book.

When you see the Old Testament connections in the Book of Revelation, much of the mystery and confusion disappears. God is not a God of confusion, so why would He have John write a book that no one could understand? In fact, much of the book refers to the Book of Daniel. Daniel was a book written for the Jewish nation, and its prophecies were fulfilled by the reign of Antiochus Epiphanes IV 150 years before

Christ. Still, John draws upon those prophecies, which his immediate 'audience' would have understood, to paint a picture for future believers.

This novel, *The Beasts*, looks at the two beasts that John portrays in Revelation 13: the beasts from the sea and from the land. The cumulative characteristics of these beasts match those of the four beasts shown in Danial. The beast from the sea (whom many label as the Antichrist) carries the characteristics of government. The beast from the land (whom many call the False Prophet) is shown as the government's cheerleader. So, today, we have what many call the Deep State acting as a global government. Its technocratic elites dictate global policy, and the various national governments (the U.S. included) carry out those dictates. And then we have the Mainstream Media, Big Pharma, Big Ag, and all of the corporate collective acting to promote what the government wants. They are the cheerleaders pushing people to believe in and trust the government. Think COVID mandates as an example.

As such, I believe we are now seeing the rise of the two beasts of Revelation 13. Their rise is not sudden and catastrophic. It is subtle, and their grip on the world and modern culture will increase over time until they have subjugated or nullified those who resist. These beasts will slowly solidify their control and then watch out. Jesus told us this time in history would be like the days of Noah. The people then were unsuspecting, and then the flood came. It will be no different today, except that the flood won't be of water.

Acknowledgments

As always, I again want to acknowledge and thank my dear wife, Paula, for her help, encouragement, and putting up with my spending time to write. With the retirement of my main proofreader, I've started using *Grammarly* for additional error checking. If you find any errors, it missed them, and let me know.

And finally, my sincerest compliments to Adrijus Guscia for his incredible covers.

About the Author

Braxton can't lay claim to wanting to be a writer all his life, although his mother and seventh grade English teacher were convinced he had what it would take. A bachelor's degree in Bio-Medical Engineering led to medical school and a residency in Emergency Medicine. He served for a decade in the U.S. Army Medical Corps with tours such as the Chief, Emergency Medical Services at Fort Campbell, KY, and as a research Flight Surgeon at Fort Rucker, AL. Who had time to write?

By the 1990s, as a civilian, his professional and family life had settled down, somewhat, and his mother once again took up her mantra, "Write a book. You're a good writer." In 1997, a Valentine's Day writing contest convinced him that maybe he could write fiction. He spent the next fifteen years learning the craft of writing.

Now, twenty-plus years after that first hesitant start, he has sixteen novels published, as well as non-fiction books and a children's book, and can't find enough time to write. As a Christian, he writes "true-life" Christian fiction (suspense and thrillers) that many call "cutting edge," as he's not afraid to take on such issues as human trafficking, racism, and more. His characters are real-life as well, with all the flaws and blemishes real people have. As such, his books are never likely to gain acceptance by the Christian Bookseller Association. But then, he never intended to tell stories just to the choir.

Books by Braxton DeGarmo:

Still Here Series:

The End Begins – 1
The Shaking – 2
The Beasts – 3
The Trumpets – 4
The Mark - 5

Non-Fiction Study Guides:

Still Here! Surviving the End Times
Still Here! The Apocalypse is Now
Still Here! Countdown Revelation

MedAir Series:

Looks that Deceive – 1
Rescued and Remembered – 2
The Silenced Shooter – 3
Wrongfully Removed – 4
A Zealot's Destiny – 5
Kidnapped Nation - 6
The Khmer Connection - 7
Resurrected Trouble - 8

Seamus O'Connor Thrillers:

The Militant Genome
Ten Seconds 'Til

Other Books:

Indebted

Children's Books:

The Toucan Who Can Can-can